Reviewers Love

"Melissa Brayden has become one ~~genre, writing hit after hit of funny, relatable, and very sexy stories for women who love women."—*Afterellen.com*

Marry Me

"A bride-to-be falls for her wedding planner in this smoking hot, emotionally mature romance from Brayden...Brayden is remarkably generous to her characters, allowing them space for self-exploration and growth."—*Publishers Weekly*

"When I open a book by Melissa Brayden, I usually know what to expect. This time, she really surprised me. In a good way."—*Rainbow Literary Society*

To the Moon and Back

"*To the Moon and Back* is all about Brayden's love of theatre, onstage and backstage, and she does a delightful job of sharing that love... Brayden set the scene so well I knew what was coming, not because it's unimaginative but because she made it obvious it was the only way things could go. She leads the reader exactly where she wants to take them, with brilliant writing as usual. Also, not everyone can make office supplies sound sexy."—*Jude in the Stars*

"Melissa Brayden does what she does best, she delivers amazing characters, witty banter, all while being fun and relatable."—*Romantic Reader Blog*

Back to September

"You can't go wrong with a Melissa Brayden romance. Seriously, you can't. Buy all of her books. Brayden sure has a way of creating an emotional type of compatibility between her leads, making you root for them against all odds. Great settings, cute interactions, and realistic dialogue."—*Bookvark*

What a Tangled Web

"[T]he happiest ending to the most amazing trilogy. Melissa Brayden pulled all of the elements together, wrapped them up in a bow, and presented the reader with Happily Ever After to the max!"—*Kitty Kat's Book Review Blog*

Beautiful Dreamer

"I love this book. I want to kiss it on its face...I'm going to stick *Beautiful Dreamer* on my to-reread-when-everything-sucks pile, because it's sure to make me happy again and again."—*Smart Bitches Trashy Books*

"*Beautiful Dreamer* is a sweet and sexy romance, with the bonus of interesting secondary characters and a cute small-town setting."—*Amanda Chapman, Librarian (Davisville Free Library, RI)*

Two to Tangle

"Melissa Brayden does it again with a sweet and sexy romance that leaves you feeling content and full of happiness. As always, the book is full of smiles, fabulous dialogue, and characters you wish were your best friends."—*The Romantic Reader*

"I loved it. I wasn't sure Brayden could beat Joey and Becca and their story, but when I started to see reviews mentioning that this was even better, I had high hopes and Brayden definitely lived up to them."—*LGBTQreader.com*

Entangled

"*Entangled* is a simmering slow burn romance, but I also fully believe it would be appealing for lovers of women's fiction. The friendships between Joey, Maddie, and Gabriella are well developed and engaging as well as incredibly entertaining...All that topped off with a deeply fulfilling happily ever after that gives all the happy sighs long after you flip the final page."—*Lily Michaels: Sassy Characters, Sizzling Romance, Sweet Endings*

"Ms. Brayden has a definite winner with this first book of the new series, and I can't wait to read the next one. If you love a great enemies-to-lovers, feel-good romance, then this is the book for you."—*Rainbow Reflections*

Love Like This

"Brayden upped her game. The characters are remarkably distinct from one another. The secondary characters are rich and wonderfully integrated into the story. The dialogue is crisp and witty."—*Frivolous Reviews*

Sparks Like Ours

"Brayden sets up a flirtatious tit-for-tat that's honest, relatable, and passionate. The women's fears are real, but the loving support from the supporting cast helps them find their way to a happy future. This enjoyable romance is sure to interest readers in the other stories from Seven Shores."—*Publishers Weekly*

Hearts Like Hers

"*Hearts Like Hers* has all the ingredients that readers can expect from Ms. Brayden: witty dialogue, heartfelt relationships, hot chemistry and passionate romance."—*Lez Review Books*

"Once again Melissa Brayden stands at the top. She unequivocally is the queen of romance."—*Front Porch Romance*

Eyes Like Those

"Brayden's story of blossoming love behind the Hollywood scenes provides the right amount of warmth, camaraderie, and drama." —*RT Book Reviews*

"Brayden's writing is just getting better and better. The story is well done, full of well-honed wit and humour, and the characters are complex and interesting."—*Lesbian Reading Room*

Strawberry Summer

"This small-town second-chance romance is full of tenderness and heart. The 10 Best Romance Books of 2017."—*Vulture*

"*Strawberry Summer* is a tribute to first love and soulmates and growing into the person you're meant to be. I feel like I say this each time I read a new Melissa Brayden offering, but I loved this book so much that I cannot wait to see what she delivers next."—*Smart Bitches, Trashy Books*

First Position

"Brayden aptly develops the growing relationship between Ana and Natalie, making the emotional payoff that much sweeter. This ably plotted, moving offering will earn its place deep in readers' hearts." —*Publishers Weekly*

By the Author

Waiting in the Wings

Heart Block

How Sweet It Is

First Position

Strawberry Summer

Beautiful Dreamer

Back to September

To the Moon and Back

Marry Me

Exclusive

Soho Loft Romances:

Kiss the Girl

Just Three Words

Ready or Not

Seven Shores Romances:

Eyes Like Those

Hearts Like Hers

Sparks Like Ours

Love Like This

Tangle Valley Romances:

Entangled

Two to Tangle

What a Tangled Web

EXCLUSIVE

by

Melissa Brayden

2022

EXCLUSIVE
© 2022 By Melissa Brayden. All Rights Reserved.

ISBN 13: 978-1-63679-112-8

This Trade Paperback Original Is Published By
Bold Strokes Books, Inc.
P.O. Box 249
Valley Falls, NY 12185

First Edition: March 2022

Credits
Editor: Ruth Sternglantz
Production Design: Stacia Seaman
Cover Design by Jeanine Henning

Acknowledgments

Not a lot of people know this about me, but I got my start in TV news. At twenty-two, I was a green reporter ready to take on the news world as I knew it. In a lot of ways, I relate to Skyler and her journey, and I hope you will, too. Writing this romance also allowed me to peek in on a few characters I first started writing many years ago. It was nice to spend a little time in their orbit again. Like putting on a favorite comfy sweatshirt.

As always, there are many people to send gratitude to and tackle with hugs. It's been an especially rocky time in my life recently, and keeping me afloat were my friends and family who picked up the slack when I couldn't. Alan, my parents and sisters, my kids, and friends like Georgia, Rey, Nikki, Carsen, Paula, Kris, and Fiona were there on the spot. I also have to send hugs and tackles to Radclyffe and everyone at Bold Strokes for their unwavering support and flexibility. I couldn't ask for a better partnership. Even in the midst of a new baby and heart attack, with Sandy Lowe's stellar project managing, we still got this book out on time. Ruth, my editor, is patient and insightful and responsible for helping me wade through the excess and find the heart of each story. Jeanine Henning turned out another cover that captured the book spectacularly. To Stacia Seaman, Toni Whitaker, Cindy Cresap, and the proofreaders who put in lots of time—THANK YOU.

To my loyal readers, and to brand new ones, I value you more than you'll ever know. I'd tackle every single one of you if I could. It's my hope that one day we'll meet, share an email exchange, or a hello on a sidewalk. We could grab a glass of wine, cup of coffee, or let's be honest, a doughnut, and talk about books. I'd love that. One day. Until then, happy reading.

For the truth seekers.

PROLOGUE

There had to be more exciting things in the world than an extra-giant squash. I was convinced and could rattle off a handful without prompting. However, everything in my demeanor screamed with enthusiasm as I held the mic and addressed the camera on my live shot from Tanner Peak's annual Squash Square Off. Cue the squash-shaped confetti.

It was midspring, and that meant the growers were out in force, celebrating their season and showing off their oversized successes in the annual competition. Today was the squash portion of the competition, and I made sure to turn up the wattage on my smile, which my small TV station's handful of viewers had listed as their favorite thing about my work on the official survey.

"We weren't sure he could pull it off, but Paul Bloomfield has done it again, ladies and gentlemen, securing the top prize at this year's Squash Square Off with this beauty right here." I grinned and gestured to Paul at my right as he proudly held up the forty-five-and-a-half pound butternut squash that had sealed his win. "Paul, I'm told you've named your squash. Can you share with us what you call it?"

Paul nodded. "It's actually a *her*, Skyler." He beamed at the folks at home. "I call her Lucy Jane after my high school sweetheart."

I placed a hand over my heart, pretending not to boil in my matching pants and jacket beneath the sweltering hot sun. "That's so sweet. The real-life Lucy Jane must be so proud."

His head swiveled back to me, his smile dimming. "I'm not allowed to contact her, but I bet so."

What the *what*? I blinked and looked straight into the camera. "And we'll leave it right there. This is Skyler Ruiz from the Squash Square Off. I know what I'm having for dinner. Felipé?"

I listened to Felipé's banter in my IFB earpiece. "Well, be sure to save some for us, Skyler."

"No promises." I grinned happily into the lens and held it.

"And we're clear," Greg, my cameraman, said and stepped out from his tripod. He sent me a look that said *Are you kidding me right now*? I sent one back that said *Paul might murder us and our families*. Greg was my guy, the person I could communicate with wordlessly. But shoots like today's made me long for the kind of journalism I'd been dreaming about since my first telecommunications class at UC San Diego. Actual news that made a difference. Giant squash were fun, but they weren't about to change the world. Unless scary Paul found his way to Lucy Jane, and that meant another kind of unfortunate coverage entirely. Speaking of drama, where *was* the real news? Crime, politics, breaking stuff. Nowhere to be found out here in the sticks. Yet, here I was. Stuck, shuffling from one small-time event to the next through the series of small towns that fed into my station's coverage area. Last night's lead story? Who was putting those ugly plastic flamingos in everyone's yard, and would that rascal one day be caught? That was my life, and nothing about it signaled change anywhere on the horizon.

"Thanks for speaking with us today, Paul," I said graciously.

He placed his thumbs under the straps of his overalls. "Anytime. And I'd be happy to sign anything for you or your viewers if they'd like an autograph. I don't mind. I'll even sign a vegetable. I don't have a single hang-up about that and have given it a lot of thought."

"Oh wow. Very generous of you." I glanced around for who these autograph clamorers might be and found no one. "I'll remember that. You have a good one, and don't get too crazy celebrating your win. No streaking across Main Street this year."

"I gotta be me." He gestured behind him as an idea hit. "Hey, now. Bunch of us are heading over to Lonesome's for a few brews. Real good bar. Feel free to stop on by. First round is on me."

Oh, a lovely bullet to dodge. "You're very kind, Paul, but I've gotta head back to the station and then home. Long day." The truth, but I tossed in a wince like a respectable human. My feet ached like a bitch, and I wasn't in the market to take out any kind of restraining order of my own.

"Suit yourself. But it's always crazy on Squash Square Off day." He laughed, and his eyes went big. "Like, a lot."

"How could it not be?" I asked good-naturedly and slid beneath my leather cross-body bag. A signal that I was out of there. *Take the signal, Paul.*

"Let's go, boys. Grab a table close to the jukebox."

Yes, Lonesome's actually had one of those. I'd seen it. Paul shot me finger-guns and dashed off with his blue ribbon, prize money, and giant squash cradled to his chest like an adored newborn.

Still wearing my work heels, I trudged to the truck with Greg, drained and dissatisfied. I was thirty years old, eight years out of college, and still working at a fledgling TV news station, covering a handful of small towns along a highway in rural California. Emphasis on rural. As one of three reporters on staff, I reported softball games, city council meetings, and—yes, wait for it!—more fruit and vegetable growing competitions than I cared to count. Why were there so many? And don't get me started on those damn plastic flamingo invasions.

"We'll be back here next week for the Peak of Berries Festival," Greg reminded me with a raise of his eyebrows. He pulled the ball cap off his mop of curly blond hair and gave it a tousle. "Hope you're ready to get your strawberry on."

I paused before hopping into the truck. Tanner Peak was a nice enough town, but I couldn't help hoping something remarkable would happen at that festival. "What are the odds someone runs off with a cash box, or a swarm of aggressive birds invades the square dancing pavilion and flies off with the mayor like the monkeys did with the Scarecrow in *Wizard of Oz*?" I nodded. "Really hoping for that monkey–mayor part."

"One can dream," Paul said with an amused smile. "But I'm betting the most exciting thing to come out of that festival is annoying rain."

"Tut-tut. Haul out the ye olde galoshes."

"Fucking A." Greg put the cap back on, silencing the curls, and slid the news van into gear. The bond between reporter and cameraperson was a unique one. You worked as a team and saw a lot of stuff together. Greg was my rock, but unlike me, he was happy with his job at the station. He got bored with the same old stories, but he didn't have the same thirst to pick up and find something better. That was me.

We headed back to the station for the evening assignment meeting where I learned that the following morning I'd be covering an uptick in parking tickets across the region. How was I going to sleep tonight now, with a parking ticket mystery looming? I had to laugh.

Once home in my small cottage along the beautiful greenbelt that came complete with all sorts of alarming nature sounds—coyotes, giant frogs, and even a snuffling armadillo once—I did what I did every night, scrolled through the TV news trades, looking for job openings. Two weeks ago, I sent in my reel for the handful of regional gigs up for grabs, not at all picky about which city I might wind up in as long as it was a step forward. All I needed was a leg up. In fact, I wasn't even particular. Any limb would do. The chance to learn from people more seasoned than I was would be fantastic. Or something where I could take on more responsibility. Extra-complicated assignments. Longer-form storytelling. I just ached for the chance to really sink my teeth into the grit and grime of breaking news, and the longer I stayed in this small-town rut, the harder it became to break out. The problem was my reel was watered down, perky and quaint at best. It lacked the killer content I needed to stand out in a sea of applicants. Plus, TV news was about who you knew, and I had to face it. I didn't know anyone of major consequence. I was Skyler Ruiz, the daughter of a hardworking immigrant who'd given me every opportunity. Now, I needed to make my own.

I lay on my couch that night with my six-pound black and tan mutt, Michelangelo, curled into a ball on my chest. Part rat terrier, part Chihuahua, he was my devoted, slightly neurotic bestie. Even Micky knew that I needed a break from the hamster wheel. A getaway, maybe. It would help me regain proper perspective and help reignite my passion. I'd have the weekend off after the parking ticket story was logged for air, so maybe I'd jet down the coastline to my hometown of San Diego for a bit and spend some time with my family. I shuffled Micky's paws. "You want to visit tía Yolanda?" I asked Michelangelo. "She's the one who gives you all the chicken when I'm not looking. She's a good aunt, but bad for your diet."

Micky lifted his paws and placed them back on my chest, energized. I was ninety-eight percent sure he spoke English and was thrilled with the news. He blinked up at me and smacked his chicken-loving lips. He was no fool.

"Yep. I thought the chicken would convince you," I said, giving his ears a hearty rub. He closed his eyes and enjoyed the massage. I reached for my phone and texted my cousin Sarah, hopeful that she'd be around and up for some hang-out time.

Thought I'd swing into town this weekend. You free? Don't say no. I'll cry.

The bouncing dots indicated an imminent response. *Stop the tears. Of course. Grace has a tuba recital Saturday, but free after. Get here already.*

I grinned. Sarah Matamoros was the sister I'd never had, and her daughter, Grace, was the sweetest, quirkiest sixteen-year-old ever. When my father died of a heart attack when I was seven, my mother moved us from Guatemala to San Diego, so we'd be closer to her sister Yolanda and her family. Sarah, eleven years older, was immediately a warm presence in my life. She took me to the park, the movies, and even to work when she needed an extra pair of hands. Now that she was a successful entrepreneur with a family of her own, Sarah continued to inspire me. As for tía Yolanda—hands down the best cook in California and God had blessed her with the best backyard barbecues in life— once she heard I was coming home, I had no doubt she would round up the family and cook her heart out. I grinned, my spirits lifted at just the thought of a weekend back in my old stomping grounds and the aroma of smoked chicken.

My phone buzzed. I studied the screen for what else Sarah had to say. But it was Kacey. My heart fluttered a little. Dammit.

You up?

I laughed at the message and shook my head at the tired line. *It's come to this?*

No. What do you take me for? her reply read.

Someone in desperate need of a hookup.

Guilty. A pause, then another message. *You up?*

I laughed. Couldn't help it. My relationship with Kacey was fun if frustrating. We could go toe-to-toe, challenging each other with zingers back and forth all night. Our chemistry between the sheets was also helpful, but at the same time, we were…complicated. Wanted different things and finally had to call a truce. We got together here and there, but our occasional with-benefits status stopped just shy of actual dating, which had always been a sore spot for me. I would have liked more and saw potential there, but Kacey just wasn't the type for anything domestic. She was a stylist who worked long hours at her own salon and kept me on speed dial for…whenever she wanted to take her clothes off. While I enjoyed the naked perks that came with our no-strings relationship, I quietly wondered what it would be like to have more from someone I really liked. She wasn't exactly perfect for me, but worth exploring.

"I'm in a fucking rut," I told Michelangelo. I pointed at my screen emphatically. "And if I meet her tonight, I'm going to stay in one. Wouldn't you say I need more?" He lifted his paws again. Solidarity. "Decided. Thank you for your sage small-dog advice. I will pay you in strawberries from the festival." More feet tapping.

I swiveled back to my phone and typed with determination. "Can't tonight. Heading out of town tomorrow. Gotta pack." I tossed my phone onto the bed and sighed, because the idea of letting off a little steam with Kacey didn't sound bad at all. I grinned, closed my eyes, and imagined her fingertips across my skin. The release it would offer, the fun we'd likely have, but to what end? I wasn't a kid anymore. God, I was tired of spinning my wheels in a job with no real challenge and a faux relationship that had hit a dead end.

Onward and upward.

❖

When I arrived on the curb outside my aunt Yolanda's house the next day, I took a moment to exhale the bad and leave room within me for the good ahead. I pulled my way too heavy hair into a ponytail and wiped the sweat from my forehead because my slightly beaten-up blue Toyota Camry had lost air-conditioning two weeks ago, and I hadn't had the money or the time to have it fixed. Bygones. I was here now and needed to enjoy it.

"Baby Skyler! Bambina!"

I whirled to my right and saw my aunt standing on the sidewalk with her hands on her hips, huge welcoming grin on her face. Her hair, once as dark as mine, had gone gray a few years back, and she'd given up on coloring it, usually keeping it pulled back in a knot at her neck. I thought it made her look wise and warm, myself. She was two years older than my mother, who would be so jealous we were getting together without her. She'd worked her way up from student to attorney and now killed it eighty hours a week for a firm in LA. We'd FaceTime her later.

"Hi, Tía. I'm here! Oh, and you look amazing." She wore white pants that hugged her round frame with the prettiest white and pink top. Healthy and vibrant. "I should take your sassy photo right now." In fact, I stopped and did just that. She struck a pose, one arm in the air.

"That's enough silliness," she yelled. "Get up to this house right now. I'm going to smooch on you."

I grinned and hurried the rest of the way to her. "Okay, but I'm hot and a little sweaty from the ride."

"Mija, please." She ignored my directive and kissed my face aggressively. "I've got cool lemonade on the counter and an ear that's eager to hear all you've been up to. Come in. Come in." She clapped. "I'm just so excited you're here."

My aunt gave me the biggest squeeze, about eight more kisses to my cheeks, and led me into the cool house I'd loved since I was a kid. The interior overflowed with *things*, tons of them, and something about the abundance of objects made the place feel homey and warm. Trinkets over here. Framed family photographs covering the side table over there. Magazines in a plentiful stack on the coffee table. A series of intricate vases along the counter that bordered the kitchen, the hub of the house where the food was made and everyone hung out. I reflected on all the laughter growing up and the amazing mingling of aromas that wafted from the room from the tall pots on the stove. Steam billowing. My mouth watered at just the memory.

Second to my own, this house had always been my safe place to fall, where I built my confidence on warm hugs and compliments, even when school wasn't the easiest place for someone acclimating to a whole new country. Luckily, I'd been a quick study and adopted a thick skin.

"Did you get new cabinets?" I asked my aunt, marveling at the beautiful white kitchen that had once been a quiet medium brown.

"Oh yes. Sarah took me shopping and your uncle Roberto installed them himself. I don't have money, but I'm rich. Pays to have a handy husband."

"Or wife," I countered with a smile. I'd followed in Sarah's footsteps in more ways than one and was beyond grateful for the inroads she'd made with our family when it came to sexuality. By the time I came out in college, my relatives were well-seasoned advocates. I needed to send her a box of cookies or something. Rainbow ones.

"Speaking of getting married, have you chosen a beloved to settle down with?" She put out a bowl of homemade fried chips and onion dip. My comfort food heaven.

I balked. "Tía, there is no one even close to beloved in my life. And I have no time to locate someone."

"They work you too hard at that news station. Your mama was telling me all about it. When are you going to move home so we can have you back?" She opened a beer for me and poured it into a glass with a lime wedge. I was never leaving this place.

"I'd need a job first."

"You could work for Sarah. Her business is booming."

Sarah had opened a home and closet organizing company, Immaculate Organization, and now managed a team of incredibly creative project managers that oversaw the construction and design for their clients. "I'd be fired. Have you seen my room? I can't even organize my sock drawer."

Yolanda frowned. "That's true. No job for you." She pulled the beer away in jest before returning it.

"Who's saying my name, and where is my adorable cousin? I demand answers!"

I grinned and turned. Sarah stood in the entryway with her hands on her hips, that infectious smile on her face, and her curly dark hair down and gorgeous. I'd always longed for her hair. Mine didn't have the curl. "I was reminding your mother that my apartment is a national disaster, and I thereby can't work for you. I'd be a disgrace. Ditched by lunch for crumbs all over the place."

Sarah winced. "I don't know about a *national* disaster, but definitely citywide. Get over here."

I did as Sarah said and pulled her into a big, rock-back-and-forth bear hug, happy to be with my family again.

"Oh, Sky-Sky. It's good to see you. How's the breaking news?" Sarah asked.

I quirked my lips in apology. "Today I informed the public about an uptick in parking tickets. Riveting stuff. I don't know how they're going to hang on until the next broadcast. I feel bad for them."

Sarah opened the fridge and found a beer. "Then you won't be mad that I put your name in the hat with a friend of mine at KTMW."

I laughed. I'd been submitting my stuff to them for years and hadn't once even netted so much as an email. The San Diego market was top thirty in the nation. Aka out of my league. "Yeah, I don't think they care. Last I checked, they had to wash their hair that night." I grabbed another lime wedge from a dish on the counter and rimmed my glass.

"Well, maybe they're free now," Yolanda said, her eyes now full of hope. "If you need a place to live, I can make up the back bedroom, and we'll have slumber parties every day." She was teasing, but my aunt had a huge heart and would most definitely open up her home to anyone who needed space.

"You are the nicest, but let's not get ahead of ourselves. How did you throw my hat in? Tell me your methods." I squinted at Sarah, curious.

"So, Emory's best friend Lucy, you remember her? Sophisticated. Kind of sassy. Runs the newswire."

"Beautiful brunette. I love the way she razzes Em mercilessly."

"Me, too. Keeps Emory in line, and she needs it. Well, her amazing girlfriend, who you have not met, is Kristin. She's a former reporter who used to work for the *Union Trib* but made the shift to TV and is now an associate producer at KTMW."

Huh. What were the odds?

Sarah pressed on. "She happened to mention over dinner that they're looking for a fresh face to fill an on-air spot at five and ten."

I sighed in resignation. "I have no anchor experience, Sar."

"Which is perfect, because they're looking for a reporter."

That got my antennae up. "They haven't advertised. Now I'm intrigued." More than that. My heart thudded and my ears itched, which always happened when I hit a surge of excitement. This was a minor development, and I cued myself to slow the hell down, but it was something, and I desperately needed something to hope for right now.

"I told her to hire you immediately, as one does, and she said to send her your stuff." Sarah pointed. "Oh, and drop our names when you do, so Kristin pays attention. Realizes it's you."

I was flabbergasted. An inside track at a top station from a very unlikely source. "I'll send everything over immediately. But the chances of getting hired in the San Diego market are next to zero with my level of experience."

"No, no, no," Yolanda said, swatting away the negative energy like an angry swarm of flies had invaded the kitchen. "We're not putting that out into the universe. You are beautiful and smart, and they need you desperately."

"I like that outlook better anyway," I said, nodding.

"Without you they are nothing," Sarah said adamantly.

My aunt picked it up from there. "I don't like the reporter they have with the spiky hair. He talks too loud. You know who I do like? That Caroline McNamara. She has class and tells it to you straight."

I sighed dreamily. I'd had a crush on her for years, which was awful of me, because Caroline McNamara was so much more than crush material. A legend in the field. I nodded to Yolanda. "She's really good at what she does. I take notes every time I watch a broadcast of hers."

"Someone has a few feelings on the topic." Sarah jokingly fanned me and with good reason. She knew all my secrets.

"I'm not afraid to swoon, okay?" Caroline McNamara had been a mainstay of San Diego news for a decade now. She had this uncanny ability to transcend the screen, sucking in the viewer entirely until you believed she was not only your most striking friend, but your most intelligent and informed. You felt like you could trust her and thereby welcomed her into your home, night after night. It's how KTMW kept their longtime viewership.

"I would kill to have a sliver of the career she's managed for herself," I said. "That's all."

My aunt smoothed the back of my hair affectionately. "Then we have to make sure you get this job. Kristin is a great place to start."

"Shall I send her cake and balloons? A singing telegram along with my reel? How does she feel about Ninja Turtles. I, for one, applaud their comeback and named my dog after one."

Sarah grinned with a twinkle in her eye. "I have a feeling your work will speak for itself, weirdo. And your face. You're gorgeous. You always seem to forget that part."

I shrugged off the compliment. "Just not exactly confident." Since when did San Diego producers care about ribbon cutting ceremonies at the newest ice cream parlor? But I was prepared to give it a shot. If I could simply land an interview, and pick up a little in-person momentum, I'd have the chance to sell myself directly. This Kristin person seemed like my first true opportunity, and I had no intention of blowing it. As my family members trickled in one at a time, the evening shifted into a festive one with lots of lively chats and our traditional soccer game in the backyard. Two goals for me and enough exercise to last all week. I had an extra spring in my step now, surrounded by the people I loved, and carrying a little bit of hope in my back pocket. This weekend had been a good choice, and I planned to keep making them.

CHAPTER ONE

The reception area at KTMW wasn't at all glamorous. Three padded gray waiting room chairs were pushed together in a row across from a friendly receptionist wearing earbuds and drinking a large iced coffee that made her hand look minuscule each time she hefted it to her perfectly glossed lips. An audio version of the morning newscast was piped into the room for us to listen to, and the low-key aroma of lemony cleaner filled my nostrils. My left leg bounced a little in anticipation of this interview, which had been so shocking to land that I still wasn't quite sure it was actually going to occur. I had trust issues when it came to exciting things happening to me because they rarely did. When I checked in, I was sure the receptionist was going to say that she didn't see me on the schedule and send me on my way. When she told me to take a seat and that Kristin would be with me shortly, everything in me sang. I looked two chairs over at the guy about my age clutching a leather portfolio and wondered if he was one of my competitors for the job. He glanced back at me and offered a nod. Good-looking, coiffed hair, tailored blue suit. Highly likely. He fit the part. Suit guy licked his bottom lip, and I decided I wasn't a fan. He was too put together. Perfect in excess. That had me nervous. My insecurities fired as I noticed a small scuff on the side of my left pump. I'd mastered the art of wearing heels over the years, tromping through tough terrain with my microphone. Anything for the right shot. If only I was as polished as Coiffed-R-Us over there—and now I had a scuff. Okay, now I was just being petty. He was likely a really nice guy, but dammit, he wasn't going to take this job from me. Scuff be damned.

"Skyler Ruiz?"

My attention snapped to a blonde standing in the doorway with a file folder in her hands. Pretty. No scuffs on *her* heels. Gray dress with a black belt. Kind eyes and a luminous smile.

"Yes, hi. That's me." I stood, knowing suit guy was watching our interaction. Hell, maybe I made *him* nervous. I passed him a grin over my shoulder that was friendly, yet confident. *Bam.* Time to get this show on the road and find myself a foothold. My only shot.

The blonde extended her hand. "Kristin James. Nice to meet you. I've heard a lot of positive things."

"Well, it's true. I excel at pool handstands, but I'm confident that's not what you mean."

Kristin laughed, and I was glad she was down for a joke. "No, no. Those come with their own merit and will be noted." She gestured to a door to the right, flanking the open newsroom. "We'll be joined today by our news director, Gilbert Tam. Right through here."

"Great," I said and followed her into the spacious, though overly cluttered, office. File folders, stacks of manuals, books piled high, and several TV monitors along an extra desk, all turned on with the sound down. The office gave off a very busy vibe, but that was the nature of news. A man with dark hair, a rumpled shirt, and a maroon tie stood as we entered. He extended one hand in my direction and in the other clutched an everything bagel with cream cheese smeared high. As he leaned, he glanced down at my résumé visible on his desk for a name prompt. "Skyler Ruiz."

"That's me. A pleasure to meet you, Mr. Tam."

"Just Tam. We're pretty informal around here. You're lucky I buttoned my shirt. Kidding. Have a seat." Except his kidding was a firm deadpan. That would take some getting used to. As I sat, Tam's eyes drifted to a TV monitor behind me. When he saw me watching him, he grabbed the remote and had the courtesy to turn them all off, giving me his undivided attention. "Sorry about that. Never stops." He gestured to the monitor with his pen. "There's a robbery in progress that we're keeping an eye on at a bank just outside of town. Could be a standoff. We have a crew on the scene now assessing the situation."

I scooted to the edge of my seat before I realized I'd done it. Now this was the kind of news that got my blood pumping. "That's great."

His brows dropped.

I heard my words. "I mean, it's not *great*. That there's a bank robbery or that someone might get hurt, just that you're on top of it."

Kristin nodded. "No worries. I don't think anyone cheers for a bank robbery."

"Depends on if we're in the middle of sweeps or not," Tam said, blank faced. He then cracked a hint of a smile that let me know he was joking again.

Kristin took over. "Skyler, as you know, we're hiring a reporter, mainly for our broadcasts at five and ten, but there would be some morning assignments here or there just depending on where our holes are."

"Understood."

"Tell us about you and your point of view. Who would we be hiring?"

I didn't hesitate. This was my elevator speech, and I'd practiced it more times than I could say. "I'm an eager, hardworking journalist who is new enough to know that I have lots to learn, but hungry enough to waste no time learning it. On the flip side, I've had time at my station to truly hone my craft and know that I want to tackle hard-hitting news that informs and transforms."

"Okay, I hear you. I like that," Kristin said with a smile.

"But what does that mean?" Tam asked, frowning. "Cut to it."

I met his gaze. "It means I'm good at my job but bored as hell out in the boonies. If you put me to work for you, I won't stop until I have the story, and you can trust that it will be the right one."

"I like that better," Tam said. He scribbled something in his notebook. "I watched your reel. It's not bad reporting, but it's not exactly what we do here."

"Which is what makes me want the job."

"But are you ready?" Kristin asked. "That's my question. This place isn't for the faint of heart." It looked to me like Kristin might have firsthand experience with that last part.

I locked eyes with her. "I'm more than ready. All I need is a chance."

Tam held up his phone. "We send you to the bank. What do you do?"

I didn't hesitate. "A statement from the PIO. Tons of B-roll and talk to the witnesses."

"They'd don't want to talk to you," Tam shot back. "Their loved one is still inside, a hostage, and they want to be left alone. Did the elementary school field day prepare you for that?"

"I explain to them that putting a plea out there, on camera, might actually help the situation. Humanize the captors and connect them to life outside the bank, to a family that loves the hostage. They'd no longer just be a number."

He tossed his pen onto the desk. "Do you believe that?"

"Yes."

"And if you didn't, would you say so to get the interview?"

I hesitated.

"So you have a moral compass. That can hold you back."

"It can also steer me toward the *right* story. I don't get caught up in sensationalism."

Tam sat back in his chair, and I couldn't tell whether my comment had resonated or offended. I opened my mouth to elaborate, but he cut me off, asking questions about the kinds of assignments I'd done at my current station, my education, my goals. Boring stuff. Nothing that would get me this job. I had a sinking feeling.

The interview seemed to end before it began, and I was left with so much I wanted to say.

"Thank you for coming in, Skyler," Kristin said. She closed her notebook and stood. "We have quite a few applicants to meet with, but we'll review your reel again and be in touch."

"It was a pleasure," Tam said and began switching on his monitors, ready to scope out the competitors' coverage on that bank, no doubt. It didn't seem like I'd left much of an impression. I had to say something, but this didn't feel like the right moment. Didn't matter. The words were on their way.

"Have you ever known deep down that you were meant to do something specific?" And there they were.

Kristin studied me. "I've felt drawn to certain things, sure."

I had a fire in me. "I've always known that I was meant to be a journalist, but I haven't been given much of a chance to prove it where I work." I shifted my gaze from Kristin to Tam. "If you hire me, you'll be hiring someone who is hungry beyond measure. I will work tirelessly for you and make sure you never regret it. When you're sleeping, I'm looking for that next story. A tiger on the hunt. I have an eagle eye for important story details and strong connections with people. I know I can do a good job here. I apologize for all the wildlife imagery, but it feels apt." I nodded and exhaled. "Thank you for speaking with me today. I hope to hear from you. Let me be the best risk you've ever taken."

I saw them exchange a look I couldn't decode as I exited the office. My feet stopped moving for a moment, however, when my eyes took in a beautiful blonde, standing at a desk across the room. Caroline McNamara. Right there in front of me. I swallowed, my skin prickling. The cameras didn't do her justice. She was quite simply striking beyond all measure. Large blue eyes, hair that fell in perfect layers just past her shoulders. She was taller than I'd realized. Maybe five seven? I wouldn't know for sure unless I got closer, which of course I wouldn't. She was concentrating on something and then shifted her focus across the room as if looking for someone specific. Her eyes landed on mine briefly before continuing to scan.

"Skyler?" Kristin said. Right. She was supposed to be walking me out.

"Coming." I thanked her again and resisted the urge to take a final look at the woman I'd long admired. Suit guy was still in the waiting room when I breezed past him, unsettled by my interview and simultaneously wondering if his perfect polish would leave a stronger impression than the farm reporter from the middle of nowhere who wasn't thrilled with her shoes and kept mentioning animals.

All I could do was hope they called.

I wasn't prepared for them to do so, however.

I'd grown used to my rut and expected to stay in it. When my phone rang three weeks later as I stood in the middle of a high school football game, waiting for the giant bird mascot to kick the festivities off with his traditional march around the field, I was nervous to slide onto the call.

"This is Skyler," I said with feigned confidence. Just me, answering any old call on a Tuesday.

"Skyler, Gilbert Tam."

"Mr. Tam, how are you?" I prayed the crowd noise wasn't too loud, but the bird was on the field now, and the people were going nuts for his blue ass.

"Just Tam, remember?" He didn't wait for a response, his tone terse, like I was one of many things on his morning to-do list. I put a finger in my ear to hear him better. "Listen, we've talked about it. You want to give this thing a shot?"

My breath caught. No buildup, no polite exchange, just *bam*. Was he saying what I thought he was saying? Was this the job offer I'd been trying to manifest, envisioning myself taking such a call every night as I lay in bed? I flipped around, away from the field. Greg was a pro and would be sure to grab the marching bird footage. He didn't need me for that. "I do. Yeah. Very much." My mouth fell open, and I swiveled around again, facing the field, because I had no idea what to do with myself in this very exciting and unlikely moment. Galloping fucking gazelles, I was getting out of the small-town news business and moving up.

Tam pressed on. "Fantastic. I can offer a six-month contract and see how things go. From there, we can decide if it's a good fit. The salary is not really negotiable."

I was supposed to speak now, given it was the customary thing to do when it was your turn. I closed my mouth and searched for words because, dammit, speaking was what I did for a living, and I needed to continue doing that, so I could eat food. "Great. Yes. All of it. The money. Six months." Way to play hard to get. I amended, "Six months is workable, I mean." It was a test. I had to prove myself in that time or they'd cut me loose. Big stations didn't blink when it came to firing reporters who weren't working out. It was the longtime personalities they held on to. People like Caroline McNamara and Rory Summerton. Rory had struck a chord with the San Diego community a few years back when he went rogue and fired off a monologue about the evils of corporate greed. I'd thought for sure he'd be axed, but to my amazement his star only rose. People felt like he'd stood up for them. I couldn't help but wonder if Caroline, being female, would have received that same treatment. The news industry was as sexist as any other, if not more so, unfortunately.

"Can you start the first of the month?" Tam asked.

I blinked. "Yeah. I can make that happen." I wished I sounded smooth. The next sentence was out of my mouth before I could stop it. "What made you decide to give me a shot?" I sounded needy. I was.

A pause. "Your reel showed a spark, presence, but I wouldn't have hired you off it. It was the last thing you said before walking out of my office, about hunger, drive. That's what I need about now. A reporter who will beg, borrow, and kill for the story. If that's you, that's the kind of change I want in my newsroom. I've gone with the seasoned hires in the past, and I wind up with complacent. I need someone with something to lose—and that's gonna be you."

"You can say that again."

He laughed. "HR will be in touch to get you set up. Don't make me regret this."

I thanked him and clicked off the call just in time for that bird to take another lap. The crowd of about two hundred began to whoop and holler even louder. I smiled at them and did a little whooping of my own. Greg glanced in my direction with his eyebrow raised because since when did I whoop on the job? I was no regular whooper. Plus, I was pretty sure my new gig wouldn't come with a lot of whooping, so it was best I lived it up now. I wanted to hug everyone I saw. Jump up and down with them. I grooved to the music on my hot drive home. It wasn't until I was alone in my kitchen that it hit me: abject terror. I was in the big leagues now, and that meant I had to get it together, remember everything I'd learned in school and at the station, and try not to embarrass myself or, worse, lose my job at the end of six months.

Then it got even more terrifying.

I'd be working on the same news team as Caroline McNamara. Reporting the news alongside a woman I considered to be the best in the business. I gripped my sink as I mulled over how to rationalize that little tidbit of information. Colleagues. Fellow journalists. Maybe even pals. Also, where had all the air gone? I gave my head a disbelieving shake. "Well, okay then. Caroline McNamara, here I come. Make some room."

CHAPTER TWO

Where do you want your kitchen thingies?" my little cousin Grace asked, carrying a box with my handwriting scrawled on the outside. I was trying to employ the organizational skills I didn't actually possess.

I quirked my lips. "The kitchen?"

"Good choice," Grace said, her approval on display. I felt like I'd just passed a new-home dweller's test as administered by a teenager. She breezed past, and I exchanged a look with Emory.

"Is there another answer?"

"It's Grace," Emory said with a grin as she sliced into a box of books, and I got it. My younger cousin was a free spirit and could easily imagine my kitchenware hanging above my bed if I expressed such an interest. "When's the big day? Kristin said they had your desk cleaned off and ready to go."

"Monday. Which will be here before I know it."

Emory blew a strand of blond hair out of her eyes and began alphabetizing the books on my newly put together bookshelf. "Well, I personally can't wait to watch you on my television."

Sarah ran a hand along Emory's back as she passed through. "We're going to watch every night. Maybe have ice cream. Or popcorn. Or both."

I frowned. "Please don't mix them."

Sarah's eyes sparkled with inspiration as Emory kissed her hand. "I might go off the snack rails. You don't know."

"But I do," Emory said. "I've seen you in action and have not recovered from the chocolate salmon experiment of two years ago."

"It was worth trying. Now we know."

Emory nodded. "It was traumatic in multiple ways, but I love you anyway."

I laughed. The two of them were my favorite couple ever. Complete opposites, with glamorous Emory serving as the conservative, stoic type and Sarah, bursting with energy, unabashedly wearing her feelings on her sleeve. My cousin was the type to take life by the horns and live every moment to the fullest. However, she was certainly rubbing off on Emory, who had really softened up over the years. It was clear she thought Sarah hung the moon. I wanted that for myself someday. Hoped for it.

In the meantime, I shrugged and absorbed the nervous jolt of energy that shot through me at the idea that I was about to take a big leap and lasso my dream job. Monday was days away. I wasn't going to sleep the night before. I could already tell. Getting my new apartment set up had certainly helped occupy my brain and kept it from going into overthinking mode. The two-bedroom located on the second floor was small but modern with a bedroom on either side of the living room, roommate style. I was planning to use the extra room as an office and had already come up with a list of recipes to try in my new kitchen. I also planned to sit on the little balcony that overlooked a glamorous paid parking lot to decompress after a long day at work. Luckily, the downtown apartment was located only a handful of blocks from the station. I could walk to work if the weather was nice enough. Then again, if the gig didn't work out, I would be forced to live in close proximity to my biggest failure and probably end up with a job as a server at a nearby dive restaurant all the while watching the news each night on the TV at the bar, and wondering desperately just where it all went wrong. Yep. That was how my brain worked.

"You guys don't have to watch," I told Emory and Sarah. "In fact, you should probably give me a few weeks to learn the ropes before tuning in. Let me fall on my face quietly. You know, without the fanfare."

"Not gonna happen," Sarah said, wiping down a lamp. "I will experience every moment."

"Me, too," Grace said coming around the corner. "And if you fall flat on your face, I can capture the spiral in a documentary about the end of your career and submit it to every festival. I'd be a decorated filmmaker before my sophomore year in college. Scholarship central. Think of the tubas I could afford."

I gasped. "Grace, I would murder you."

Grace nodded. "Well, that documentary certainly took a twist. Make that my freshman year."

I laughed, reveling in the wash of warmth that came with being back here, among the people I loved. "You can thank me later."

I spent the weekend decorating the apartment with little touches, finding just the right spot for this painting or that lamp, relishing the details that were already making the place feel like mine, wearing myself out with work. Then, it arrived.

Monday.

❖

I'd been right. I hadn't slept. I had my ironed suit all laid out and timed my short drive in advance. I was told there was a nine a.m. story meeting, so I made sure to arrive at KTMW by eight. I waited in the lobby as my heart thudded and palms sweated until an assistant from the assignment desk, Mila, showed up moments later to walk me in. I hadn't been given my electronic badge just yet.

"Welcome to KTMW." She beamed. "What station are you coming from?"

I met her friendly gaze. Dark hair like mine. Similar age. Shorter. "I was at WBBA before this."

"Oh yeah, up the highway a few hours."

"That's the one."

"Very cool. You'll be over here."

She had an interesting look on her face as she led me to a desk toward the back of the newsroom, probably trying to piece together how I'd gone from a small-time station to this one without anything in between. Same, Mila. Same.

The newsroom was already hopping with people moving around, asking each other questions across the open space. The morning broadcast had been on air since six and would carry through until nine. A good portion of staff who'd been there since the wee hours would hang on for a bit and then shuffle home as the evening folks arrived to prep their day and the newscasts ahead.

I eyed the spot next to me. "Whoever sits there is incredibly neat," I said to Mila with a laugh. The desk was full of supplies, all sectioned off and in their own spots around the perimeter with the help of actual dividers, leaving the main portion of the desk completely empty. I'd never been that put together in my entire life. Someone had taken the time.

Mila laughed. "That's Carrie for you. I have to get back to the phones, but is there anything you need?"

I looked at the boxes of office supplies and the laptop that had been left on my desk for me. "Nope. I'll just get myself set up and then head to the story meeting soon."

Mila nodded, walking backward, the incessant ringing of the phones acting as her beacon. "Great. Conference room right over there. Meeting's at nine. There'll be coffee and pastries. All the good stuff."

"Awesome." Already an upgrade from the bring-your-own policy at my old station. I got to slicing open the packages of Post-its, staples, pens, and more when my overly meticulous neighbor arrived in my peripheral.

"Hi, I'm Sky—" The words died on my lips, and I squeezed the pad of blue Post-its way too hard, bending them into a wonky shape. It wasn't Carrie, my obscure desk neighbor, who'd arrived. It was Caroline McNamara who—I sighed internally—clearly went by Carrie. That meant I now sat next to Caroline McNamara on a daily basis. My brain wasn't quite sure what to do with that information. I was equal parts thrilled and terrified. Maybe we'd be friends. I'd bring an extra coffee for her. She'd tell me the latest anecdote from her drive to work. We'd laugh over little things.

"Sky?" She seemed puzzled. "You're a new reporter?" She said it as if we happened a lot, which jibed with the revolving door Tam had alluded to.

"Skyler, actually, and yes. First day. But you can call me Sky. If you want."

"Do most people?"

"Well…no."

"Skyler then. Welcome," she said, her attention already on her screen. Of course it was. It was Monday morning, and there was surely a lot to catch up on. I stayed out of her way, stealing glances here and there until it was time for the morning story meeting. I arrived in the conference room with my laptop open, my coffee doctored, and my excitement level dialed to high. The room filled up over the next ten minutes, and I went out of my way to introduce myself to everyone I could. They seemed busy, but friendly enough. There were three other reporters that I recognized in attendance, and probably others I needed to learn about. A handful of producers filed in already in quiet conversation with one another, and just before we got going, Caroline and Rory, the evening anchors, joined us, taking the seats at the center of the table. While they wouldn't go out on stories themselves, they likely wanted to be in the loop about what kinds of stories were in the works. I also knew from my time as a viewer that Caroline occasionally took on special feature stories that they'd advertise ahead of time. Interviews with high-profile people. Celebrities. An intimate look at pertinent subject matter. All good stuff.

"All right. Let's go ahead and get started. It's looking to be a busy day ahead," Kristin said, offering me a smile before kicking things off. "First of all, good morning, everyone, and a warm welcome to our newest reporter joining our team today, Skyler Ruiz." The room collectively nodded in my direction and smiled.

"Thank you. Happy to be on board." I smiled, but the moment quickly passed, and we moved on to the objective, mapping out the day's stories.

Kristin raised her eyebrows in expectation. "What do we have today? Carlos, let's start with you."

Carlos Benavides. I'd seen him on air. He was good, but a bit too presentational in his style, in my opinion. He came with a lot of hair, though, styled into a very impressive swirl. He sat forward. "Those giant birds are invading the area around Mission Bay again. Egrets. They smell awful, and the residents are over it."

"If you can get me good B-roll of the birds in large groups, then it's a maybe," Kristin said with a shrug. She didn't seem all that jazzed. As a general rule, the station would have way more stories in the works than would ever make it to air that day. Some stories wouldn't pan out. Others would be bumped when something last-minute broke. In sculpting a broadcast, especially one that was changing by the minute, more was more. It was important, as a reporter, that my story made it to air each day, and I would work tirelessly to make that happen.

"On it."

She consulted her laptop screen. "There was a robbery on Eighth this morning. Shots were fired, but no one was hit."

"Boring," Rory said, and he looked it. Huh. Where was the passionate guy I'd seen so many times on air? "We get ten of those a week."

"Doesn't mean we don't check them out," Kristin said calmly. I could see why she produced, the picture of calm and collected over there. She ran through a few more of the city's overnight happenings. A congressman with a vandalized home. Snatched up immediately. A press conference held by a gubernatorial hopeful. Grabbed. I was missing out. Two more stories were nabbed, and I was left wondering what I would do with my afternoon. I hadn't wanted to seem overzealous on the first day, but maybe I'd blown it.

"I could take the robbery story," I said, raising my hand. "See if there are any details that might make it more compelling."

Caroline raised her gaze and studied me as if perplexed. I was now very aware of myself and wondered if I'd somehow said something wrong or strange. Maybe I had lipstick on my chin. I slyly swiped at it.

Kristin, however, nodded in support, so whatever it was couldn't have been that bad. "Thank you, Skyler. Give it a shot, and let me know. Take Ty. Your photog. You'll work primarily with him. He knows the city well." I nodded, took down his name, and would find him when the meeting concluded. I listened as the fifteen or so people in the room went back and forth, pitching ideas, updating the producers on what they had in the works. Even Tam stepped into the space before the meeting concluded.

"Carrie, where are we on the home-invasion segment?" he asked. He turned to Kristin. "Weren't we looking to slot it at the end of the five o'clock next Thursday?"

Caroline didn't hesitate. Her eyes flashed. "I need a tighter edit on the reenactment footage, and I've asked for it four times, even left my notes."

"Let me look into the delay," Kristin said. "We'll get it turned around."

I blinked. This was a side of Caroline McNamara I'd yet to see. Calm. Confident. Pointed. Gone was the overt on-air warmth I'd come to identify her with. This version was kind of a badass, and I liked it. I grinned as I took in the rest of the story meeting, feeling like one of the pack. It was a whirlwind of fast-paced planning and organization, and I couldn't have been happier. When I arrived back at my desk, Carrie was just a few seconds behind me. I heard her heels clicking across the floor. She took a seat at her desk and looked over.

"Can I ask a question?" She didn't wait for a reply "Why take the robbery story? It's a dud."

I thought on it, intimidated. "Just trying to be a team player."

She nodded. "Admirable. But who is that going to benefit in the end?" She raised an eyebrow. "Not you."

I opened my mouth, but she was up and moving already, having moved on from our interaction, probably off to see about that re-edit she needed. I felt silly now for laying up in the meeting. She was right. I had six months to make my mark or be shipped out and needed to step up more and back up the hunger I'd professed to Tam.

"Are you Ty?" I asked one of the camera guys hanging out near the editing bays.

"Nope. Over there," the man said. I followed his gaze to a guy with an athletic build, a backward baseball cap, and a pair of cargo shorts. His hair was a mixed mop of blond, brown, and strawberry sticking out from underneath the cap in a variety of directions.

"What can I do for you?" he asked with a big smile.

"I'm Skyler Ruiz. New reporter."

"Another one," Ty said and exchanged a look with the first guy. "Revolving door of you guys around here. Luckily, you seem friendly. Do you like food? I'm a big eater."

"I'm not opposed to it."

"Awesome. We'll be buds. What's up?"

"Kristin said I should grab you. I'm headed out to cover an early morning robbery on Eighth. A 7-Eleven."

"And you want me to tag along. Snag some shots."

"I was hoping you'd be game. She said we'd be working together."

"We will. Just wanted to make you ask." He grabbed a backpack and car keys from the wall. "Let's ride. Maybe I can score a midmorning Slurpee. They better have lime, man. Those places always have cherry and cola only, and I don't get that. The world is bigger than that, ya know? We need the green. And not apple either. Lime."

"I will hope for lime on your behalf."

"Hey, I appreciate that."

Ty meant it, too. Twenty minutes later, while I located the manager at 7-Eleven who'd been on duty when the place was robbed, Ty made a dash for the back of the store and filled up an obscenely large cup with a bright blue slushy drink.

"Tell me exactly what happened last night," I said to the young guy who'd agreed to speak with me. Brown spiky hair and a nose ring. Once I got his story, we could record some B-roll footage of the store and get a few sound bites from him that could be edited into a short package later.

"Right. So a kid came in wearing a gray hoodie, closed up tight. I could barely see his eyes. No one was in the store but me."

I jotted a few notes. "Tell me about your interactions with him."

"He put a Snickers on the counter and then said that if I wanted to live I should give him all the money in the register."

"He held a gun on you?"

"No, but there was one in his pocket. I thought he was faking me out, so I told him to go to hell. Next thing I know there's a bullet in the floor, and I'm tap-dancing."

I looked behind me at the very noticeable mar in the black and white linoleum. "How'd that happen?"

"Got me." He scratched the back of his head. "Thing went off, I guess. Shit. I about jumped out of my shorts."

Ty took a long pull from his straw as he sidled up next to me. "No lime."

"I gathered."

"Blueberry works, though." He held it up to the manager. "Pumped you have more than cherry, bud. Good lookin' out."

The employee offered a fist bump, which Ty reciprocated. "I got you."

I broke up the new bromance. "Okay, so the gun went off. There's the hole in the floor. Then what happened?"

"Once he shot, the kid took off. I think he scared himself to death. Ran down the street like a little bitch. Didn't even take the Snickers."

"So a botched robbery. Anything stand out to you?" This was going nowhere, which was to be expected, but I was really hoping to come back with something for Kristin. Prove myself on my first time out.

"Other than the fact that his name was stitched on his damn backpack. Who does that? Robs a store with their name on their bag?"

Interesting. "What was the name?"

"Seth. Big letters. I bet he runs with a group of kids that are in here a lot. They don't have much to do and get into trouble. It's a fucked-up cycle that really speaks to the decline of our community in the face of near recession. *Freakonomics* at work."

Huh. I hadn't seen the insight coming. And Seth was such an innocuous name. Why couldn't he have been Razorblade or Muppet Man or Mooch. Anything memorable. "Mind if we talk to you on camera now?"

He puffed up like a D-list celebrity who'd just been recognized. "Not at all. Think the other stations will be by?"

I didn't. There was no story here. For a city the size of San Diego, an accidental bullet in the floor of a would-be robbery scene was not a big deal. Caroline was right. I should have fought for something meatier. That was on me. My only chance of salvaging this thing was to play up the emotion of the incident, get the manager to explain his fear, and focus on the happy ending tied in a neat little bow with a Snickers on top. Even then, the only chance the piece would see air was if it was the slowest news day ever.

"Anything good?" Mila from assignments asked when I called in. She'd be gathering up all potentials and helping the producers understand what stories they had coming in.

"Not a lot here. No," I told her honestly.

"Okay. I'm gonna send you to the council meeting, then. You have maybe thirty minutes to get over to City Hall. Room three. Can you swing it?"

"Yep." I closed my eyes and nodded, cringing because of the mundane nature of the coverage. Hell, they didn't even need a reporter there, just Ty with a question or two in his back pocket should they need a sound bite. I pushed through the afternoon, feeling defeated and silly for arriving with a whimper.

"Hey, new kid. You'll get 'em next time," Ty said and bopped me on the shoulder. He lifted his camera. "Gonna get started editing the convenience store footage, just in case."

"I wouldn't waste too much time on it," I said with a sigh. There was something about his energy that I liked, though. Goofy, but at the same time steady and confident. I felt like I could count on Ty, which was what you wanted in a partnership.

"How'd that robbery thing go?" Carlos asked with a grin, leaning against my desk as I sat with a sigh.

"Not much there," I said honestly. "And the smelly birds?"

"Total infestation. Great visuals of the flocks hanging in the trees, bird crap everywhere, and some testimony from some really irate homeowners, one in a bathrobe. They're running with it at five and likely ten, too."

"Nice," I said, half-heartedly.

He bopped off into the newsroom and looked back. "My first day? I went blank on a live shot from a car dealership fire. Four seconds of silence on air. I kid you not."

"Really?" It felt like a warm hug. Maybe Carlos wasn't so bad.

"Tell me more." I touched my desk, offering him his seat back like Mrs. Claus beckoning an adorable child.

He returned, his voice quiet. "This is the thing. First days are supposed to suck." He looked around. "Especially in this cutthroat business, where you never know who's gunning for you."

"I'm not used to a competitive newsroom."

"Well, I'm afraid you just got tossed into the deep end without a life jacket." He stood. "Now we see if you can swim, little guppy."

I swallowed because, dammit, I wanted to swim. I just needed to figure out where my confidence had dashed off to. It had come to work with me that morning and drifted away slowly, a lost student on a field trip.

"I didn't see your robbery on our story board," Carrie said, sliding into her chair. I looked up from my newly installed email account on my newly issued laptop, which had clearly seen better days. The *N* key had been completely worn down.

"No. Wasn't much there."

"A shame." She said it without much inflection, almost as if it wasn't worth her attention. I was a gnat in the middle point of her day. I exhaled slowly, not letting it get to me. It did.

"Back at it tomorrow." I offered a smile. She was camera ready in a gorgeous blue suit that matched her eyes, a cream-colored blouse underneath.

She shot me a glance and said nothing as she moved to apply her lipstick in a mirror on a stand she'd produced from her drawer. Still a gnat. I should have left the conversation there. Taken the cue. I didn't.

"That's a great color. The suit."

"Thank you."

"I haven't been down to the studio yet. Maybe I'll check out the broadcast."

"Are you going to try and make conversation there, too?" Her gaze never left the mirror.

"Oh." A pause as I searched for my ego. "No. Not a word." I went back to my email, feeling stepped on and annoyed that I was letting it get to me. This business was not for the weak.

Just then I heard the click, click, click of Caroline's heels on the floor behind me, but I remained in my chair.

I'd see the studio another time.

❖

"It wasn't an awful week at all," Sarah said and dropped a slice of piping hot pepperoni pizza onto her plate. "I'm gonna devour you," she told the pizza. "You had two stories on air."

I bit into a breadstick as I sat at her kitchen table. The view of the pool from this spot was breathtaking. Emory and Sarah had such a gorgeous house. Sprawling white, open floor plan, breathtaking outdoor space, and right on the beach. I felt better just being there. "It was a wake-up call. That was for sure. I'm not in Oklahoma anymore."

Sarah squinted. "You've never lived in Oklahoma."

"What? No. I was referencing *The Wizard of Oz*."

Sarah's mouth fell open and closed. "Kansas. That's Kansas. How do you not know that? We've failed you. Your mother trusted us and we didn't deliver."

I waved her off. "I preferred Ninja Turtles."

She blinked. "You are a unique snowflake, Skyler. But I love you all the same."

"As much as Dorothy loved Dodo?"

She closed her eyes, and I grinned proudly.

Emory joined us with a salad in a giant ceramic bowl that felt criminal when there was fantastic cheesy pizza to eat. Apparently, she was training for a half marathon with Kristin, another health nut. Who had the fortitude for that? Emory was a combination of too many badass traits working together to make us all feel like we'd overslept. Rich, athletic, good-looking, and smart. Didn't seem fair. She looked over at me around a bite of avocado. "Kristin told me on our run that you're finding your stride at the station."

"Well, that's nice to hear." I sat taller. The week *had* improved from that first day. I'd learned where the break room was, managed to get two of my stories to air, and Caroline McNamara had yet to murder me in my chair for existing. I couldn't help but notice how friendly she was to our other coworkers, warm even. Laughing with them. Shooting the breeze in slower moments. Everyone looked to her as a leader and a friend. Yet everything I did just seemed to annoy her.

"Morning, Carrie," I'd said the day before.

"Morning," she said, without looking up. Then louder, "Hey, did we hear from the guy with the snake?"

I searched my brain. "Um. Hmm. I don't think I know about a guy with a snake." I laughed and met her eyes. "I feel like I should, though. That sounds intriguing."

She blinked. "What? No. That was a question for Bruce." Ah, the assistant producer two desks over. I nodded and tried to appear smaller.

"Kristin is kind," I told Emory. "I'm still mildly floundering, like a fish on land, but I'm flopping around less than I was on Monday. The less flopping means progress."

Sarah pointed at me. "That's what I'm talking about. Rome wasn't built in a day. You're gonna be a star reporter soon, but you have to work your way there. Learn everything you can. Be a sponge, *querida*. Flit around and make yourself useful. And bring food. Tons of it. People love it when there's food." She sat back in her chair, wisdom imparted. "Now I'll enjoy this pepperoni gift from heaven."

I laughed. "Pepperoni, then the pool? Is there a chance of that?" I eyed their gorgeous outdoor oasis.

"God, yes," Emory said. "Swimming as the sun goes down is good for the soul."

And swim we did. And laugh. And talk. And even had a little white wine that I might have tossed an ice cube into.

"Pool wine," Sarah said, when I passed her a guilty look. She plopped an ice cube in her glass and we clinked them in cheers.

The next day was Sunday, and I used it to decompress, walking the sidewalk perimeter of my apartment complex with Michelangelo that evening as I texted with Kacey. Bad idea. Alert. Back the hell off. But the familiarity was like a security blanket after a week that had taken its toll. Some lighthearted flirting helped lighten my mood, advised or not. When my phone rang, I slid onto the call. "You're *calling* me now? This has taken a turn."

"Tell me what you're wearing, and don't leave out details." Kacey's voice was a little raspy, which meant I had turned her on with our back and forth. Not surprising. I knew her well enough to know exactly how.

"Oh, you're bad. I can't just hop on to phone sex with you. Nope."

"Why not? I'm off work, and you're my favorite way to unwind." I could tell she was smiling through the phone, envision the sparkle in her brown eyes that she used to charm the ladies. And there were other ladies. She didn't hide that.

"Because then we fall right back into our old habits, and I've already taken things too far with you tonight."

"I'm not the one who had a problem with those habits." Her tone was light, playful, just as it always was. She never offered anything deeper, and I had a feeling that was part of the allure. Her being just out of reach. My self-awareness had to count for something, right?

"Yeah, well, maybe I'm ready to move on from the fun." My smile faltered. "Ground myself in reality."

"You've always been the more mature one." She paused. "So no phone sex. Want to meet up, then? You drive an hour. I drive an hour. I'll even pay for the room. Hell, it's the weekend. We should party, Sky."

A two-person party. I closed my eyes, halting my walk. Micky looked up at me. I couldn't believe I was even considering the offer, but I definitely was. *Stay strong. Be the moose of strength.* I'd always admired moose as a kid and latched on to them as my kindred spirit. I had to be the moose right now and stay brave and steadfast. Had to. *Say the correct words, Skyler.* "I'm afraid I'm too tired to party at a highway hotel tonight. And maybe too old, too."

"I had a feeling you would say that. You break my heart."

"We both know that's not true. Swing by Lonesome's. Maybe a wayward woman will wander in on a pony with a strawberry between her teeth."

"Wayward women in small towns are a myth, Skyler."

"Don't give up hope."

"Yeah, yeah."

I clicked off the call, proud of myself. Look at me, turning pages and looking ahead. My career had taken a giant step forward, and now it was time to take control of my growth as a human. Respect myself more. I rolled my shoulders, energized. Look into having an actual love life at some point. I looked down at Micky as we resumed our walk. "But who even has time for one of those these days?"

He picked up his feet in a jaunty little trot, and I mimicked him.

"Exactly. You get me."

CHAPTER THREE

On the way to glory, there had to be a little grunt work. I hoped that was true and that I didn't make it up just to make myself feel better. I was sent to cover another council budget meeting because I hadn't been scrappy enough in the morning editorial grab-and-go. I did throw my hat in for an arcade that had been caught scamming its customers and rigging the games, but I'd been edged out by seniority. Renee, a glamorous, seasoned reporter who spent more time worrying about her hair and nails than I thought important, insisted she had an inside track and a source. Something I very much doubted. What could I do?

The meeting was drama free, and all motions were approved without much fanfare.

But it was on my way out of the courthouse that my ear was tugged. Not far from the stairs, I heard a loud conversation among a group of police officers shooting the breeze.

"Nah, dude. The money for the cruisers is a done deal. The commissioner is gonna shit a brick when she hears."

Another officer laughed. "Wish I could be there to see the look on her face when she does."

"This is just the beginning, man," a third said with authority. "You think those two are at war now? Gear up. The hatchets are about to start fucking flying."

Huh. I took a seat on the half wall in front of the building and pretended to be interested in my phone as I latched on to bits of the story, assembling the narrative one piece at a time. Apparently, the sheriff had requested funds for three new police cruisers from the commissioner in a public meeting, but for whatever reason, the request was later denied in a closed-door session. If I understood what I was hearing correctly, the money for the cruisers was then donated by a local steak house, which seemed bizarre. Apparently the owner hated the commissioner. I pulled up Kendall Steakhouse's Facebook page, surprised to see the number of posts blasting the commissioner for the cruiser decision, putting them right in the center of what seemed to be a local political feud. Why was no one paying attention? I scanned the page. Because the steak house hadn't tagged anyone directly, and the public figures had kept their views off social media. Who would be keeping tabs on a steak house? Yet this was unique. How often did you have local businesses jumping in the middle of a dispute between two county officials and actually making a difference? I was amazed.

I waited until the group of officers disbanded, leaving just one, who I followed to the café on the first floor of the courthouse. He got in line to pay for his coffee, and hey, look at that, I did, too.

"Hi." I flashed my most winsome smile.

He turned, paused, latched onto my gaze and smiled back. Nailed it. "Hey."

"Officer Blackwell?" I found his name tag easily enough. "Skyler Ruiz."

"Do we know each other?" He was still smiling that easy smile, probably trying to place me.

"No, but I'm a new reporter at KTMW. I wondered if you had a moment to talk about the disagreement over the police cruisers. I heard that Kendall's Steakhouse has agreed to fund the purchase. Would you be willing to chat?"

His eyebrows shot up. He couldn't have been more than twenty-five, and a reporter peppering him with questions he wasn't allowed to answer was likely intimidating. "No comment, ma'am."

I made a point of relaxing. Taking off the reporter hat. "Cool. I get it." A pause. "Well, then can we just have coffee together? New in town." I grinned, holding up my own full cup and doing my best to show off the dimple that had gotten me through closed doors in the past. He passed me a relenting smile back. Score.

"Just coffee would be fine. Yeah." His ears turned red.

"Deal," I said.

We grabbed a table in the courthouse café, and he let me know that his name was Jake and he was waiting to testify about a drunk-driving stop he'd made. I let him know that I was learning the ropes at the station and struggling to get a foothold on a good story. After establishing my—truthful—vulnerability, I eased a strand of hair behind my ear, leaned in, and went for it. "You know, if you were to tell me more about the tension between the sheriff and commissioner, I wouldn't have to use your name in the story. But it might help get me noticed at work where I'm currently crashing and burning. No one ever has to know, and you would be doing me a huge favor."

He looked to the side, nervous. Maybe trying to see who was nearby. Luckily, no one was. We were between mealtimes, and the café was pretty lifeless.

"No interview required," I assured him. "Just point me in the right direction. Help fill in the backstory and maybe give me the name of someone you know from Kendall's who might be willing to talk on record." I sat back. "The thing is, this story is going to happen regardless of you or me. I was just hoping to be the one to bring it home."

He didn't say anything. Neither did I. But I held eye contact and waited, watching as his resolve began to crumble before my eyes. He seemed like a nice guy who wanted to help.

Finally, "Okay, so this is what I know. But keep my name out of it."

"You have my word. I'm just looking for the information that will help me move forward. Just trying to keep my job." Also true.

Jake went on to detail a slowly eroding relationship between Sheriff Patrick Denison and Commissioner Roz Harlow, who had apparently been working behind the scenes to discredit the sheriff. Madame Commissioner had subsequently been caught on video at a Christmas party calling him a petty mama's boy born without balls. Ouch. The video had circulated throughout the police department, humiliating Sheriff Pat, whose son's best friend happened to own Kendall's Steakhouse. The best friend wanted to stick it to the commissioner by undermining *her* for a change, resulting in the police department getting those new cruisers. Kendall's looked like the hero, and the commissioner looked like the big meanie, unwilling to help the city get what it needed to fight crime properly.

I sat back. This was a story the people of San Diego would be interested in. I still couldn't believe no one was reporting on it until now. "This sounds like it's been a crash-and-burn relationship."

"That's what I've seen. Sheriff was pissed, but now he's happy as a tick in a tar bucket." He winced. "Grew up in the South."

"See, now that would be a great quote."

He smiled. "No can do, but I have a feeling the assistant manager over at Kendall's would talk to you. Her name is Essie, and she hates her job. Has one foot out the door already."

I scribbled down the information and smiled at Jake. "You've been such a big help. If there's ever anything I can do for you…"

He stood, his coffee gone. "Have dinner with me. You're really pretty."

"Oh." I winced. "If I wasn't gay, I'd totally be into it."

He rocked back on his heels. "Dammit. Fuck me. My loss."

"But I'd love a new friend."

He nodded. "Fair enough, Ms. Skyler. You've got one. See you around?"

"You will. Take care, Jake. You saved me today, and I will not forget it."

My adrenaline pumped and I bounced on my heels like a prizefighter. This was the kind of work I'd been dreaming about as I twiddled my thumbs at produce festivals. I was finally chasing a *story*, and it felt good. I closed my notebook and pulled out my phone, ready to place a call to one Essie at Kendall's Steakhouse.

"What's going on? You look like a happy little reporter," Carlos said as he rounded the corner from the break room. The traffic pattern flowed around the perimeter of the newsroom, almost like a highway, and my desk offered the perfect rest stop on the curve. People stopped to chat, eat their snack, and shoot the breeze before they carried on. It was actually dumb luck because it gave me the chance to get to know everyone and keep an ear to the ground for what kinds of stories were in the works. The downside was I was a target for idle conversation when I should really be chasing my own stories.

"I am happy. I finally have something in the works." I got back to typing with verve.

"And that would be…?"

I paused. I was still early and maybe spilling to Carlos would be shooting myself in the foot. We worked for the same station, so he wasn't exactly competition. Yet I felt the need to guard what I had like an alert junkyard dog on a gravy mission. "I've got some intel that there's some drama at the sheriff's office."

His eyes went wide and he came closer. "Denison?"

"Yeah. It's actually sounding pretty juicy."

"Tell me what you have, and maybe I can contribute."

I recounted the gist of what I'd learned eavesdropping and the rest from Jake. As I spoke, I caught a glimpse of Carrie passing on the way to her desk. She'd be going live soon for the five o'clock. She was dressed and already through hair and makeup, most of which she did herself. As much as I didn't want to be, I was always acutely aware of her presence. The back of my neck prickled as she got closer, and when she sat down, everything in me tightened just a little bit.

"That does sound juicy," Carlos said. "Have you pitched it to Kristin and co?"

"Not yet. I need attribution. Someone on record. But I have a lead."

"Couldn't hurt to let Kristin know what you have working, though. Keep me posted." Carlos offered me a fist bump, took a bite of his apple, and carried on his way.

A moment of silence passed. "I'd be careful if I was you," Caroline said.

I turned to my right. "Oh. Why do you say that?"

"Well, because this isn't WBBA." She knew where I'd worked last? I filed that away. "The reporters here are cutthroat. They have to be."

My high came crumbling down like the walls of Jericho. I felt warmth hit my cheeks. That always happened when I was embarrassed, dating all the way back to third grade when I'd been asked by Mrs. Middleton to explain why Mars was red but had not read the chapter as assigned.

"Carlos seems harmless. He's actually been the friendliest out of everyone." I said it with a smile, but sure, there was a hint in there. A nod in her less-than-friendly direction.

"And he is. Mostly. But you just gave him a week's worth of information to do with what he wants. He's a story hound, and you're discounting that."

I balked. "Yeah...but I don't get the feeling he'd step on my toes in any way."

She offered me a beautiful smile that said I was so very naive. It made me angry. The know-it-all condescension. "Okay. Then carry on."

"I will."

She studied her screen, and I focused on my social media scour, checking out any interaction between cast members of my burgeoning story. When Caroline headed to the studio, I picked up the phone and placed a call to Essie.

"Interesting," she said, when I explained who I was. "I'll be honest with you, Ms. Ruiz. I'm not a fan of my boss or what went down. The sheriff is an ass and a misogynist." Her voice was loud, brash. Like she didn't care who heard her. This was a woman with an axe to grind, and that made her helpful to my cause.

"I had a feeling, which is why I gave you a call."

A long pause. "Yeah, I'll talk to you."

I hopped in my seat. "Great. Can we set something up for tonight?"

"I can meet you tomorrow."

"Would you be willing to go on camera?" I tried not to hold my breath, but I did scrunch my eyes closed. If she said no, there were ways around it. Change her voice. Use a silhouette.

"Hell, yeah, I would. I have a lot to say, too."

I opened my eyes and nearly dropped my forehead into my hand in relief. Thank God for this woman. "Fantastic," I said, instead of weeping. The desperation I'd been feeling began to evaporate slowly, and I could breathe. A part of me also couldn't wait to show Caroline McNamara that I knew what the hell I was doing and was worthy of this job.

When I arrived home that night with a bag containing a big juicy cheeseburger, Micky's whole body wagged in greeting, and only half of it was for me. I scooped him up and headed to the kitchen. "It's a good day, little guy. And you're getting a few french fries in celebration. Maybe even a bite of this burger. That's right, I said it. French fry heaven awaits us both."

In the morning, I'd meet with Kristin and see if I could shake anything loose at the commissioner's office before moving on to the sheriff's. Time to be the moose I always knew I could be.

I fell asleep full, satisfied, and excited for the next day. Micky the wonder mutt curled into the back of my knees. Not only were things falling into place, but they were happening in the right way. I was working hard. And, damn, it felt good.

CHAPTER FOUR

It was one of those mornings where everything seemed to happen in fast-motion. My breakfast was a rushed banana nut muffin as I scurried to my car. I'd taken the shortcut on my hairstyle, opting for a simple clip in the back, and every traffic light had been green, zipping me into work in a flash.

The story meeting was no different, on fire. Rapid back-and-forths as my brain struggled to stay in the mix.

There was a lot happening in the city that morning, and we were grabbing assignments from Kristin like raindrops in a storm. She studied her iPad, looking smart in a light gray pantsuit and heels. "There's a home dedication in honor of the mayor's wife. Do we want it?" She frowned at Devante, her assistant producer. He nodded.

Renee looked up. "I can cover it. I did that piece on her philanthropy while battling cancer. Could be a full circle follow-up."

Kristin nodded. "Good point." She studied the clock. "You'd have to leave. It's scheduled for half an hour from now. We just got the press release."

Renee stood and gathered her things. "Not a problem. I'll grab Liam." Her camera guy.

"Skyler, can you be on standby to grab a live shot for the five, most likely from the house stabbing from earlier, unless something more timely pops up."

"Yeah, on it," I said, excited and nervous to go live for the first time. Butterflies hit. I'd have to text Yolanda and Sarah and let them know that this was a broadcast to watch. They still got so excited to see me on television. It made me feel ten feet tall, kinda important.

As the meeting concluded, I lingered. "Kristin, can I grab you for a second?"

"Only if you can walk and talk. I have a meeting with Tam and a new sponsor."

I fell into step with her down the long hallway back to her office. "I wanted to let you know about a story I have in the pipeline."

"I love news stories. Tell me more."

I launched into what I knew so far and watched as she raised her eyebrow. "That sounds amazing."

I nodded, pumped just telling the story again. "I thought so, too. It has a lot of interesting angles."

"Except I already gave Carlos the green light."

I opened my mouth and closed it again. Confused. "I don't understand how that's possible. He didn't even know about it yesterday morning."

"I don't know. He pitched it yesterday afternoon."

After we talked, my brain supplied: *Fuck. Me.* Kristin must have seen the look on my face. "Hey, follow me in here."

I was too numb to do anything but obey her very basic command. She closed the door to her office, which was a lot smaller than Tam's. She regarded me with a gentle expression on her face. "Did he take what you were working on and run with it?"

I swallowed. "I think so." I felt the blood drain from my face, my happy little balloon popped.

"Okay. As your assistant news director, I want you to continue working on it, and we'll see who comes up with the best story."

"All right," I answered, digging my fingernails into the palm of my hand painfully.

"But between us? As your friend, I want your story to beat his ass and take this thing home, okay? I'm rooting for *you*. You can do this." She gave my shoulder a little shake of encouragement and opened the door, her blue eyes meeting mine. "I need to get to that meeting. Don't give up. Bust this thing wide open."

"I'm gonna try."

I stood outside Kristin's office for a few moments, letting it all sink in. He'd duped me. That son of a bitch Carlos had made me feel like we were friends, that he was my cheerleader, when all the while he was snaking my story. I shook my head, cursing myself for falling for it. I heard Carrie's warning echo in my head and hated that she'd been right all along. Didn't matter. I shoved it aside and stormed back to my desk, hell-bent on bagging this story.

I was scheduled to meet Essie near the steak house in under an hour, and I needed to grab my belongings and my goofy camera guy and get on the road.

"Everything okay?" Carrie asked. Probably because I'd been slamming things from my desk into my bag without regard for discretion or peace. With each second that passed, my blood boiled hotter. I scanned the newsroom for Carlos, my newest nemesis. He was missing, probably hunting down my story, and as someone who'd worked in this city for longer, he already had plenty of contacts and sources.

I turned to Carrie reluctantly, tail between my legs. "Carlos pitched my story to Kristin."

She sighed and rolled her lips in. "Of course he did." She paused. "I'm sorry, for what it's worth, but hopefully you'll remember this moving forward. Keep the good ones close until the story is yours officially."

I closed my eyes briefly. The last thing I needed was an *I told you so* moment, and that's what this felt like. I wished I could be gracious, accept the wisdom of someone I looked up to. It would have been the humble approach. Instead, I nodded curtly, slung my bag onto my shoulder, and hightailed it out of there.

"You ready, Sky Blue?" Ty asked, turning in his chair as I approached his editing bay.

I ignored the nickname because I didn't mind it and popped my sunglasses onto my face, ready to take control of this situation and reclaim what was mine. "Let's ride."

On the drive over, I seethed and planned. My phone pinged with a message from Kacey. *What color is your bra? I need a distraction.*

I exhaled slowly. There was no space in my brain. Kacey wanted to extract what she needed in the moment and then flit away again, ignoring everything I'd said just a few nights prior. Annoying.

Not going there with you. Please respect my request. I hit send and stared out the window at the gorgeous day, offering a way too pretty backdrop to the city on a morning that felt fraught.

Yep. Later.

The chilly response hit me harder than I would have predicted, hanging over me like a pesky cloud, but I had to shove it all aside and focus on the day in front of me. There was work to do, and now it was more important than ever.

Ty and I arrived at Harbor Park and set up near the picnic tables in the spot Essie and I had agreed to meet. I took a moment to bask in its beauty overlooking the Bay, the sun's rays sparkling on the distant water's surface. The shoreline path would make for such a gorgeous morning walk. I made a note to come back someday and spend more time here. Bask. As we waited, I pored over my questions, rearranging their order in a strategy I hoped would encourage more detailed answers. Always best to warm them up first with some softballs. In the midst, I checked my watch, scanned the surrounding area. She was late.

Ty was mid-handstand next to a tree. He glanced over at it. "Do we look alike?" he called.

"Twins," I shot back and searched the nearby trail for any sign of a woman who could be Essie. Nothing. Ty then climbed the tree and picked out a nice branch to chill on. "I don't see your woman, and I got a great view. She message you?"

I checked my phone for the eighty-fourth time. "Nope. I'll call her."

But she didn't pick up. We waited an hour. Ty made friends with the local squirrels, and I wondered if he'd join them and serve as their leader. At the ninety-minute mark, I had to call it, gutted. As we drove back to the station, I grappled with defeat, holding back frustrated tears.

"Hey, don't sweat it, kid," Ty said affectionately, though he had to be close to my age. "Maybe she just got her times confused. I do that a lot."

"No. I think she stood us up on purpose." I exhaled slowly. "Had a change of heart." I looked over at him, unkempt strawberry-blond hair bouncing as he bopped his head to the music. "Ever have a day that just absolutely sucks?"

"Only like every Thursday. You gotta buck up on days like that. Go extra hard. Take no prisoners and then smile later with a cold one and maybe a game of pool. You know, if that's your thing."

"Not bad advice. Go hard. Have a cold one."

When I arrived back at the newsroom, it was busier than when I left. The clock was ticking, and as stories fell into place, copy needed to be written for the broadcast. The various producers had their noses down and their fingers typing. The phone lines at the assignment desk rang incessantly, providing a shrill soundtrack as reporters put final touches on whatever they had in the works for the five o'clock.

Devante popped his head up from his workstation. "Skyler, you're a go on the live shot from that home stabbing, which has since turned into a murder. The victim died an hour ago, and police are still processing the scene. Just messaged you all the details we have so far."

I nodded, switching gears. "Got it. I'll take a look and get out there." Thank God I'd worn my nicest blue pants and jacket combo. The station didn't provide a clothing allowance to reporters, so it was up to me to make sure I could keep up with my colleagues, and suits weren't cheap.

Ty and I were on the scene with the live truck operator an hour before the broadcast. I spoke with the public information officer on the scene, the handful of neighbors who'd gathered near the home. I spent the remaining minutes practicing the bumper, which would tease the segment and the lead-in I'd offer live, once the anchors tossed it to me. I'd done these kind of shots a million times, but this one felt more important. Given the nature of the crime and the number of viewers who would tune in, it was.

The IFB in my ear allowed me to hear the audio of the broadcast as well as Kristin's voice in the booth. "About to toss to you, Skyler," she said. "Stand by."

"Ready."

Caroline's voice transitioned us. "Unfortunate news on the west side this morning when a mother of two was stabbed to death in her home. We're going live to Skyler Ruiz for the latest."

That was my cue, and I looked straight into Ty's lens. "Thank you, Caroline. I'm in front of the home of thirty-four-year-old Delores Menders, who was stabbed multiple times in what police now believe was a home invasion gone wrong. It's believed that the perpetrators entered from the rear of the home. The screen was cut and the lock broken." I paused there for the short narrated package full of B-roll footage to run. When it finished, I nodded at the camera. "From the west side, Skyler Ruiz."

"Skyler, thank you." We should have been finished but Carrie didn't transition. "So there were two intruders or was it more?"

I blinked. "At this time, the police are unsure of how many entered the home."

"You said *perpetrators*. Plural."

"Carrie, what the hell?" Kristin said in our ears. "Hand it to weather."

I nodded, holding steady. "I did, Caroline, but the truth is we just don't know."

"I see. Thank you for clarifying that detail for our viewers. Now let's turn to Genevieve with what sounds like a wet week ahead. How soon are we gonna need our umbrellas?"

"We're out," Ty said, stepping back from his camera and dropping his arms.

I stared at the ground, feeling blindsided. "I said *perpetrators*. The default should have been *perpetrator* if we didn't know how many. Why did I do that?"

Ty shook his head. "It doesn't matter. That was fucking uncalled for. She didn't need to put you on the spot. I've never heard her do that before."

I hadn't either, and I'd watched her for years. "Doesn't matter." I let my arm still holding the microphone drop to my side. I didn't like the stunt Carrie had just pulled, but at the same time, the error was mine. I'd misspoken. I thought about my family watching at home, the viewers who were just getting to know me. Embarrassment bullied its way on the scene, followed by frustration, anger, and the feeling that I was just done with today. I'd been swindled, stood up, and now humiliated.

Stick a fork in me.

❖

I didn't go home. I should have, but I didn't.

It was pouring. The storm came out of nowhere with big dark clouds and made itself known with ominous rumbling. I couldn't help but feel the parallel to my own life's trajectory. Though I was upset and worn down, I was also hungry. Luckily, I had some chips in my desk. For now, a warm cup of coffee would help wake me up, so I could come up with what the hell I was going to do now that I'd pretty much lost the heart of my story. I was dead in the water, with Carlos likely racing around town, gathering all the pieces I couldn't seem to grab hold of. I was near tears about it.

Checked the clock. It was well after eleven, and only a skeleton crew remained in the newsroom, working in the now dimly lit office space to prep for the morning broadcast and cover whatever breaking news happened overnight. When I arrived in the break room searching for coffee, it was empty with the exception of Caroline, who'd come off the ten o'clock broadcast that night. I paused, letting that realization wash over me. Fabulous. She usually headed home after the ten wrapped, so I was surprised to run into her now, knowing better than to make small talk. She'd only say something snarky disguised as helpful about my live shot, and I didn't have thick enough skin for it tonight.

What I needed desperately was java. Caffeine. A slap across the face to wake me up. I brought my own each morning and therefore had never had to master the station's contraption before. I quietly bypassed Carrie, made my way to the machine, scanned the knobs and buttons, and sighed internally at how complicated the thing looked. What happened to the kind with the easy little carafe at the bottom? Why did everything have to be so hard? I held back frustrated tears and stared at the diagram on the side of the machine, attempting to mimic its instructions, pressing the required buttons, which just caused more lights to blink angrily. I opened the cabinet above, searching for an instruction manual, only to have a ton of insulated paper cups tumble out onto my head in a full-on attack. "Fuck," I said, slamming the cabinet closed and watching it bounce a few times, cups hitting the floor all around me. I angrily picked up the cups, returned them to the cabinet, and slammed the door again. Hard.

"Something wrong?" Carrie asked from her spot at one of the round break tables. She had her laptop open and a cup of coffee because *she* apparently knew how to work space-age machines.

I swallowed. Regained my composure. "It's fine. It's been a day."

"Oh yeah?" She was watching me, giving me her full attention. "Something happen beyond Carlos?"

"Well, the live shot thing." She nodded and winced. That was something. "Plus, a source I thought would pan out didn't show, and I'm dead in the water. Again."

"About the dispute with the sheriff over the cruisers?"

I nodded. "I had a woman from Kendall's ready to talk in depth about the feud. After Kristin gave me the go-ahead, I went to meet the woman, who must have gotten cold feet." I still couldn't believe I'd lost my shot at my first big story for the station. And now the coffee machine wanted to go a round with me, too, like the little bitch it was. I glared at it, sitting there smugly across the room.

Carrie took it all in. "Okay. Well, that happens. Do the cabinets really have to pay for it?"

I whirled around, my anger taking hold. "Yeah, I think they do, because you know what? It's too much. All of it." I kicked the bottom of the counter and instantly regretted it as pain shot through my big toe, fueling my anger. "The damn coffee machine won't work, sources lie about what they're offering, reporters blatantly steal, you and your condescending high horse, and stupid Kacey, and do you know what else?" I was on a roll. "The hot water in my apartment was out this morning, and I took a cold shower. It's too much, okay?" I opened and slammed the cabinet again, even though I didn't need anything inside. "Too, too much."

"Wow," I heard her say.

I stalked past Carrie on my way out of the room *without* coffee only to have my right foot catch the leg of one of the empty chairs, catapulting me forward. I collided headfirst with the edge of the counter on the opposite side of the room with a sickening thud. For a moment everything went black. Not good. That was before the searing pain hit. I took stock. I was flat on my ass on the floor. That much I could tell. The black I'd seen had now turned red and that was because there was apparently blood running into my eye from somewhere on my forehead in a drizzle. My stomach turned, and I pressed my hand to my head to try to stop it, which just got blood on my hand and on the sleeve of my good suit jacket. Not good, again.

"Shit. Skyler." I was vaguely aware of Carrie kneeling in front of me, though I was too stunned by the force of the collision to process much else. She quickly scanned the room and came back with a dry rag that she pressed to a spot near my eyebrow. That hurt, and I hissed. "Just hold still. You're going to be okay." I could smell her perfume or lotion or something amazing. Probably expensive. Definitely memorable. Like a meadow full of flowers. I tried to imagine myself there. She bit her bottom lip as she removed the rag and surveyed the damage. "Oh yeah. You might need a stitch. You've got a little gash."

"Nah, no stitches. I'll be okay." A lump rose in my throat. I took over, pressing the rag against my head and attempting to stand. When it came to embarrassment and pain, embarrassment won out every time, and it was my goal to save face and not cry, dammit. Unfortunately, I was buzzed, either from the collision with the counter or Carrie's proximity and display of warmth. Either way, the room went sideways for a moment, and I grabbed the wall for support. "Whoa. Okay."

That did it. Carrie immediately pulled out a chair for me. "You know what? We need to sit for a bit."

We? I wasn't going to argue. I was still angry at her for the hard time on air and ongoing judgment that she always seemed to level at me, but she was the only one present. I took a seat and studied her. She was studying me right back with a creased brow. I found her beauty annoying now. In fact, I found everything annoying.

"How many fingers am I holding up?" Carrie asked.

"Four," I said blandly. "Which is better than just the middle one

I'd have predicted." Yeah, I was apparently just saying any old thing I wanted to now. Interesting.

She smothered a smile. "Didn't feel appropriate."

Was she trying for levity? That was new, at least with me. I couldn't get over how stupid I felt, careening into the countertop in the midst of what was supposed to be my big angry exit. Who screws up their own big angry exit?

"You hit pretty hard," she said, taking my hand away from the wound and lowering the rag again. Her eyes carried concern. "The bleeding has slowed way down, so you might get your wish about dodging that stitch. We need to clean you up, though. You look like the victim in a horror movie." She tapped my knee which made me go still and warm. "Sit tight. I'll be right back." I was too interested in what was about to happen to go anywhere. When she returned, she carried a small first-aid kit. "Behind the assignment desk, should you ever need it. I let the night shift know about your fall. There will be paperwork to fill out."

I winced, wishing to have kept this whole thing a secret. Workplace accidents didn't really play out that way, though.

"You doing okay in here, Trip?" Eddie, one of the editors, asked, poking his head in. "Heard you took out a counter with your face."

I held up a sarcastic thumb, and he shot me one back. I was beginning to feel like part of the crew, at least. Razzed just like the rest of 'em. Just a more clumsy one.

I turned my attention back to Caroline to find her applying antiseptic from a small packet onto a cotton swab. She met my eyes with her crystal blue ones. Why was her skin so flawless? Her voice was quiet. "This is going to sting like a bitch, but you got this. Deep breath."

I nodded, braced, and inhaled. To my shock, she took my hand in her free one and squeezed gently as she applied the medicine. If the stuff hurt, I couldn't tell. In fact, I held that deep breath, forgetting to exhale entirely. My brain was preoccupied. Hijacked. The room felt small as I studied Carrie's jawline, her chin, her perfect lips, as I held her hand in mine. Unfair that anyone had lips like those, nearly heart-shaped, like they were drawn by an artist. She leaned in closer as she tore into the packaging of a bandage. I missed the warmth of her hand in mine. "Just want to make sure I angle this right."

"I'm sure you could just slap it on there. It'll be fine."

"No, no. I want to do this correctly."

"Why are you being nice to me?"

The comment must have caught her off guard. It surprised me as well, but my nerves were worn down and my coping skills nonexistent. To her credit, Carrie seemed to take it in stride. "Because you seem like you could really use it." A pause. "And maybe I'm a little guilt-ridden that I wasn't so friendly before. I should have been. I also want to apologize for the challenge on air tonight. I'm not proud of how I behaved."

She leaned in again, sharing my space as she applied the small bandage. I had not seen this coming. "Thank you," I said quietly. It was about all I could manage in the midst of my mystification. The night had taken an unexpected turn. The woman I'd looked up to and crushed on for years was not only reclaiming a little bit of her stock but was doing so while wildly inside my personal space. I could never have imagined a moment like this one five years ago. Yet here we were. Alone after hours in the break room.

"And all done." She sat back. "You'll probably want to take a couple Tylenol and refrain from storming out of any more kitchens."

I stood, feeling sheepish for my angry display earlier. "Sound advice."

"And about that source. I have a contact in the sheriff's office who might be able to help you."

"Seriously?"

"Yeah." She pulled a pad from her bag and scribbled a name and number. "An old friend from when I walked in your shoes."

I tried to imagine Caroline McNamara pounding the pavement, hunting down a story. It sent a shiver. "This is fantastic. Thank you."

"I figure I owe you for…you know."

"Well, if anyone was going to haze me a little…I guess I'd like it to have been you."

"Fair enough, Skyler Ruiz. Take care of that head of yours. It's apparently pretty hard."

I did something dumb and knocked on it. Why? "I'll give them a call," I said, holding up the piece of paper.

"Who's Kacey?" she asked, turning back.

I frowned, caught off guard. "What?"

"You said the name Kacey in the midst of your tirade. Stupid Kacey."

Right. I had. "Oh. Um, just someone I see on occasion."

"Well, I hope he's a good guy."

"*She*, actually. Kacey's a good person. It's just…complicated."

I saw something subtle shift in her expression. "Gotcha. One of those. Take care of yourself." And then she was gone. My head throbbed, my stomach *still* rumbled, and my brain couldn't seem to get back on track. As I sat at my desk, lamp on, attempting to make notes, all I could do was replay the last thirty minutes of my life over and over again. Carrie's unexpected caretaking, the way her fingertips brushed the hair from my forehead, the concern in her eyes. It had affected me.

"Yeah, this isn't gonna happen tonight," I said and tossed my pen onto my desk, giving in to the universe that seemed to want nothing more than to keep me guessing. But I wasn't going to complain about the events of this evening, because even with a busted head, it had ended on a high note. I'd snagged both a phone number for a tried-and-true source and taken a small step forward in my working relationship with Caroline McNamara.

Tomorrow was a new day. A clean slate. A small smile made its way onto my lips as I switched off my desk lamp and grabbed my bag. "'Night, guys," I said to the two assistants behind the assignment desk. I might have hummed a little tune as I made my way to the parking lot. Two thoughts. First, the tide felt like it just might be changing. Next, Caroline McNamara was a definite enigma. Call it the reporter in me, but when it came to her, I wanted to find out more.

CHAPTER FIVE

I was the moose, dammit. At long last!

Caroline's guy at the sheriff's office was not only talkative but got me a moment on camera with Sheriff Denison himself, who—of course—downplayed any rift with the commissioner but confirmed she'd denied his cruiser request and that Kendall's had picked up the tab. All on the record. Having his face as part of my story anchored the narrative and gave it credibility. After several well-thought-out voice mails to Essie, she also agreed to meet with me, going on camera with how much Kendall's owner hated the commissioner and why. The story took off from there. The more I established on record, the more other people with information were willing to contribute to the piece.

"Gotta hand it to you. This is good stuff," Kristin said, shaking her head after watching the finished package in the editing bay. "A note. Cut the last sentence of the sound bite from Essie. Tighter that way, and keeps the focus narrow. But overall, you guys killed it."

I looked back at Ty and grinned. "Thanks. We can do that. What about Carlos?"

She shrugged. "Couldn't get a comment from either side officially, so the story's yours. We'll run it at both five and ten tonight."

I shot a fist in the air, feeling like I'd finally hit a home run. Once Kristin headed back to the office, Ty and I celebrated the only way two people should, with a silent victory dance in front of the monitor frozen on the sheriff's frowning face. "One down, a zillion more to go. You might be a news shark in rookie's clothing," Ty said, offering me a final fist bump as I left him to finish up those edits Kristin asked for. "Go Sky Blue, go!"

"I see your story's on for tonight," Carrie said later that afternoon while she applied a final coat of lipstick before going on air. I tried not to stare. Her hair seemed softer today, sporting a natural wave. My mouth went dry, and I stared at my desk a moment to shake free of the not unpleasant sensation the image brought on. It was like every time she entered a room, she dared me to notice her a little bit more. Oh, I did.

I smothered a smile. "That's right. It all worked out."

"Congratulations."

"Well, if it wasn't for your guy, I'm not sure any of it would have happened. I owe you a drink. A box of doughnuts. A car."

She pointed at me and stood on her way to the studio. "Holding you to the first one. I like free drinks."

How did such an innocuous comment make my whole body go numb and tingly and back again. I nodded, words failing. I watched her walk away because I had to. When Caroline McNamara was in a room, that room was charged. Unlike any other. I spent the rest of the night, even the part when they sent me on a live shot from the Laundromat on strike for the ten o'clock, smiling from ear to ear. When I said, "Back to you, Caroline," my spidey sense flared. I felt like something important was about to happen to me.

And I was scared but more than a little bit ready.

The weekend came at long last, and I rejoiced. The week had just about done me in. I slept a little longer, snuggled Mr. Micky, and then clipped him into his leash to visit Sarah.

"You're too skinny. You need food." She shoved a plate of chocolate, fruit, and cheese closer to where I sat along her kitchen counter on that cheerful Saturday.

"I do not," I told her. "The camera isn't kind."

"You are being ridiculous. Eat. Have you heard from Aunt Carla this week?"

I shook my head at her mention of my mother. "She's off being a superlawyer in LA."

"She's ridiculously proud of you."

I nodded. "She said so last we spoke, but that was literally a six-minute conversation. She's always on the go."

I watched the smile slide off Sarah's face before she thought enough to replace it. She knew my mother didn't always come through on the warm and fuzzies. But that's why I had her and Yolanda. They'd been there when she wasn't able to be. School events, holidays when she didn't make it back into town quite in time.

"Well, I'll tell you who else says you're killing it. Kristin. Well, Lucy said Kristin said that. And Emory told me. Follow?"

"Surprisingly, yes. I'm definitely not the superstar in the newsroom, but I no longer feel like I need to run screaming for the countryside again. I might be able to hold my own with these people." I popped a chocolate-drizzled banana slice.

Sarah frowned. "You're selling yourself short again, Sky-Sky. I know you, and you are capable of so much more than holding your own."

"That means a lot, coming from you." I paused. "I'm not sure you know how much I look up to you, Sar. Always have. When I was a kid, I obsessively copied your hairstyles."

"The hair part I knew. Even the unfortunate bangs. I apologize for that one."

"Was hoping you might."

"Hey, since I have a moment with you, I wanted to talk to you about something," Sarah said, pouring me a glass of amazing-looking strawberry lemonade, which I was pretty sure she'd made from scratch.

"Okay. Everything all right? Do I need to sit down again?" I was smiling, joking with her as we so often did.

She slid her hands out flat across the white granite countertop, her gaze falling to the gray pattern. "I hope so." She looked up with a careful smile. "The thing is, Emory is sick." I paused my glass on its way to my mouth. Sarah's eyes brimmed with tears.

"What? No." My stomach plummeted, and my limbs went warm as I waited for more information.

"She found a lump in her breast, and a biopsy has confirmed it's cancer."

I didn't know what to say. Emory Owen was the strongest person I knew, and it didn't seem possible that something like this could happen to *her*. In my brain, she was untouchable. My emotions bubbled to the surface. "Sarah, I hate this. This is awful." I closed my eyes, trying to remain steady. "No, it fucking sucks."

She held up a hand. "We caught it early, so say a prayer of gratitude for that. Luckily, it hasn't spread to her lymph nodes. That's big."

"So now what?"

"Now we treat it. They're going to take the lump and treat her with radiation a month later, after she's healed from the surgery."

"God. Okay. What does that look like?"

"She'll go five days a week for six weeks for whole breast radiation. After that, they'll do another week or so and target the tumor bed. A boost. Aim everything at the spot they took the lump." Sarah placed her hands on her cheeks, probably still absorbing the enormity of it all herself. "The doctor thinks that might be enough. We're going to hope that it is."

"God, and here I am, going on about stupid work stuff that doesn't even matter. How is she?"

"Who are we talking about?" I turned as Emory entered the room. "That businesswoman-turned-artist who was just diagnosed with the Big C? Certainly not her." She looked from me to Sarah, serious expression on her face that luckily dissolved into a smile. "It's okay. People have been speaking in hushed tones around me all week. You should have seen the look on my sister's face. You'd have thought I had died already. Not that I'm going to." I immediately moved into her arms and held on tight.

"You forgot devastatingly beautiful," Sarah said. "But yes, that would be you. Just giving Skyler our official update."

Emory lifted my chin and looked down at me. "I'm doing okay. Not the greatest week I've ever had, but I'm feeling ready to take this on. Don't worry, okay?" I nodded and released her. "I'm going to be just fine."

In my peripheral, I saw Sarah wipe away a stray tear as if she hoped no one had noticed. It tore at me. "You guys, what can I do? Do you need help with Grace? I'm an excellent shuttle service. I can pick her up from school or practice or pitch in around here."

Emory waved me off. "We're fine. But you get points for the offer. I'm going to take this one day at a time and not let a diagnosis consume me. Because that's all it is. A jumping-off point. I'll have the surgery and go from there."

I had to hand it to her. She seemed so put together and ready to take on the world. I would have been a wreck and angry at life. "You two continue to amaze me."

They shared a smile, and I was grateful they had each other.

"Will you be at Kristin's tonight?" Emory asked, pulling herself away from Sarah's gaze. She kissed my cheek with an affectionate smack as she rounded the counter.

I nodded, surprised to have received Kristin's verbal invitation the day before, but happy to have been thought of. "Yes, she says she wants to get to know me better now that we work together and have, ya know, you people in common."

Sarah placed a hand over her heart, touched. "I love being *you people*."

"Me, too," Emory said with a far-off look in her eye. "Dreams do come true."

"What does one wear to an adult dinner party in a large city?" I asked. "I don't want to wear one of my businessy work outfits, but jeans and a tank don't exactly seem the way to go either."

Sarah smoothed my hair from behind. "You're too cute for anyone to care. God, Skyler, when did you grow up? I wasn't looking, and you're a stunner." She turned to Emory. "Have you seen how beautiful my little cousin is? Look at this model face." She grabbed me by the chin and squeezed my cheeks. "Great big eyes and a gorgeous smile. I could eat your face."

I laughed and shook free. "Stop being nice to me and tell me what to wear."

"Do you have a cocktail dress?" Emory asked.

"Do I have a cocktail dress?" I had several and kept them reserved for swankier events, but I wasn't sure if this one qualified. Kristin hadn't been specific.

"They're usually pretty nice dinners," Sarah said. "You've met Lucy, right? She does everything first class. Expect place cards. Long-stemmed glasses. That kind of thing."

I grinned, loving the idea of attending a fancy-sounding party. "Oh, I'm all in on this. Plus, it will give me a chance to see Kristin and Lucy together, which honestly, I'm trying to imagine." Lucy, who I'd met a handful of times, was Emory's best friend in the world. She was charismatic, talkative, and the life of any party. Kristin, on the other hand, was friendly but definitely more conservative in her demeanor. Thoughtful, which made sense coming from her writing background.

"Kristin grounds Lucy, and Lucy inspires Kristin to let go."

"Like you do for me," Emory said, grinning.

"Now you're just trying to score points."

Emory mimed a jump shot. "And?"

"At least ten," Sarah said and raised a seductive eyebrow. I felt like a voyeur just being in the room.

I waited, but they were still looking at each other like soap opera characters. "And that's my cue to get the hell out of here and let you two be in love." I pointed at Emory as I backed out of the kitchen. "I love you. And I'm serious about pitching in." I turned my focus to Sarah. "Anything you two need, you call me, or I'll be royally pissed off."

Emory winced. "Can't have an angry cousin-in-law."

I stared at her. "I'm a bulldog with a reporter's microphone. I'll chew you up and take a quote."

"Chilling," Sarah said, hugging me with the protective arms of an older cousin. "You be good to the world, little Sky. I'll see you at my mom's for dinner on Sunday, okay?"

I grinned, enjoying the fact that I no longer had to miss out on those kinds of family gatherings. "I'll be there with my stomach and its friend, my other stomach."

"Good, because my mother wouldn't have you otherwise. You'd be on the curb, thinking about what you've done." She touched her chest. "Speaking from experience."

Before I left, I raced back and gave Emory one last firm hug, tearing up in the process, and hoping that I communicated in that embrace all the love and respect I had for her. "You're going to be okay," I said in her ear.

"Thank you," she whispered back, emotion choking her voice in a manner so uncharacteristic that it forced a lump in my throat. It was a startling reminder of the universe's power when the strongest person you knew was the one shown vulnerable to an illness. It made me stop and take stock and say a little prayer of gratitude for all that I had. She gave me a little shove. "Now get out of here and go kick ass at the station. I'm going to need something good to watch when I'm stuck on the couch soon."

I grinned through my tears. "I love a good challenge, and I won't let you down."

❖

Sarah had been right. Blessed Betty. When I pulled up to the two-story home along Mission Beach, it stole my breath and made me stare. Not just the house—white, modern, and with a lot of large windows—but the surrounding landscape. Palm trees loomed in front, and the gentle sound of the ocean floated in from the back. My heart squeezed. I loved the ocean and couldn't imagine getting to live in such close proximity. Kristin and Lucy's driveway was short and small, which left cars lining the road. I searched for a spot, took a deep breath, and walked in my heels and my short black dress up the walk, taking in the last sliver of sunlight as it waned pink and orange on the horizon.

The door swung open as I made my way up the curve of the sidewalk, and Lucy beamed at me, stunning in a white dress off one shoulder. She matched the house beautifully. Her dark hair had been pulled into a knot at her neck, and her blue eyes sparkled. "I haven't seen you in I don't know how long, and now look at you! And a reporter in a market like this one?"

She held open her arms, and I stepped into them and kissed her cheek. "I don't live in a house as stunning as this one, but I'm doing okay. Hi. It's great to see you."

"Skyler. Kristin gushes about you. Daily. It makes me so proud to say I knew you when you were just a kid."

Kristin gushed about me? That was news, and it bolstered my confidence instantly. My boss was happy with my performance. I could rest a little easier. "Well, I could easily gush right back and do, nightly, to my dog, who's now the biggest Kristin fan." I switched to sincerity. "Seriously, though, she's great at her job. The calm in the storm."

"I couldn't agree more." She stepped back. "Well, come in and mingle, grab a drink. We have everything. Make yourself at home, and you'll find everyone gathering in the living area."

"Perfect. I'll see you in there. Oh, and Lucy, thank you for having me." I handed over a bottle of wine because my mother had taught me manners.

"Are you kidding? I'm thrilled to have grown-up little Skyler at my dinner party."

I left her at the door to greet the other arriving guests and made my way inside. Quiet music played from somewhere unseen as I made my way through the foyer, the *click click click* of my heels following me. The table, in what seemed to be the formal dining room, was set beautifully for twelve, folded white cloth napkins and all. I didn't see Emory or Sarah in the small handful of people mingling in the large living room, but my gaze landed on someone I did recognize, Carrie. She turned in that moment and met my gaze, breaking into a soft smile. She wore black pants and killer stilettos along with a sleeveless flowing blue top. How she managed to look both dressy and beachy at the same time, I had no idea. But that was Caroline. Her hair was down, soft and kind of wavy in the gentle sense. Out of her anchor attire and fancy hair and makeup she looked even more stunning. Before this moment, I had been sure that would have been impossible, but this woman was born with natural beauty. She moved in my direction, and I straightened, preparing to speak or listen or a combination of both. *Just relax. Smile.*

"Well, you look fabulous." That was not the opening line I was expecting and swallowed, my plan shot. "I didn't know you'd be here."

"Thank you." I smiled, keeping it cool. "Lucy is a family friend, and of course, I know Kristin from work, so…"

"Small world."

"Isn't it?" Lucy said, handing me a glass of white wine as she whisked past on her way to play hostess. I held it up to her in gratitude. Carrie sipped from a glass of red, holding it by the stem, which was a normal thing for any human to do, but the way she did so sent a flutter through my midsection. She had feminine hands, slender fingers. She had a way of giving new meaning to mundane tasks.

"No Kacey tonight?" she asked.

"No. No Kacey. And you look beautiful, too." It felt weird to say, and now my cheeks were warm, but she didn't seem to notice.

"Thanks," she said quietly and glanced at her drink. If I didn't know better, I would have said that I'd caught a hint of vulnerability there. As if my simple compliment had mattered. Huh. And maybe it had. "The buzz about your story has been really positive. I don't know how much Tam has shared, but it's garnered us quite a bit of attention. You scooped every other station."

I grinned because I was aware. Since they'd run it earlier in the week, my inbox had been filling up. Suddenly, I was on the map, and the people of San Diego either wanted to share their strong opinions on my story or pitch me my next one. I felt bolder in the morning story meetings with some clout beneath me, and the other reporters now knew I could hold my own. Even Carlos had apologized for underestimating me. One story was not going to make or break me, but it was certainly a step in the right direction. "I have to admit that the response has been nice. You know how badly I wanted it to pan out."

"And so do the break room cabinets." She sipped from her glass, and I caught the faint lip print.

I winced. "I should probably write them a note of apology."

"Might inflate their ego."

"Oh." A pause. "We can't have conceited cabinets."

"We're in agreement on that." She touched her glass to mine, and we grinned at each other, with me enjoying the new give-and-take dynamic. Ever since my unfortunate counter careening, the chilly tension between us had evaporated, not that I fully understood its origins to begin with.

Maybe one day I'd get the courage to ask.

But seeing Carrie outside the station was surreal and more than a little exciting. Like running into your hot teacher outside of school. Yet that wasn't how I saw her. I looked up to Carrie, sure, but I wanted to be seen as her colleague, her equal, not the little puppy that ran along behind her.

"Carrie, have you seen the view from the back deck? It's gorg. Come see."

I blinked at the woman who slipped her hand into Caroline's and stood just a little too close. I felt a muscle in my jaw tense at the recognizable energy between the two. I knew exactly what I was seeing, even though my brain was too stunned to fully process it.

"Skyler Ruiz, this is Audra Kline. She's an architect. Skyler is the newest reporter at KTMW."

"Oh yes," Audra said. She was pretty. Dark blond hair and hazel eyes. Her tan was impressive. I tended to burn. Not that I had time to lounge in the sun anyway. "You did the story on the police cars that steak house paid for."

"That was me. Carrie was instrumental in my success, I should add."

"As for your story, I'm sure it's only the beginning," Carrie said. She turned to Audra. "Now show me this view you're so excited about."

I watched the two of them, a gorgeous couple, if that's what they were, make their way to the set of sliding glass doors. My mind was essentially blown by this new information. Carrie wasn't happily married to some guy with a beard and a tie?

"Skyler, you're here. You made it!" Kristin. But my brain was still busy.

"Is Carrie…in a relationship with that woman?" I had to ask and felt like I knew Kristin well enough for it to be off the record.

Kristin's face took on understanding, and I followed her gaze to Audra and Carrie out on the deck. "She used to be. Yeah. I think they're just friends now."

Why hadn't the public been notified, and by public, I meant *me*. Carrie dated women? Everything I thought I knew about life had just been tossed out the window, and I was going to have to start fresh. Probably learn English again. Did I even like pizza? "Interesting."

The side of Kristin's mouth tugged. She was well aware that I was a lesbian. "I know. It's a lot to take in."

"Right?" I asked in a hushed tone. "Because...*right*?"

Kristin laughed, patted me on the head, and was whisked away by a guest asking where they could find green olives.

Shock aside, the evening was just what I needed. A group of kind adults enjoying a fantastic dinner prepared by a hired chef, over intelligent conversation. I felt like I'd been invited to the big kids' table and never wanted to leave. Did I spend a good part of dinner staring across the table at Carrie, who ate her food slowly, as if taking the time to enjoy each bite? Perhaps. Now that the ice had melted off her, I saw her in a whole new light. The journalist I'd long admired and the woman who was maybe on the way to becoming my friend. The introduction of the ex-girlfriend added more to my understanding of who Carrie was, and it turned out we weren't so different.

"I agree with the point you made at dinner," Carrie told me later as we lounged on the couch in the living room. The guests were down to about half, and the formality of the evening had fallen completely away with the late hour. I sat with my shoes off and my feet curled beneath me, facing Carrie on the other end of the couch. "About how much the industry has changed with the rise of social media. It's hard to keep up. The station wants me to start learning TikTok. What am I supposed to do with that? Create lighthearted videos? I'm a newswoman."

I squinted. "Why would they want you on TikTok? What does that have to do with the station?"

Carrie shook her head and watched the room for a moment. Lucy and Kristin smiled sweetly at each other in the kitchen. Emory nodded sagely at something Kristin's neighbor was explaining. "I think they're struggling for a foothold to keep the ratings where they want them to be. To keep us *relevant*. Younger people are getting their news from the internet rather than television." She shrugged. "And let's be honest, I'm not getting any younger."

"Who needs you to?"

"Well, the network would love it." She sipped from her champagne glass. A champagne kind of girl. I liked that. Oh, and I'd had two-point-five glasses of wine and no shame. God, she was stunning. If the camera could see her now, makeup faded, no shoes, and her blond hair framing her face as the ocean breeze floated in from the open back door, they'd be just as captivated as I was.

"Well, the network can fuck right off." Had I said that?

She smiled at me, seemingly touched. "Well, thanks for that. But maybe not so loud. We are at our assistant news director's home."

"Good point. Still."

She was studying me with soft eyes. I liked it. I wanted to live here. "You want to come over sometime next week?"

I couldn't have been more stunned. "Me?"

"You're the only one on the couch." She smiled from behind her glass, regarding me, amused.

"Yeah, I mean, yeah."

"I will accept *yeah, I mean, yeah.*"

"Maybe you can tell me more about working at the station, your career."

Her eyes laughed, even if the rest of her didn't. She thought I was cute, the way one would a sweet kitten. I wasn't sure how I felt about that. "Sure, if you want. I can do that."

"But we don't have to. We can just have a drink or eat something. At the same time." These were stellar ideas I was throwing out there. Incredible, really.

"Might be weird if we took turns."

I nodded. "Given."

"I thought so."

The tone was light, and I couldn't help but wonder if there was the smallest amount of flirting hovering in our back-and-forth. Was I crazy? I had to be. There was no way Caroline McNamara was flirting with me, whether she was into women or not. I paused. But maybe *Carrie* was, the woman beneath the intimidating persona. Even *that* seemed ludicrous, given the fact that I was…me. No one important.

"When?" I asked, apparently feeling the need to nail this down.

"Oh, um…what about Saturday. I'm off."

"Me, too."

"Swing by late afternoon. We can hang out." She caught sight of something across the room. Maybe Audra signaling her. "I'll text you my address. Better go. 'Night, Skyler. Tonight was fun."

"'Night," I said, but nothing could have pulled my attention from the small details that came with Carrie's exit. She gave Audra's hand a squeeze and let go, located her clutch, and spoke quietly to Lucy and Kristin, exchanging a laugh followed by cheek kisses. She quietly slipped out the front door, and I was left on that couch, grappling with all the new information that overloaded my very intrigued brain.

Sarah sat down and said something casual about the dinner. Maybe that the garlic mash had been set on fire. I absently agreed, vaguely aware of Emory joining us.

She looked at me. "What's going on with this one?"

Sarah tapped her cheek. "I don't know, but she looks kinda happy about it and will agree with practically anything I say."

I pulled myself off the cloud I was floating on. "She's a lesbian, you guys. Or fluid, it's hard to say which. And it's more than a little surprising. Are you feeling all right?" I asked, my eyes flying to Emory. I'd been wondering all night, but we'd not had a moment.

"I'm fine. But what is it you're going on about?"

"Have you ever found out someone you thought was straight is not so straight, and your world feels very weird all of a sudden?"

"Ah. Carrie." Emory rolled her lips in, but her eyes danced with knowledge.

Sarah simply smiled.

"Wait. You knew?" I looked from one of them to the other. How had they not shared this information the second I got the job? Because they'd been busy with *actual life stuff*, I reminded myself.

Sarah raised a nonchalant shoulder. "Kristin's had her over before, and she had that same woman with her, so yes, it was pretty easy to surmise."

Emory nodded. "The covers on books don't always tell their whole story."

My mind raced. "So I am finding."

Sarah leaned in. "Are you crushing on Carrie?"

"What if I am?" It wasn't anything new. The crush just took on new meaning now.

They exchanged another look. My pseudo-parents were checking in with each other. They seemed to decide that Sarah would take this one. "But let me ask this. Is it wise to get involved with someone you work with?"

"Involved? No. Are you crazy? There's no way we're involved or even on our way. This is Caroline McNamara we're talking about here. And me, a rando reporter, trying to keep my eyeballs above water in a major market I have no business working in."

"Rando?"

I grappled to explain. "A nobody. Inconsequential in her orbit. Aka me."

They looked at each other.

I sighed, exasperated. "Why do you keep doing that? No more secret couple's-knowing-look eye things."

"That's really not something you can police," Emory said simply. "It just happens. Like the wind."

Sarah turned to me. "But you can look out for yourself. That's something you can do. You can also stop selling yourself short. You're every bit as important as Carrie. Just as smart and just as beautiful."

She was crazy but came from a good place. "Bless you for thinking so."

"Hermosa, I know what I know." She placed a hand on my forearm. "Just keep your wits about you. This job is all you ever wanted."

"Well, I don't plan to blow it." A pause because my brain was stuck like a record with a scratch on it. "She dates women, you guys."

Emory laughed. "You should see the smile on your face. Want us to walk you to your car?"

"Yes, please. I have a car, right?"

"You do," Sarah reassured me.

As I drove home, I danced. Excited about the evening, going to work that Monday, and the invitation to Carrie's house. It was what I did when good things happened. With the windows down and the San Diego night air in my hair, I drove along the shoreline, soaking it all in. This was my new life, and it felt like things were finally starting to happen. I heard Sarah's words in my head: *Just keep your wits about you.* But for tonight, I wanted to feel.

On impulse, I looped my car around, parked in one of those paid lots, and made my way down to the beach. I slipped my shoes off, and with heels dangling from my fingertips, I walked through the sand, squishing my toes into it as the cool tide rolled across the tops of my feet. Then and there, I nodded up at the sky full of stars overhead, granting the universe permission to take me on whatever journey seemed to be beckoning me.

"Let's do this," I said quietly.

CHAPTER SIX

S eth had struck again. Sweet Betsy.
When I heard the traffic on the police scanners, that was my first thought. "Whoa. Wait a sec. Did you hear that?" I asked Mila, who was manning the assignment desk. I'd stopped by to see if there was anything interesting in the works that I could grab hold of early when I caught the chatter. Mila had become a great resource, and the more interest I showed in what went on behind the assignments desk, the more she kept me in the loop about possible stories in the pipeline.

Mila squinted, which I'd learned was what she did when concentrating. "Something about a botched robbery," she said and turned up the volume on the channel. We listened to the back-and-forth conversation between officers, most of it in police code I'd gotten pretty good at unscrambling. Someone had attempted to rob a 7-Eleven and had ended up firing their gun into the shelf full of chips, sending Cheetos, Funyuns, and Ruffles flying into oblivion. The guy fled on foot, making away with absolutely nothing. I checked the address on the map Mila had on her screen.

"This sounds eerily familiar," I told her. "I'm gonna grab Ty and head over."

"Got it. Let me know if you have anything, and I'll keep Devante posted."

The cops were just finishing up their report when we arrived. I grinned to see my police pal Jake exiting the store wearing his hat and going over his notes. "Hey, you."

He looked up, stared, and broke into a smile. "Skyler the coffee-swilling reporter."

"Just here for a gas station hot dog."

"Sure you are." He glanced behind him. "Not much of a story here unless there's wasted-chip outrage. Does your station cover that kind of thing?"

"It does. When I heard the chips were caught up in all this, I raced over to fight for justice."

He nodded, not at all buying it and catching me looking at his notes. "Something I can help you with, nosy?"

"Do we know the perp's name, and is it Seth?"

"We do not. And Seth?" He studied me. "What do you know?"

"Between you and me, there was a similar incident about three miles from here a few weeks ago. Perp got scared and fired his gun into the floor. Young white guy, goes by the name of Seth, which is a fantastic criminal name if you ask me. It's what I would choose."

I could tell from the look on his face that the description likely matched. "Seth, huh?" He made a note in the margin of his little pad. "Interesting." As my eyes scanned his unreadable scribbles, he flipped the notebook closed before I could get much. "Saw your story. You kept your word."

"Always. I promised you anonymity. I would never go back on that. In fact, I owe you for the intel." I leaned in. "I know where to find free chips. You don't even have to open the bag."

He grinned. "You're pretty good at this reporter thing."

"Aww, shucks, Jake. Anything you can tell me?"

"Nope."

"Fair enough. Until next time?"

"You bet."

I headed inside and joined Ty, who'd already gotten B-roll of the store and the chip fiasco. We were luckily there just in time for crumbs galore. The story on its own wouldn't likely make the broadcast, but I had a feeling it would feed into a larger narrative if I was patient enough. I could play the long game. One of my strengths. I turned to the clerk. "Could we get just a few moments with you on camera? We want to hear your story."

He straightened his T-shirt and stood three inches taller. I smothered a grin. Everyone loved being on TV.

"And where have you been?" Carrie asked when I arrived back at my desk an hour later.

"Quirky robberies are afoot. Chips are paying the price. I must right this wrong."

"Quirky, you say?"

"It's too early to talk about, but it could be interesting." I paused.

"Your eyes look extra blue today, and you seem energized. Why is that?"

"Hmm. Maybe I'm just in a good mood."

I opened my laptop. "Hot date?"

"Jury is still out on that one." She didn't linger. Picked up her makeup bag and left for the studio while I tried to figure out exactly what our last exchange had meant. Was she talking about us? Some other person she was seeing this week? So many possibilities. I wasn't complaining. Because when Carrie was around these days, my skin tingled and my world hummed pleasantly with the kind of electricity that made everything feel purposeful and fun. Plus, a little mystery never hurt anyone.

❖

When the weekend came, I was surprised to see that Carrie's house was smaller than I would have guessed, given her fame and reputation. She was San Diego elite, appearing on billboard ads and serving as the face of a number of different charities. Her home, however, was a modest one-story stucco, not on the beach, but two blocks in. It did come with some pretty fantastic landscaping, though. I'd give her that. I followed the winding sidewalk through all sorts of greenery of varying heights with little pops of color coming from flowers I couldn't name if I tried. I wondered if Carrie had done all this herself, and then remembered how busy she was and likely rich.

"What's caught your interest out there?"

I looked up, the sweating bottle of wine I carried by the neck dropped at my side. My offering. "I was just admiring your curvy garden walk. It's beautiful." I'd worn a casual purple sundress and flat sandals, which thankfully seemed to line up with her red halter top and cropped faded jeans. I took a minute to absorb the very casual version of her. She had ten years on me, but today, you'd never know it. Today, she appeared youthful and bright-eyed, her blond hair down with the longest layers falling well beyond her shoulders.

"Thank you. Little passion project."

I gestured to the plant with the palmlike leaves. "This was you?"

"And these." She held up her hands, signaling they'd done the work. Two rings and a bracelet adorned. My stomach went tight. Oh, I liked her hands very much. "Come in. Let's relax. I have the back door open. You can't see the ocean, but you can hear it."

"What smells so amazing?" My senses went into overload as I entered the home. She was baking something. Or had. And it was heavenly. My eyes scanned her living room—gray furniture arranged in a U-shape, open to three towering bookshelves full of not just books, but elegant looking objects. Vases, a small lamp, a series of awards, a photograph of her accepting one. She was such a fucking grown-up and impressive person. One of the reasons I'd forgiven her so quickly after our early missteps. I wanted to know this woman. I craved knowledge of her.

"Rosemary bread." I turned and saw her in the open kitchen, slicing into a loaf with a large bread knife. "How about a warm slice with some butter?"

"If you greet all your guests this way, you're going to have a line."

"Who says I don't?"

"Not me. I swear. Do I still get the bread?"

She slid a small plate my way. That's when I realized I had no small plates at home. I needed to get on that because I suddenly felt like a hospitality heathen. "The rosemary is fresh from that garden you were just admiring."

"Wow. Thank you." I stared at the thick buttery slice, and my mouth watered. I heard the splash of liquid in a glass and grinned as I saw her pouring rosé into two oversized wineglasses. "You're spoiling me now."

She raised a shoulder. "It's the weekend. We all need a little extra care."

"I like the philosophy."

She met my gaze. A smile. She looked away. "So, what do you think?"

I paused, unsure of the subject matter. "About the bread? It's probably the most wonderful thing I've tasted in years." Not a lie. Hot, fresh bread needed some kind of medal for its contributions to society, and Carrie needed to be thanked in the speech.

"KTMW. You're beyond the brand-new zone at this point. How are you liking the job?" She sipped her wine and waited for my reply.

"Well, now that all hazing has come to an end…"

She raised a finger. "That statement might be premature."

"Now that all hazing has tapered off, I'm starting to feel at home. I understand how the place works."

"And that's different than WBBA?"

"They're different *planets*. The competition for just a bite at a good story is not something I dealt with there. Everyone played nice in the sandbox and brought brownies."

Carrie slid a piece of the warm bread into her mouth and took a bite. I had trouble deciphering her words for a moment. "Brownies could be nice."

"I prefer a career that's actually going somewhere."

She came around the kitchen island and paused next to me, hip kicked against the counter. "I think you're more than on your way. I've never in my life seen Tam hire someone from such a small market. You skipped about four steps."

"Trust me. I'm well aware. I'm still not sure why he took a chance on me."

She lifted her chin. "There's something about you."

"What?"

She shook her head looking at me. Unabashed. "I'm still not sure."

"Is that why you made my first couple of weeks difficult? Because you thought I hadn't earned it?"

Carrie exhaled slowly and reached for her wine, signaling that she might need it to tackle this question. "I've actually thought about it a lot because it's very much out of character for me."

I winced. "That bad, huh?"

"I think the answer is a two-parter. You're young, beautiful, and you have this really noticeable presence. The trifecta had me—how should I say this? Intimidated."

I stepped back and drew an *X* in the air. "No. I refuse to believe that *you*"—I gestured up and down her body—"being who you are, could experience even an ounce of intimidation at the hands of some new puppy of a reporter."

"Well, you have to, because it's true." She shrugged. "I'm human. I'm also not twenty anymore and am well aware of shelf life when there are cameras involved. A newer model walks in the door? Sure, I'm aware that she might be here to replace me."

"That's crazy." I shook my head, mystified. I folded my arms. "What's the second part?"

"Kind of a replay of the first part but with a more personal angle thrown in."

I frowned. "Define personal." Because I really, really needed to know that part.

She sighed as if I was forcing her to explain, and I was. "Young, beautiful, and that presence again. But it affected...*me*."

"I don't understand." Was I following correctly? I surely wasn't. My insides were going warm, though.

"Outside the job." She just stared at me. Waiting.

"Oh." My brain stuttered and tried to process the realization. "Are you saying…"

"I noticed you, and it had me on my toes for a whole separate reason. It wasn't until I allowed myself to get to know you, to *like* you, that the intimidation seemed stupid and then faded. Well, a little."

I didn't have words, so I gulped my wine. Chugged it, in fact, and then extended my arm all the way out for a refill. I was going to need it.

Carrie laughed and reached for the bottle. "Okay, that was adorable."

I reemphasized my request with a second bounce of my arm, and Carrie obliged with a laugh.

"Well, if you were intimidated by me, I was terrified of you. And in awe. I've been watching you on television for years, looking up to you."

"Since you were, what? A child? A toddler?"

"Stop that. I'll be thirty in March. Thank you very much."

"March, huh? Nine and a half years."

"See? We're contemporaries."

She laughed out loud at that one. "Sure." A glance around as if remembering her hostess duties. "Want to see the house?"

Did I ever. "Very much. I can already tell that your skills extend to decorating. Your house looks like one of those model homes. The nine and a half years is showing in a really good way. I need to work on adulting at a much higher level."

"You'll get there. Decorating is another hobby. On weekends, I love to shop for this place. A rug here. A clock there. It feels like each room is always shifting with me and my style."

She had style in spades. I was working on distinguishing mine from hodgepodge. She led me from the expansive main living and kitchen area to three bedrooms on the left side of the house, each ridiculously comfortable looking but with its own chic color combination and crisp lines. A soft lavender and gray bedroom. A blue and cream one next door. The third was clearly a study set up for Carrie with an elegant mahogany desk that brought out the flecks of brown in the tile flooring. Large windows without curtains looked out on her backyard, which was much bigger than I would have imagined. She nodded at the window. "I'm a huge sun bunny. I have to have the natural light. Gets me going."

"I'm surprised you don't live on the beach."

"It's close enough, and this way I can spread out a bit more. Garden. Set up my hammock. It's close enough if I want it."

I nodded and wrapped my arms around myself. "I hope to live right on the beach one day. It's a dream of mine." The idea of waking up early, taking my coffee outside as the ocean breeze lifted my hair and woke my senses, sounded like heaven on earth. Just the sound of the ocean gave me goose bumps.

She paused as if saving the declaration. "I think you're going to have that. Goals are hugely important. Dreams beget dreams. They keep you hungry."

"Is that how you did it?"

She nodded and turned off the light in the study. "I worked my ass off to put myself on the map, but even now, I can't be complacent. There's always someone waiting in the wings for my job."

She made a valid point. One I'd not really ever considered. I just figured once you were Caroline McNamara, you had it made. In reality, she had a lot to lose, and the industry could be brutal. "There's no one like you, though."

"True. But there are younger versions." She winked and led me through the living area to the other side of the house. "The primary retreat."

I stared in awe at the mostly white and cream room. Retreat it was. A huge California king sat in the middle of the room with a large skylight overhead. Just beyond it sat an entire sitting area with a small sofa and two curvy chairs that I could imagine her curling up in with a book. On the side of the room, closest to the door, stood a built-in granite counter with an actual refrigerator and coffee station. "You are wildly set up in here. You don't have to leave."

She raised a proud shoulder. "I like to be comfortable."

I met her gaze. "I'm learning a lot."

"Good."

"And this house is much larger than it looks. From the outside, I never would have known you had all this going on." I followed her out of the room. "You have a coffee station in your bedroom, Carrie."

"My little secret hideout. Now tell me more about you."

It was a broad question, and while I wanted to dazzle this woman and show her that I was every bit as capable, creative, and smart as she was, it was strangely more important to me to be completely honest. "I think I'm a woman still figuring it all out."

She sat on the living room sofa with her legs folded beneath her, and I joined her on the opposite end, keeping my feet on the floor. "I think that's identifiable. What are some things you want for yourself?"

"A career that I'm proud of, someone to share it all with. A family one day."

"And that house on the beach."

I grinned, enjoying the thought. "Can't forget the beach." I paused. "Tell me something that you'd wished you'd known as a reporter."

"To enjoy every second of the hunt for your story." She shrugged. "I miss it now."

I frowned. "You're in the anchor chair and you miss the field? Unheard of."

"Don't get me wrong. There are perks to air-conditioning and studio lighting." She winked at me. "But I do miss interacting with people, crafting the narrative. The journey. Now I'm a talking head for the most part. Not that I dislike my job. I don't."

"Well, you're certainly more than a talking head. More like the quarterback."

"Thank you." She lit up, and so did the entire room. "I like that. I'm going to hold on to the analogy."

"Please do." I finished the last of my drink and stood. "And because I want to be invited back to this deceivingly large home someday, I'm going to go." It was close to dinnertime, and I didn't want to make her feel obligated to cook or order food for us. Plus, she likely had other plans, and the leave 'em wanting more move felt like a good way to play it. It's something I'd actually decided on before arriving. I hated the idea of wearing out my welcome.

"You don't have to go," she said, watching me from the couch.

"I'm sure you have somewhere exciting to be. It's the weekend."

"Oh, I don't know about that." She nodded and an unreadable expression crossed her features. "But I'm glad you came by. It's nice getting to hear more about you. Make a new friend."

"Yeah," I said, hearing the softness in my voice. She did that to me. "I mean it when I say I'd like to do it again. Another drink. Another slice of homemade bread."

"Now I've done it."

"The bar is so high."

We locked eyes and suddenly I didn't want to go anywhere. Was it too late to take it back?

"I will relieve you of that," she said of my glass. "And I'm sending the rest of the bread home with you."

"Then it must be Christmas."

"Just call me Mrs. Claus."

Nope. Mrs. Claus had never been this sexy. And that's what Carrie did to me. Sex comparisons with beloved childhood characters. She was that potent. "Well, since I have permission." We walked to the front door and I rocked back on my heels. "See you soon?"

"Monday. Bright and early for you. A little later in the day for me." She opened her arms and leaned in, pulling me against her. Was it wrong that I delayed letting go for probably a second longer than reasonable? She smelled amazing, like that same meadow of flowers I'd envisioned when I'd hit my head. I could get drunk on it. When I pulled back, there were her blue eyes looking back at me. Our faces were noticeably close and neither of us went out of our way to amend that. *Steady yourself.* I'd seen moments like this in movies but had never experienced one for myself. Time suspended, leaving Carrie and me, breathing in the same air, hovering somewhere close to perfect for just a select few seconds of wonder. She adjusted a strand of hair on my shoulder and took a step back. She'd noticed it, too. That little move proved it. I lifted my hand in farewell and wordlessly headed back down the sidewalk in an unfortunate careening to the humdrum of my normal life. I relived that last lingering moment over and over, a little slice of heaven for me to take out and hold whenever I wanted. And I did lots of wanting. Of all varieties.

CHAPTER SEVEN

"Who in the world is talking?" Grace asked, blinking at me from the passenger seat in my car. She had her dark hair in two french braids and a picture of SpongeBob at a disco on her purple T-shirt. My little cousin was brilliant, kind, and adorable. Because of that combination, she easily pulled off her own quirky fashion and even made it look great. All she was missing was the tuba she'd mastered in the marching band.

I pointed to my new car addition. "A police scanner. The station hooked me up with one when I asked. That way I can make sure that I don't miss anything I could be covering."

"This is all very Kristen Welker of you."

I quirked an eyebrow. She was sixteen. "You know who Kristen Welker is?"

"Skyler, I watch the news. You know I'm in debate, right? Welker is my hero. She's goals."

I did know the debate part. The kid had more after-school activities than an actual school bus, which was why I was playing shuttle service. Emory, recovering from her lumpectomy, had her second round of radiation that day, and Sarah was with her. I was glad that they'd finally taken me up on my offer for backup help with Grace. She had her license, but no one exactly trusted her behind the wheel just yet. There was rumor of a lead foot and a fascination with race cars that I could one hundred percent imagine. That was Grace, future valedictorian who would also smoke you in a drag race and laugh about it. Fearless.

As we drove, the scanner kicked on, and I turned it up just to check in. Another robbery. This time the suspect made off with sixty dollars in fives from the register. He'd grabbed the one stack and had taken off before grabbing the rest. Huh. You'd think he'd at least grab the twenties if he was going to take one. I looked over at Grace. "How would you feel about a detour to check on a robber who was too terrified to take what he came for?"

She nodded in the direction of the road ahead of us. "I say, take me to this place."

It wasn't a convenience store this time, but rather a small grocery store with a large assortment of fruit. Grace snagged an apple and handed over a dollar to the cashier. The police had come and gone, but the owner was incredibly eager to speak with me. I got Ty on the phone and had him video the guy as he ranted about the youth of today and the boy who'd stolen his fives. The description matched. A kid who was nervous as hell.

"Could you see his face?" I asked.

"He's a rugrat hooligan. A child," the man practically bellowed as Ty rolled. "He was waving a pistol around and had no idea what to do with it. I saw tufts of blond hair under his hood. Barking at me to hand over the cash. Someone could have been hurt or worse. We need this guy off the street. Now!"

"That's a great sound bite," Grace whispered, and I was proud of her for recognizing that. This was the first time someone had mentioned the danger this kid posed. I had Ty bank the footage and thought it was time I talked with Kristin about the story. We might have enough, and it was time to get this guy off the street, which just might happen if I could get the stores to release stills of the guy from surveillance.

"Wait, so there's a kid named Seth botching robberies all over the city?" Kristin stirred her coffee as she mulled over my pitch.

I was pumped, on a high, and probably talking too fast. "That's what it's starting to look like. A young kid who is clearly out of his depth is showing up at small stores, misfiring his gun, and running out of the place with next to nothing. Then does it all again in a week."

"Seth?"

"Right? It's not the toughest name, which is why it gives the story a hook." I was bouncing and could feel it. "Can I formally move forward? Thoughts?"

She waved her spoon at me. "Sure. Can you get it to me for tonight?"

I winced. "Maybe."

"Make it happen."

Gah! I dashed off, fled the office like a felon, and got to work. I grabbed Ty. "We gotta move. Can you start work on the Seth package? I'll get on the phone to get surveillance. We can shoot my stand-up in front of the first convenience store and then cut to Seth footage, intermixing sound bites. I don't know why I'm telling you this. You know what you're doing. I'll leave the room. Are you good?"

Ty grinned and his eyes crinkled. No sign of pressure or urgency, which helped me relax. "Yeah, buddy, we got this. I'm wearing my lucky cutoffs." He offered me a high five and then ambled into the editing bay. I turned and barreled to my phone to see about that surveillance video, except I didn't. I barreled right into Carrie as she came around the corner instead.

"Whoa." She caught me by the shoulders. "Skyler."

"Sorry," I said, meeting crisp blue eyes. "Didn't mean to go all linebacker on you." That's when I saw what she was wearing—a sleeveless blouse with quite a dip in the front. "Now I have a *whoa* of my own."

She straightened, released me, and slid her hair behind her ear. "New from the wardrobe people. The higher-ups have requested edgier."

It was definitely that. Carrie looked amazing, but more like she was on a date than delivering the news. They were definitely moving in a new direction. "Well, you look fantastic."

She dropped her tone. "It feels wrong, but apparently we're warring for ratings with Channel Twelve." I didn't want to encourage the ideology behind the choice, but I would definitely tune in to see Caroline McNamara looking like that. I realized I was going to hell. I would enjoy every moment of her until my descent. "What's with the rushing?"

"Oh. I have a potential story airing tonight if we can turn it around in time."

"Go, go, go. I won't keep you." But she could. I'd make up the time later if it meant more time talking to Carrie. We'd not really seen much of each other this week, and after that moment outside her house, I craved more time. Okay, I craved a lot of things, but they all involved her.

"But can we catch up later?"

She smiled softly. "I would love that."

"Good. Great." I was feeling brave. "What time are you off?" I said it half in jest.

"Ten forty-five tonight. You free?"

"Yeah," I said automatically, shocked. "Let's get that drink." I loved adrenaline and the way it allowed me to act on every whimsical thought.

"Meet me at Jack's across the street? It's quiet enough. We can unwind."

"I'll be there."

"Bye, Skyler. Stop running into things."

"No promises." Yes, I turned and watched her walk down the hall, taking in the subtle movements of her hips and trying my damnedest to smother my grin. I'd seen Jack's before and colleagues from the station going in and out. It was an unofficial hangout, and I was excited to experience it. But honestly, I'd have driven to Texas with her if Carrie'd asked.

"Oh, you got it bad, bad, bad. Look at your hound dog face."

I turned to see Ty watching me watch Carrie.

I smacked him in the stomach. "You don't know that. Maybe I was working through the story."

"Sure, buddy." He walked away again. "Do you always drool over robberies?"

"Maybe."

There was nothing more exhilarating than sliding a story in under the wire, just in time for broadcast. Devante had watched the Seth package twice before tapping his pencil to his chin and requesting two minor changes that had Ty editing like a bat outta hell. When Kristin approved the final version, Ty and I stood and fell into each other in a celebratory hug before happy dancing through the editing bay. Conga line was next.

"I see you two are already quite the duo." Kristin wasn't wrong. I missed my old camera guy Greg and our steady partnership, but working with Ty was fun and energizing in a whole new sense. He kept me grounded and calm when I took things too seriously and reminded me that sometimes you had to take time for a damned lime Slurpee and dance session.

Ty shrugged. "She's all right. A little eager for my taste."

"He's okay, too. A little dopey for mine."

We nodded in agreement and hip bumped.

"Yeah. Okay. Just as I thought." Kristin shook her head and left for the control room. She'd be on headset for the broadcast.

"Go watch," Ty said. "You know you want to."

I hesitated. "No." Then, "I think I'm gonna." Giddy. I scrunched my shoulders.

Who would have thought that the very story I'd gotten stuck with on my first day at the station would lead to a larger package? One I was immensely proud of. I rolled my shoulders, standing in the back of the cold studio midbroadcast, watching as Carrie teed up my story. I gave myself a little squeeze. The daily reporting I did was great, but when a story of my very own hit air, a different kind of pride hit like a drug.

"A string of botched robberies has police on their toes, chasing a suspect that just can't seem to get his act together. Skyler Ruiz has more." I watched the monitor as my face appeared and the package played, a series of clips from witnesses, and my voice under the surveillance footage of Seth.

"Know anyone named Seth?" Rory asked as the broadcast shifted back to the news desk.

"Thankfully, no," Carrie said with a laugh. "Let's just hope the police get to know him shortly. Don, I hear there's reasons for Padres fans to rejoice."

I was smiling, marinating in the satisfaction that I'd done my job and excited to come to work and do it all over again. For now, I had a drink to look forward to. With a quick hair fluff and lipstick application in the station restroom, I was on my way.

Jack's was actually a really cozy bar, dark woods, dim lighting, and a menu full of cocktails I wasn't entirely unfamiliar with. I was first by design and took a moment to catch my breath before the outside door opened and Carrie appeared. She made it approximately 2.3 steps before a couple exchanged glances and paused their exit. She'd been recognized. I watched as she smiled and nodded and posed for a selfie with the couple. As they exited, I watched her anchor smile dim. She exhaled, now the woman once again, and scanned the room. I smiled and lifted a hand when her gaze landed on mine. She approached and slid into the booth across from me. "Now that was a day."

"Wasn't it?" I exhaled. "I didn't order yet. I wanted to wait for you."

"Oh, that was thoughtful. But you didn't have to do that."

"Glass of the Zingari Toscana for you, Carrie?" the server asked with a smile. She had a pencil behind her ear and one arm full of tattoos. Impressive. I'd never have the courage for such a permanent decision, but the ink worked for her.

"I'd love one, Johanna."

"For you?"

"Oh. I'll have a glass, too." Johanna nodded and headed off. "They know your order. You're a Jack's regular."

She winced. "I've had a few here. It's true." She sat back. "Seth, huh?"

"*Seth.*"

"What the hell? Kristin said you made the connection before the police even tied the crimes together."

I shrugged. "Different officers taking the reports. I was lucky enough to be the commonality."

"Oh, don't do that." She shook her head. "Don't downplay your skills or the power of your observations. Women so often gloss over their achievements when we should be hanging banners about all we accomplish. No one does those things for us. So I'm celebrating you on your behalf."

Our drinks arrived and I lifted my glass. "You're right. To how fucking brilliant I am."

"And to getting Seth the help he needs."

We touched our glasses and she regarded me. "You look really pretty tonight."

This was not the first time she'd complimented my appearance, but for some reason, it felt like the most…intimate. It was just the two of us, sitting in a dimly lit booth late at night. It wasn't just a pleasantry. It couldn't have been. I let that settle.

"Thank you."

"Skyler?"

"Yes?"

"The blushing at compliments is also a nice touch."

I rolled my lips in, trying to squash the heat on my cheeks, but I felt her gaze on my skin, and that upped the difficulty. Finally, I decided to just roll with it. "I'm glad we're doing this. Spending time together." I still wasn't sure what it all meant, what her intentions were, because it was hard for me to believe they were anything beyond those of a friendly colleague. However, the evidence was beginning to suggest otherwise. I liked the evidence very much.

"Yeah." She bit the inside of her lip and my middle section went tight. "There's something I want to show you. Follow me."

"Okay, sure." We left our glasses and I followed her down a little hallway off the main room that was lined with a series of framed photos on the wall. I perused the selection as we walked, noticing one of her and Rory with their arms around a guy I imagined to be Jack himself. I pointed at the photo and turned to her, ready to comment, only to have my shoulders gently pressed against the opposite wall and Carrie step into my space. "Oh," was all I managed as my eyes dropped to her lips a split second before they were on mine. I was instantly warm and alive and beyond turned-on. I kissed her back, savoring the experience of the warmth of her mouth. Her lips parted, granting me entrance, and I slipped my tongue into her mouth, tasting. The hallway was dark and private enough that I let myself get lost in her and the haze of kissing the most intoxicating woman I'd ever known. How was this my life? I sank into that kiss with all I had. Her hands cupped my face, and when she pressed her body up against mine, it pulled a moan from the back of my throat. She was every bit as confident at kissing as she was on air, and it was hot as fuck. A door at the end of the hallway opened, and Caroline took a reflexive step back. Calm. Cool. One of the servers passed us, and we nodded. Meanwhile, everything in me screamed out at the loss because all I wanted to do in this world was reverse our positions, press her against that damn wall, and pick up where we left off with the kind of dedication kissing Carrie demanded.

The server disappeared around the corner and we were left alone in the hallway. We watched each other for a beat. Our breathing tracked noticeably faster, and we came back together again without a word. My fingers slid into her hair and her hands landed at my waist, hauling me in, hips to hips. Our eyes met. Hers flashed. The tension of those first few encounters, the flirtatious energy of the last few, the compliments, stolen looks all came together in an explosion of passion. My fantasies had been good, but nothing compared to the reality of this moment, this woman.

"I didn't know that was gonna happen," I said, apparently embracing my honest side.

She touched her lips and rolled them in. I wondered if she tasted the gloss from my lips. "I surprised myself. Should I apologize? I will if—"

"God, no."

A pause. She softened. "Good. I just…you have an effect on me." Her mouth was so close to mine. "That's the best way to put it."

I didn't know how that was possible, but after the last five minutes, I was starting to believe in my power. Was a little drunk with it now. "I had no idea, but I will say that I can definitely identify. Well, now that you're nicer."

That pulled a smile. "It's paying off."

I asked what I had to. "When we leave this hallway, is this whole thing going to disappear? Back to business as usual tomorrow?" Quite simply, I didn't want the spell to break.

"I think that's up to us."

I nodded. Absorbing. "I like options."

"Me, too." She inclined her head back down the hallway. "I propose we take the *option* to finish that wine before Johanna thinks we ditched it."

I exhaled, trying to remember what a simple task like wine drinking might entail because my world had been wonderfully disrupted. "I think I can manage that."

It turned out to be harder than I thought. We attempted to muddle our way through conversation.

"Tell me about your mom," Carrie said. "You said she raised you alone."

I nodded and swirled the wine in my glass. My heart still thudded. *Focus.* "She worked long hours and put herself through law school, trying to provide for me. So she wasn't around a lot, but when she was, she was always this bright light in my life. I spent a lot of time with my aunt and uncle, lived with them for months at a time. And Sarah, my cousin, who you've met. She was at the dinner party."

"The sweetest human on the planet." The way she was looking at me, though, said her mind wasn't on Sarah or her sweet qualities. It was where mine was, trapped back down that hallway and wanting to kiss her again.

"She's pretty great."

"I can tell."

"Me, too."

"A lot."

We were no longer making sense. What we were doing was losing ourselves in each other's eyes like a couple of lustful cartoon characters. I'd never experienced this kind of physical tug to another person and savored every moment of it.

"Speaking of the dinner party, you in that dress." Carrie shook her head. "I could not stop looking. I thought you were beautiful the first moment I laid eyes on you, but that night…" She grinned into her drink and took a sip.

"Yeah, well, you weren't the only one making discoveries. I had no idea you…"

"What?"

I dropped my voice. "Weren't exactly straight." I still didn't know how she identified, but after that kiss, I could certainly rule out one option.

"Well, I've not taken out a billboard."

"Is it something you keep quiet?"

"There was probably a time when I did. But these days, no. I'm not interested in bottling up who I am. But I'm sure there are executives who would prefer it."

I blinked. That one snagged my attention, because this was the second mention today about what the higher-ups might want. "It seems like you get a lot of pressure from above."

She laughed. "Understatement. I'm sure they would love it if I lost ten pounds and ten years, but I'm not a magician. So they control the things they *can*, like my clothes, my PR framing."

"God." Carrie didn't strike me as the kind of woman who would bow to those kinds of demands, so it made me wonder if she feared for her job. The idea seemed ludicrous to me. She was a staple in this city. Her face was everywhere, and in my experience, she was universally adored. "I can't say I've received the same kind of scrutiny. I think that just means I'm a nobody."

"Give it time." She shook her head. "You're not going to be a nobody forever. Your star is already climbing. Trust me."

I was nervous to ask for more, but I valued her perspective. "What makes you think so?"

"You have that spark. It's unteachable. People are born with it or they aren't. Others just can't look away. Do you think Tam hired you for your experience?"

"I was covering softball games and the mayor getting a pie in the face for charity."

"See? He knows the spark when he sees it."

"He saw it in you."

"Back in the day, yes. I'd only worked in two other markets before landing as a reporter at KTMW."

"You were me. And maybe I'll be you one day." I looked off into the distance wistfully, only halfway serious.

She nodded. "But be careful what you wish for."

"But it's the dream, that anchor desk."

"And I get why. The power seat, the attention, and there are quite a few perks. I'll be honest about that. But it comes with the scrutiny and expectations that aren't so easy to meet."

I might have loved kissing Carrie, but I liked talking with her like this, candidly, nearly as much. She was full of wisdom and knew the station better than anyone else. "You'd never know it. You handle the pressure well."

"Yeah." But something shifted behind her eyes, and the smile that had been there moments before had waned. I wanted it back, and my brain was already trying to figure out how to make that happen.

"Well, you have a fan over here." I looked skyward. "In maybe more ways than one."

Her lips parted, and I remembered how sexy they were all over again. "We're dangerous, aren't we?"

I nodded.

She shook her head as if to say: *What have I gotten myself into?*

"I don't think I could wrap my brain around everything that's happened today if I tried." That's when the exhaustion hit, having been buried for hours by the excitement of the drinks, the story, the kissing.

She took a deep breath, mirroring my fatigue. "Then let's leave it for tomorrow's version of us. They're much better equipped."

"If we walk out together…"

"Who knows where we'd end up?"

We let that linger between us a moment as the angel and devil on my shoulders waged a war for the ages. I had a feeling I could persuade her to go home with me or to take me back to her gorgeous landscaped compound. But was that the right way to go about this? I wanted to be thoughtful and was literally in no position. My brain was missing in action. Had ghosted me.

Here went nothing. "I can't believe I'm about to say this, and I'm one hundred percent certain I'm going to regret it later, but you go. I'm going to do the levelheaded thing and sit right here and pay the check."

She raised an eyebrow. "Gonna fulfill that IOU, huh?"

"It's the least I can do," I deadpanned.

That pulled a laugh. "Skyler, Skyler, Skyler. You're pretty adorable." She tapped the table. "But I will graciously accept the drink." She reached for her bag. "Congrats on the Seth story."

"Thank you. It was a good day."

She sent me one last smile and, with a wave to Johanna, headed for the door. Part of me wondered if we'd slipped into some sort of alternate universe and the world would return to normal tomorrow. Would we see each other at work and pretend none of this happened once the light of day hit? I sighed and leaned against the back of the booth, allowing my mind to revel in each delicious moment of tonight. As a sea of rapid thoughts overwhelmed, I knew one thing for certain. If I died in my sleep that night, I'd leave this earth a very happy woman.

"Was everything to your liking?" Johanna asked as she picked up the leather portfolio containing my credit card.

"Oh, very much," I said without hesitation. "Five stars."

CHAPTER EIGHT

The air felt different now. So did even the smallest interactions with Carrie. They carried new weight. Had a whole new meaning.

I'd kissed her. She'd kissed me. Passionately.

There was also the element of secrecy that wrapped everything up in an exciting little knot. I grinned to myself more than I didn't. I relished sharing that little stolen bit of information between us.

Carlos walked by and paused to chat with Carrie about the story meeting, looping me into the conversation, too. He had no idea what we'd done the night before. *I made out with her, Carlos. Yesterday.*

"Have you seen Tam around today?" Carrie asked later, swiveling in her chair as if pulled from a moment of intense concentration.

I turned from my spot at my desk. "He was in the break room half an hour ago, so he's gotta be around here somewhere." We stared at each other for a beat too long. It felt purposeful and awesome.

"That's great. Thank you." She stood and headed off to find him. "And blue is a great color on you."

I smiled at my computer, my cheeks hot, my morning made.

I was out on stories most of the day, tracking down sound bites from the mayor and covering a feature about a group of kids raising money for their classmate with a life-threatening diagnosis. None of it required a live shot, so I was back at the station before the five. Carrie had a mirror out and was giving her hair a fluff, something she did daily before walking down to the studio. She regarded me out of the corner of her eye.

"Good stuff today?"

"Medium stuff. Sweet stuff." I shrugged. "It was a good day."

"Now what?"

"Now is the best part. I get to watch you bring it all to the people." Her eyes lit up, and it stole the air. "You're really going to watch? Here?"

"I'll watch the five here and the ten from home. With popcorn. And my dog, Micky. Micky adores popcorn. Catches it in the air. You'd like him."

"Maybe I'll meet him?"

"Oh, I think you definitely will." The thought gave me such a rush of energy that I couldn't contain myself. "Hey, can I show you something in bay three?" It was empty. I'd just passed it moments before.

She checked her watch, likely making sure she wouldn't be late to the studio, and nodded. "Of course. A story?"

"Yeah, I need your opinion." I led her into the tiny dimly lit room, closed the door, and turned. "Hi."

She grinned. Gave me a head shake. "You're sneaky."

"A little." And with a confidence that might be fleeting, I seized the moment and kissed her with all the desire I'd had building in me for the past eighteen hours. She might have had me against that hallway wall the night before, but I had her against the door of the editing bay, my tongue in her mouth, my hands creeping up from her waist closer to the undercurves of her breasts, which without even seeing them had to be the most fantastic breasts on the planet. Round. Medium in size. My hands itched to hold their weight and then run my thumbs across her nipples. My tongue longed to lick circles. The idea alone had me wet.

"Good God," she murmured as I kissed off the gloss she'd likely just applied. She apparently didn't mind and came back for more, capturing my mouth and running her tongue along my bottom lip. My shirt was being untucked, and her warm hands were on my back. I heard myself moan at the simple touch. I'd never felt my responses so intense. My knees shook.

"You have to get to the studio," I said around a kiss. "I really, really don't want you to go." Another kiss. "But you can't get fired for standing up"—a kiss—"all of San Diego. That would really dampen the mood."

"Mm-hmm," she said, her lips clinging to mine as if savoring this last moment.

"But you'll"—kissing—"need more"—kissing—"lip gloss. I kissed it off."

She pulled her face back. "Good thing I have some. Come here," she said and hauled me in for one last toe-curling go round. Who taught this woman how to kiss, and could I get an amen in their honor?

"Praise God."

"What's that?" she asked, smoothing her hair back in place.

"Reflex celebration."

She touched my chin. "We have to stop kissing in dimly lit small spaces."

"I'm fully in favor of exploring larger ones. And medium. More of the small is fine, too. Did I say praise God a minute ago? Meant it."

"You're so cute. Have I told you that?"

I took a breath, letting my heart rate settle. "You have. I don't mind it at all. Would sex kitten be better? Sure. But I can work with cute."

She opened the door and looked back at me. "You're just proving my point." She dropped to a whisper. "And sex kitten is definitely in there, too."

The door closed and I was left hot and bothered and wondering what was next.

"Hey!" Ty yelled, popping his head in and scaring the life out of me. "You in here editing something?"

"What?" I placed a hand on my terrified chest. "You can't just walk in on someone and scream."

"Yes, I can," he said and looked around, taking in the blank monitors. Caught. "What are you doing?"

"Nothing," I said, pushing past him into the hallway.

He laughed. "Does nothing deliver the news at five and ten?"

"Shut up," I said, without looking back.

Lasagna noodles were so weird. Who invented them and what must that have been like? I sat on a barstool watching Sarah make dinner and felt like I was twelve again, admiring my big cousin doing something cool. I'd swung by to catch up, see how everyone was doing, but I also selfishly wanted to talk to someone about the new development in my life. My head was spinning in an excited, terrified sense, and I needed to find balance.

"Seems quiet today," I said.

Sarah nodded and I could tell her spirits were low. "Grace is at a debate tournament. Walter is snoozing in his doughnut bed." I glanced behind me at the family dog, curled into a big ball. "And Emory's lying down in the bedroom. She's been a little down. Low energy."

My heart sank. The reality of her situation still didn't seem real. I hated every second of it. "So, she's struggling. I get that."

Sarah took a moment. "She acts like none of this is a big deal and that she's feeling fine, and while that might be true physically, she's not herself. I wish she'd just admit that this whole thing, being sick, it's taking its toll." She tossed the spatula onto the countertop and placed her hands on the back of her hips in a frustrated move.

I nodded. "But she's Emory."

"Pillar of strength and unbreakable in the face of adversity. Yeah, I'm familiar." She nodded too many times, battling something inside herself. "But there's a time when it's okay to drop all that and admit that things are hard," she said, clearly worked up.

"Not how she was raised," I said, reminding Sarah of Emory's less-than-warm upbringing. "She was groomed to be the best and show no cracks in the armor."

"But that can only go so far. I need her to speak up more. Let me know what she needs, so I can be all those things for her." She was beyond rattled, and who wouldn't be? The woman she was in love with was very sick, and it likely felt like her world was spinning out of control without any brakes. I couldn't imagine the stress.

I took Sarah's hand and gave it a squeeze. "But listen, there's *you*, too. I'm here for you, okay? On days where you just need to cry or vent or throw back a shot of the good stuff because it's been a day, you call *me*. We'll throw 'em back together."

The tiniest of smiles appeared, the kind that came with encouragement. Sarah picked up the spatula and smoothed the sauce again. "Well, I can't get you drunk and send you off to TV land."

"Sure you can," I said automatically. "Drunk reporters are in. People love it when the news goes off the rails. It's the best, really."

"My cousin, the slurring town crier."

I nodded along. "Has quite the ring. You're welcome." I glanced at the staircase that led up to their bedroom. I'd come over with the idea I'd dish with Sarah, tell her everything, but now I was ready to pivot. "Can I go in and see Emory? Or would that be pushing it?"

Sarah nodded. "No, I actually think it would be good for her. She hasn't been going out as much and needs to see humans other than me, Grace, or Lucy, who barges in on her and barks orders. It's the greatest. I need her on payroll."

"Taking a page from Lucy's book then." It was all the permission I needed. I made my way up the stairs and knocked quietly. "Hey, Em. It's Skyler, your favorite cousin-in-law. You free?"

"Oh." A pause. "Yeah, yeah. Of course. Come in."

She was sitting up on top of the rumpled covers, which probably meant she scrambled there when she heard me coming in. Her hair was down and her face pale, but she was still Emory. Radiant even when less than herself.

"Hi, you. I'm here for your brain."

She sat up taller as if to prove herself. "And here I am with it. Convenient, no?"

I nodded. "Most definitely."

"I didn't even know you were here. What's new? Hit me."

I sat cross-legged opposite her. "My head is spinning, and all I think about is kissing."

"Well." Her eyes went wide. "That is not what I expected to come out of your mouth." She winced and leaned in. "Aren't you still fifteen?"

"You'd think, but no. I'm nearly thirty and saw two gray hairs last week."

"No."

"I keep telling you, I'm old. Let's get back to the kissing and its impact on my productivity. How do I get the dishes done?"

She waved an arm back and forth and closed her eyes. "We've skipped a step. I didn't even know you were dating anyone."

"Exactly. I'm not. I'm just doing the kissing."

"Huh." She nodded, absorbing. "And enjoying it apparently."

"Immensely. I look forward to more."

"Skyler. Who are you kissing?"

I paused. "Carrie. Caroline McNamara of TV fame."

"Oh, man. Does Sarah know?"

"She does not. You're first. Honored?"

"Gloating. Sarah's always first." A smile. She was more energetic now, which felt like a win. While I was happy to add a little spice to what might have been an otherwise depressing day, everything I'd said was wholeheartedly genuine, and I welcomed any girl talk, advice, or even admonishment. Though I couldn't imagine why.

"There have been two instances of the kissing, if you can even call it that. Making out is probably more appropriate, and now I'm not normal anymore. I'm a hyperexaggerated version of myself that smiles and exhales a lot."

Emory pointed at me. "Well, you're doing it right now."

"Of course I am. It's my new look. Is there an angle I'm missing, though?"

She paused. "Well, definition, for one. You said you're not dating, just kissing. As someone who places a lot of value on you and thinks you're a fantastic person, I question her intentions and want to protect your heart like a guard dog."

"There is that."

"So you have real feelings for her?"

"It's early, but yeah…I think I could. Not that I'm ready to declare to her officially." I shook my head, trying to dissect it all. "I don't want to come off as someone not able to handle a little no-strings-attached entanglement, but at the same time? I've been there, done that with Kacey, and that only works for so long."

Emory's eyes took on fire. "See? You're already very aware of what your needs are and what does not work for you. Don't be afraid to voice those things. Sooner rather than later would be good."

The idea, while incredibly practical, was terrifying. "I think I'll just play things by ear. See where it takes us."

Emory marinated on this for a beat. "Promise one thing. Don't let her status cloud your perspective. This is a woman with more life experience than you, who you've looked up to for quite some time."

"You should see her very grown-up garden. I could never."

She smiled. "That doesn't mean she gets the upper hand, okay?"

I nodded.

She closed one eye. "Can I say one last thing?"

"Yes. I'm paying attention to everything you're throwing at me."

She took my hand. "You're very excited about all this, but don't confuse your excitement for feelings. They're different."

Okay, that was sobering, but also a valid point.

"Give yourself time to get to know the true her before deciding this is right."

"Fair enough. I like it. I will channel my inner reporter and get the whole story before reaching any kind of conclusion." It actually sounded like the best kind of project, and I wanted to get started right away. I fell back onto the bed and threw my arm over my head. "Did I mention the kissing, though?"

She grabbed my cheeks and gave my face an affectionate shake. "I think you said something about it."

"Am I missing important details in here?" Sarah. She stood at the door with her hands on her hips as she studied us.

Emory beamed. "*A*, I was first and *B*, We're going to need to make out later. It's all the rage."

She laughed. "Well, I always chase trends."

"Here we go again." I covered my eyes. "Stop being cuter than the rest of the population. It's not fair. Give the rest of us a shot, please."

"Nothing we can do about that," Sarah said. "Want to help me set the table?" She was using her extra-sweet voice, so they would definitely be making out later.

"I thought you'd never ask," Emory said, seeming to forget that I was in the room. Sarah had this way of simply dazzling her. Plus, there seemed to be a light in her eyes again, and that made me happy.

"And you," Sarah said, breaking away and pointing at me. "You're staying for dinner. No arguments. Grace will sob if you try to leave before she's home."

"I never flee from homemade lasagna."

"And she has a bit of news," Emory said, slinging her arm around my shoulders as we left the room together.

Sarah beamed. "Oh, and I can't wait to hear all about it."

Emory looked over at her. "Just remember, I was first."

CHAPTER NINE

The next weekend brought the annual station picnic where the various teams that made the news happen at KTMW came together to hang out and eat a lot of food. Verdict? Michelangelo looked really cute in a bow tie. Because it was warm out, I limited his outfit to just that one accessory so the folks at the station picnic would see him at his sassiest but also at his most comfortable and relaxed. A versatile Micky was the best Micky.

As for me, I went with navy shorts and a white and navy shirt tied at the waist. A matching white sandal said, *I'm fashionable but also here for sandwiches*. I pulled my hair into a singular barrette, leaving much of it on my shoulders, and hoped that I'd both blend in and maybe pull a little attention from a dazzling blonde.

When I arrived at the park close to lunchtime that Saturday afternoon, the aroma of hot dogs and hamburgers wafting from the nearby grill nearly brought me to my knees. I'd not eaten breakfast, and that made the food that much more fantastic smelling. The picnic grounds were already crowded, and what I thought might be nineties music floated from the DJ booth in the distance. There was a ring toss game for kids, face painting, and even a couple of guys twisting balloon animals. That atmosphere was easily festive and lively.

"Can I interest you in a green giraffe? My treat." I smiled at the sound of Carrie's voice as it tickled my ear. My whole body said hello.

"I have a feeling they're free. And green?" I turned to find her standing there in a sky-blue sundress, slightly off the shoulder. Her blond hair carried lazy waves. The flip-flops on her feet were less fancy than mine, which made me absorb how relaxed and all-around gorgeous she looked. I swallowed. My palms itched. I loved it.

"I prefer a little less realism in my balloon animals, or what's the point?"

I grinned. "I'm just amazed you've thought about it enough to formulate a balloon-animal philosophy."

"Not my first network picnic."

I pretend-gasped. "Then you know where the good food lives."

She leaned in, and I could smell her perfume. Fresh flowers on a spring day. "Tam's grillwork is superior to Devante's who leans more toward an outer char."

I nodded. "This is valuable intel."

"Who is this dapper dog?"

I looked down and grinned at my prancing pup. "This is Michelangelo. He doesn't mind a little char."

Carrie knelt down with the look of someone literally melting. I'd never seen her so utterly vulnerable. "Hi there, adorable puppy." She beamed at him, and I realized that I was, perhaps, no longer present. Micky, attention hog that he was, shook his entire back end and picked up his feet as if marching in place. After he gave her hand a few good licks, she leaned closer and allowed him to lick her cheek.

"Now you've done it."

"We're just saying hello." She straightened, but when she did so, she brought Micky up with her. "We're really good friends now," she informed me and kissed his cheek right back. "I like his tie." Another kiss. I could see where this was going, and it made me smile. Especially since my dog was clearly in heaven and stared at me with such victory that I had to laugh.

"Caroline? Do you have a moment?"

She beamed at the man who'd approached us. "Of course."

"My wife's a big fan, and I'd love to introduce you."

She looked down at Micky and back at me. "We're going on a field trip. That okay?"

I laughed, surprised at her commitment. "By all means."

I searched out a beverage, stoked to find a large dispenser of fresh lemonade, and watched from a distance as Carrie and my dog posed for the photo. Once that happened, it was like she'd opened the floodgates, and there was an informal line of staff family members who wanted to say hello and grab a selfie with her. Her job was never really done. To her credit, she didn't seem to mind and smiled and laughed at all the right moments. I remembered her body pressed to mine in the editing bay, and my cheeks went red-hot.

"How's it going, Skyler? Enjoying yourself?" Carlos rocked back on his heels, wearing plaid shorts and a white polo.

"I am. Steal any stories lately?" I said it with a wide, friendly grin so he knew we were okay, but that I also saw him for who he was and what he was willing to do.

He considered my question. "I don't know. Any more Seth spottings I could get in on?" He was ribbing me, but in a playful way. "What about Thomas, or Kenneth? Got any of those?"

"I'll have you know that they caught Seth. My story got his photo out there, and the tip line blew up." Apparently, the whole neighborhood knew Seth and his ineptness and just needed a little prompting to call in. I loved it when my work made a difference somewhere. It made the job all the more gratifying.

"Job well done," he said sincerely and touched his beer can to my cup. "It's rough out there, and you're holding your own. The world is noticing. Trust me. Tam sure is."

I squinted. "How do you know that?" I hadn't received much feedback from the man himself, outside of a polite nod or small talk before he headed back to his office with the army of television screens. I imagined him mainlining popcorn and taking furious notes on all the other stations, sacrificing sleep and sanity.

"Easy." Carlos widened his eyes. "Because you're still here. They don't wait too long before deciding someone isn't the right fit. You seem to have made the cut." He raised his can at me a final time and trotted off because they'd called for anyone who wanted to play touch football.

I stood on my own and absorbed what he'd said. *I made the cut.* Understanding and relief flooded, and I bopped my head to the music, on a high. I was safe. Thus far in my new life, I was doing okay. Better than okay, really. It was in that moment that Carrie turned her head, midconversation with one of the studio camera guys and his wife. She met my gaze and latched, Micky now sitting patiently wrapped around her ankle. The exchange was private, and colored by the knowledge of all we'd done together and all the things I still wanted to do. She broke into a soft smile, and I longed to do them then and there. Instead, I sipped my lemonade, exercising patience I didn't know I had. She was already changing my life.

An hour later, after we'd both been stolen away into conversations with other people, I found myself, at last, free. I scanned the grounds and found her alone at the condiments table assembling a burger. "Lettuce placement is important," she said as I approached.

"Define."

She gestured to the leafy green in her hand. "Can't have soggy lettuce. You have to keep it away from the ketchup. Give it its own side of the burger where it can hang out in peace. Crunchy. Leafy." She placed the lettuce on the opposite bun from the one she'd already added ketchup and mayonnaise to. "Follow me for more tips." She winked.

"You make a compelling case. You might have a shadow," I said, touching her wrist and causing her to go still. She rolled her lips in. I removed my hand. Just a little reminder of our sizzle, which seemed to have had the effect I'd intended.

"I'm not sure I mind that sentence," she said. More of that torturous prolonged eye contact. How long until I could touch her again the way I wanted to? She had other plans. "Come on. Let's check out the egg toss. Important picnic component. I'd hate for you to miss out on the basics."

"There's an egg toss?"

"Every year." She grabbed her plate, and we headed out. "I used to partner with Rory, but we broke up over a difference in strategy. He's too aggressive out there. This whole thing depends on the throw-catch relationship. Looking for a new partner now. Game?"

I paused, understanding. "Are you suggesting *we enter* the egg tossing competition? What if the egg I throw breaks all over you?" I stared in abject terror at her perfectly fitting sundress that was best egg-free. How could I live with myself if I changed that?

"Then I'm sure you'll find a way to make it up to me," she said quietly. "Won't you, Skyler?"

I sucked in air. Point taken. I definitely could.

As we waited for our official number to be called, Lucy appeared in picnic glamour. A red plaid sleeveless top and white shorts. She scooped up Micky and agreed to babysit during the competition. As we chatted, I watched Carrie attempt to eat her cheeseburger amid several interruptions. A bite here. A handshake and introduction to someone. A bite there. A photo with a well-wisher. Another bite. Oh, to be that burger.

"Gonna bring it home this year, Carrie?" Kip from sports asked as he stretched. Literally stretched. Apparently, these people took egg tossing way more seriously than I would have guessed.

"You know it," she said, dabbing the ketchup daintily from the side of her mouth after a hearty bite. She was like one of those judges on a reality competition who dove into food with gusto, but at the same time made eating it look easy. Controlled. How? I would have made a mess of that burger. Ketchup dribbling down my chin in hapless disaster. She was a goddamned sexy pro. "Ms. Skyler Ruiz is my teammate this year."

"Oh yeah?" Kip asked, turning to me. "Feeling lucky?"

"Not especially," I said blandly, my nerves bleeding into my voice. Carrie raised an eyebrow, and I laughed at her subtle correction. "I take it back. I'm feeling like we have this thing all sealed up. No question of our imminent victory. Get ready to cry, sports guy." I looked to Carrie. She nodded. Who knew she was this competitive?

"See you out there," Kip said, stretching his quads one last time before jogging out onto the makeshift competition field.

With the last bite of her burger popped into her mouth, Carrie dusted off her hands and grinned. They called our number. This was it. "Ready to do this?"

"I guess?"

She leaned in and whispered, "Don't worry, Skyler. If your hands are half as good with this egg as they were the last time they were on me, we're going to do just fine." I was left to pick up my jaw as she sashayed after Kip onto the egg battlefield, her ass looking simply magnificent, her legs beneath the dress toned and perfect. My mouth watered, and it had nothing to do with the food. Why was the world keeping me from what I wanted to do so very badly? I imagined what she sounded like when she came, and my whole body experienced a toe-curling shiver.

It turned out I wasn't awful at egg catching and throwing. I thanked my mother for suggesting softball as a way to meet people when I was a third grader. Not only had I met my best childhood friend—Brittany Minor, who now sold Mary Kay and drove a pink Cadillac—but I now had advanced hand–eye coordination that helped me impress San Diego's beloved anchorwoman who I'd been kissing in dark, small spaces. A win.

"Everyone, take another step back," Kristin said into her portable microphone. She was serving as the contest manager and took her job very seriously. Blond hair pulled back and shorts-top combo that showed off the fact that she was a runner. The four remaining teams, which included Carrie and me, did as we were told. "And…throw."

With a deep breath, I tossed the egg, making sure to give it a good conservative arc that would allow Carrie to catch it with soft hands. Nothing out of control. Next to me, Rory threw his egg with a little too much gusto, and Kip paid for it with yolk splattered all over his arms. "My bad," Rory yelled. They exited the field. Another one down.

We pressed on. Carrie threw the egg to me as my heart thudded. Just then, out of the corner of my eye, I saw Micky break free from Lucy's grip and come barreling toward me, leash trailing. By the time my gaze flitted back to Carrie, the egg was well on its way to my chest and with a sickening thud landed on my collarbone and splattered across my chest and upper arms. Micky was now at my ankles, celebrating our reunion with a few vertical springs.

"I'm so sorry," Lucy said, arriving moments after him. "He took off like a shot when he finally located you."

Carrie was in front of me next. She took in the eggy scene with a grimace. "Oh no. Look at you. I'm so sorry."

I held up a hand. "No, I am. I lost focus."

"No, *I* am," Lucy insisted. "I made you lose it."

We laughed as Kristin looked on. "When you three are done, I'll kindly ask you to exit the field."

"Let them stay," Lucy argued with her girlfriend, hands on hips. "Totally my fault for unleashing an adorable dog on them. I cry for mercy upon this innocent team."

"The judge's ruling is nope." Kristin dropped the mic to her side. "But you look cute asking."

Lucy offered an imaginary curtsy to the side of her shorts and fired back a wink. We left the field and looked on as two of the marketing assistants took the win and a gift certificate for admission for two to the nearby movie theater, complete with a built-in snack budget.

"That could have been us," I said somberly to Carrie. "Free snacks. We have to pay for them."

"I don't know how we'll recover," she said, handing me another handful of paper towels. "And I'm really sorry about the shirt. I've been admiring it on you all afternoon." I glanced down at the tragedy. My shirt was temporarily ruined, but because I worked on a variety of unpredictable stories, I always traveled with a change of clothes.

"Not to worry. Back in a few."

"I'll keep my best friend safe while you're gone," she said, scooping up Micky, ruiner of egg tosses, and peppering him with more kisses. He looked at me gleefully. I glared back, jealous and not afraid to show it. "We'll be just fine."

"Mm-hmm."

When I returned, the margarita truck had arrived, and Carrie had secured frozen drinks for both of us. "I took the liberty," she said. "You and a straw sounded kinda fun."

"You did good." It was getting warmer out as the sun moved lower in the sky. The frozen margarita felt cool on my tongue and lowered my body temperature. Heaven-sent, like everything about this day. The fun, flirtatious vibe that bounced between us was the kind of drug I urgently craved. The bonding with my new coworkers had me feeling victorious, and to top it off, Michelangelo was a hit. Especially with the person who mattered most. Egg-bombing aside, this was shaping up to be my day.

"What are you doing after this?" Carrie said and sucked ever so gently from her margarita straw. I now saw her point about these things. Holy hell. Heaven help me.

"I have no plans that I can think of." My eyes were still on her lips and the way they worked that straw.

We were alone. That hadn't happened a lot today. "I was just remarking to myself—you've seen my place, but I've never seen yours."

"You were remarking?" I loved the way she constructed sentences. My center went tight, and I shifted, ordering myself to stop that.

"I was. I was doing that. Thoughts?" Her eyes sparkled, and my heart rate sped up.

"I think your proposal is the best idea I've heard today." It had been a long afternoon, and the sun had almost disappeared behind the trees. I imagined us relaxing on the couch together. Maybe opening a bottle of wine. Her go-to. Maybe my hands had a way of wandering to her thigh. I looked around. About half the crowd had already left. "I think it would be okay if we left now."

"I'll follow you this time. *Your* shadow."

I smiled. "We have a theme."

"It works."

I led the way home with Carrie following not far behind. I met her on the sidewalk out front, nervous energy abounding. "Disclaimer. There's no incredible landscaping on the way in, and it's not a deceptively huge apartment. No false walls or big rooms hiding in the back."

"Disclaimer. I wasn't expecting anything in particular, Sky. I just wanted to see where you live."

Sky. She'd only called me that once before, but I liked it very much on her lips. I had to pause to absorb all the feelings it brought on. I'd have to unpack that later along with the newfound urgency she'd shuffled into my agenda. "Right this way." I led her inside, now hyperaware of every little detail of my decorating, and grateful I kept a relatively clean apartment. "This is it. This is the place."

She smiled and perused the living room that opened to the small serviceable white kitchen, separated by an oversized island that would have been super-helpful for someone with more advanced culinary aspirations than my own. These days I came home so exhausted, I was lucky to have the energy to pop a bag of microwave popcorn or heat a bowl of Campbell's. "You have cultivated a very nice place for yourself in the world. This looks like a great apartment to come home to." She sat down on my lavender couch and gave it a bounce. "Comfortable, too."

I rolled my lips in. I liked the look of her on it. "The walls could use a bit more decor. I haven't had the time to shop." She looked around at the framed art I did have and pointed to the painting of a cat reading a book on a bench. I liked quirky things.

"I don't know how you're going to beat this one."

"Well, I can't. It's one of the reasons I resist the effort. Can I interest you in something to drink?"

"Mm-hmm." She stood and made her way over to me. "Can I just do this first?" She wrapped an arm around the small of my back, angled her head, and kissed me like the expert at it she was. She knew how to push my buttons in just this short time. I sank into the warmth of her mouth and the way she held me close, like she couldn't bear there to be distance any longer and she was here to change that. The swell of her breasts pressed against mine made me dizzy. Not a complaint. I wanted every part of her pressed against me. I pushed my tongue into her mouth and took her face in my hands, angling more for better access. She murmured her appreciation, and a shot of something potent hit between my legs and then upward. This was the moment I'd been dreaming about all day. Our third kissing session, which now came with a familiarity and, dare I say, even more heat than before. We were looser. Hungrier. It felt like the sexual tension between us continued to climb, and I was pretty sure we were about to rocket right off the scale altogether.

She stepped back, and I almost cried out in protest, needing those lips. That kiss had been too good to end. "Let's have that wine now." Her voice was smooth, low, like she'd been good and turned-on.

I blinked, trying to remember how to open a bottle and where to find one. All my brain cared about were her swollen lips and the pleased look she had on her face. She should be pleased. My body was on fire, longing to be touched, sexually aroused to a level I wasn't used to, while at the same time wanting nothing more than to take this woman to heights of pleasure while she wore not a single stitch of clothing. My head swam at the image. Maybe even on my new lavender couch.

"What's wine?" I asked.

She laughed and placed a hand on my head.

"Don't say adorable," I warned. "Not right now."

"I was merely going to say that I see a bottle back there. May I?"

I exhaled slowly, steadying myself. "You can do whatever you want, and I mean that."

I heard her laugh quietly behind me. Moments later, the cork popped, and I heard the splash of wine in glasses. "For you." I accepted and touched my glass to hers.

"To getting acquainted."

She smiled. "I like that." She wandered down the hall and peeked in on my bedroom. I leaned back against the kitchen counter and watched with the kind of permission that kiss had afforded me.

"I wasn't expecting a moose." She was referencing the framed painting across from my bed.

"Not many people do, but it's my inspiration. Gives me strength when I need it. Like now, by the way."

She made her way back to me. "Whyever would you need strength now?" she asked, amused. She traced a fingertip across my stomach to the underside of my breast as she passed. I sucked in air, and my breasts woke the hell up.

"Because you keep doing things like that, and I'm just…"

"Hot and bothered." Her blue eyes had gone dark. She was hot and bothered, too. If someone tossed a match in the center of the room between us, the whole place would have gone up in flames in under a second. She sipped her wine. "What do you want to do about that? We should probably come up with something." Her gazed moved down my body, and I felt every second of it.

"Are you kidding?" I watched. Waited.

"I have ideas, but you're too far away. Come here." I wasn't feeling shy in the least bit.

Wouldn't be a problem. I was ready to take control and go after what it was I wanted. I set my glass on the end table and watched as she slowly approached. Drunk on power and desire, I reached for her, pulled her in, my focus on the front of the sundress. She'd been on top of that neckline all day, adjusting her dress so it never dipped too low in front, that little line of cleavage peeking out and then disappearing again when she noticed. Not anymore. She'd abandoned the mission and showed a generous amount. I prayed it was on purpose.

"Hi," she whispered as she leaned in and softly kissed my neck. Gasoline on the fire. My eyes closed automatically, and I leaned my head back, allowing access. Her left hand was working to open my shirt's bottom button. Success. I inhaled. Then another button, higher. Air tickled my newly exposed skin. Distantly, I heard music. She had me hearing things. This was that good. Except the music got louder. It wasn't in my head. I ignored it, shoving it to the side, waiting for her to reveal my breasts and take them into her hands. I swallowed my arousal, refocused, and kissed Carrie with renewed vigor, only to hear what I now recognized as a Timbaland song. Could that be right?

"Do you hear that?" Carrie asked, pulling back and looking behind her. The music had become oppressively loud, and now my phone was ringing in my bag. What was happening?

"I do. Let me see what's going on." I cursed whatever neighbor was ruining such an important moment for me. I swung open the front door and peered down the outdoor landing to the sidewalk below, shocked to see Kacey standing there with a bouquet of flowers and a Bluetooth speaker strapped to her ankle, blasting the song.

For a moment, I didn't say anything. I gaped, speechless and trying to piece together what was going on.

Kacey beat me to the words. "Before you say anything, hear me out. I've heard everything you've been saying and gave it some thought. Like, I stayed up."

I hurried down the stairs. "Kacey. No, can we not—"

"And I know now that you were right. Dead-on as always. This isn't a fling. I want what you want. The on-demand hookups were great, but you want us to be more, and now I want that, too. We need to formalize this."

I couldn't believe what was happening. I could feel Carrie watching from above. I cringed. "This is not the time to do this."

"Yes, it is, because I don't want to waste another moment that we could be spending together. I was just stuck in this senseless loop of nonsense. A roller coaster never leaving the tracks. But I've caught up to you now. You knew all along that we belonged together, and now I do, too."

"Things are different now." I was speaking quietly, as if it could keep Carrie from hearing. Ridiculous. "Can I call you? This is all too much, and I have neighbors."

She dropped the flowers and moved to me, taking both of my hands in hers. "But they don't have to be different." She looked around. "And I want your neighbors to know what I do. That I love you, Skyler, and I know you love me, too." She shook her head as if the desperation was overtaking her. This was not the Kacey I knew. "I'm willing to do whatever it takes to be yours."

"Kacey," Carrie said, descending the stairs. She had her bag on her shoulder and paused next to us. God, no, this wasn't at all good. "It's nice to meet you. I've heard about you."

Kacie nodded, still on the high of the mission. "Hi."

I turned to Carrie. "It's fine. This will just take a minute. Please don't go."

She scoffed but in that calm unflappable way of hers. "Oh, I definitely think I have to do that. I hope you two figure out your troubles. 'Night, now." I felt the chill as she passed me on the sidewalk without so much as a look back. This wasn't good.

My heart sank, and I dropped my hands. "You should go, too," I told Kacey, who glanced behind her at Carrie's retreating form.

"Was that the woman from the news? Why is she here?" Then understanding hit. "Oh."

"Yeah." A pause. "Look, I'm really sorry, but I can't do this with you. I care about you a lot, but things in my life have shifted."

Her fervor had quieted, and Kacey looked sad. "And you're dating the anchor from your station."

I sighed. "I'm not really sure but need to find out."

"Fuck me. I'm too late."

"Kace. No. It's just not the path we're supposed to be on. We're friends. We had a good time, but it's probably best for us to both move forward."

She nodded, attempting to accept my words. "Are you sure? Because I just feel like I'm ready for more. You made me think about the bigger scheme."

"And maybe you are. Find the woman for you. She's out there."

We stared at each other as she worked through it. Her brown eyes carried such shock. "I thought for sure this is what you wanted."

"Well, now you get to find what it is *you* want."

She nodded. "So…I guess I'm not staying over."

We shared a laugh. "No staying over."

"The couch? The anchor lady won't mind." She passed me a smile.

I grinned back. "Good night, Kacey. Drive safe."

CHAPTER TEN

Carrie didn't return my messages that night. Or my calls.

I hadn't done anything wrong but was still consumed with horror at what had occurred. It still didn't feel quite real, as if a bad dream I could just shake off. Only it hadn't been.

I couldn't sleep. Images played back in my head on repeat. I vacillated between Carrie smiling at me at the picnic and the confusion in her eyes on the sidewalk and then back to the hunger in them when she'd walked toward me in my living room. All of it underscored by a distorted version of the Timbaland music that played from Kacey's speaker in a garish taunt.

Finally, I gave in to my sleep failure and headed to the station. At least playing the role of early bird might get me top pick at the incoming stories from overnight. I was desperate for any worthy distraction.

The newsroom was a quiet bustle when I arrived, but different than what I'd grown used to. The lights were dimmer, and the morning folks so much quieter than the evening team. It felt like something important but secretive was underway. Coffee showed up in excess, and the aroma of fresh pastries hung in the air. Not bad.

As I shuffled through email, I stared at Carrie's empty desk, organized and perfect as always. My heart tugged at what was not to be the night before, and I felt completely off balance. Plus, there was the sidecar of guilt that came with rejecting Kacey's grand gesture. Two months ago, I would have grinned and invited her in to see where things between us might lead. I'd been ready for more, eager for a shot.

Two months now felt like two years. I couldn't imagine going backward.

The feelings I had percolating for Carrie felt entirely different.

They affected every aspect of my life. I woke up thinking about the next moment I'd get to see her, share a laugh, or simply learn from her on the job. I had nothing in my life prior to compare them to. I blew out a breath and absorbed my very real set of circumstances. Yep, I had it bad.

The day took off early, and Ty and I hit the road singing to Shawn Mendes, him on lead and me on backup. We covered a school board protest, a hospital overrun with an outbreak of RSV in infants, then went live at five for a shooting in the park. It was the first contact I'd had with Carrie since she'd headed down my sidewalk, and it was live on air for thousands to watch.

Her voice tickled my ear. "Skyler Ruiz is on scene at Murray Ridge Park to tell us about a near-death experience for a local teen earlier today. Skyler, what's the latest?"

"Caroline, Eddie Meyers is a typical kid. He likes hanging out with his friends and figuring out which pizza joint has the best slice. What he didn't expect was to come face-to-face with a gunman in the very park where he grew up."

From there, the broadcast rolled over to the package we'd put together just an hour earlier. I waited for my wrap up, anxious to get back to the station where I could put the final touches on my hospital package, which would run at ten. After that, I could bring my long day to a close. But more than anything, I was also hoping to put things right with Carrie, because being this off balance with her felt awful. I couldn't face another night of tossing and turning.

The package came to a close and I was back live. "In the end, Eddie is grateful for 9-1-1, his good friends, and his life. Caroline."

"Well, we're happy to hear he's okay. What a terrifying ordeal."

"Isn't that the truth," I heard Rory say.

"Next we'll take a look at all the ways you can step up for Saturday's blood drive. Stay tuned."

"We're clear," Ty said. He scurried over and offered me a high five and a hip bump, which had become our two-pronged custom. "Crushed it, as always. I gotta run. My anniversary. I need to put a bow tie on over this T-shirt and eat the fancy grub with my lovely lady."

I grinned. Ty and his wife were celebrating fifteen years, which meant Sandra had put up with his puppylike antics for a long time now. "Bless that woman for loving your bow tie T-shirt combo."

"I say that every damn day." He popped on his neon-green

sunglasses, did a little shoulder dance, and slid into his truck. I'd ride back with Charlie, the live truck operator, who was every bit as kind but not nearly as much fun.

When we got back to the station, I finished up what work I had with one of the other editors, who would submit the story for final review before it aired, and then went about shuffling things around on my desk. Mindless. All a tactic to stall. Next, I took a walk around the newsroom. Stared at the decor on the wall. Awards. Photos. Policies. At last, there she was. Everything in me went quiet to make room for her. Still wearing a red dress from the broadcast and now back at her desk, Carrie studied her screen.

"Nice handoff earlier." I was referencing our exchange on the live shot from the five.

She lifted her gaze and found mine. "It was smooth. Good job today."

I looked behind me. No one in the newsroom was in earshot. "Can we talk? About last night." My stomach balled itself into an uncomfortable knot. But I had to get through this part.

She relaxed into her chair. The expression on her face told me that I wasn't allowed in anymore. The door was closed, and I hated every second of it. "I'm not sure we need to. No hard feelings, okay? I mean that. You have a lot going on, and that's okay."

"No hard feelings," I repeated. "Okay, great. But I want a reset. The whole thing was a giant misunderstanding, and I'm just sorry you were there to witness it."

"Maybe it was. What do I know?" She smiled at me, but it wasn't the kind I'd grown used to. Not her real smile, the one she snuck me when no one was watching. Not even the sweet one she offered when they were. She had a barrier between us now. "I wish you guys the best, figuring it out. I'm sure you will."

I sighed. "So that's it? I haven't even explained it all yet."

She took her hands off her keyboard. "I know, but let's keep things simple, okay? Focus on our work relationship. Stay friends. I'd really like that. Probably less messy in the end." She offered another obligatory smile.

I'd given her too much time to think this through. She was laying up, playing it safe. "Yeah. Okay." I attempted a smile of my own, but my success was debatable. She was taking a pointed step back, and that was that. What was I supposed to do? My mind went blank. Numb.

And then sad. Also, I wasn't willing to stand here and let her watch my disappointment play out. Dammit.

Without another word, I gathered my things and headed home for the night. Comfy pants and a couple of shots of Crown would hopefully dull the acute pain of today. I'd have to worry about the long-term later. Develop strategies, tactics, for not dwelling on what felt like a gaping loss. I didn't know what had Carrie running away with such determination, but I had a feeling it had very little to do with me. If only that knowledge helped even a little bit. Fuck my life.

❖

There were a lot of things in life you couldn't plan for. Breaking news was certainly one of them. As a reporter handed an assignment, you generally had a few scant details when you headed out to snag a story, but the reality of the situation might be entirely different once you arrived on scene.

I'd buried myself in work the week following the station's picnic. Anything to keep me from falling into a pit of self pity over what I'd now dubbed the Kacey-Carrie travesty. The more hours I put in scouring the tips that came in, listening to the scanners, and staying in constant contact with the assignments desk, the more stories came my way. I was learning fast how to stay ahead of my colleagues, and that was to work harder.

The domestic dispute I'd heard chattered about over the scanner was still very much in progress when Ty and I arrived at the small home in a residential neighborhood belonging to the Sorenson family. I had that part established before arriving. I'd also expected the issue to be under control by the time we drove the ten minutes required. I was dead wrong.

When we approached, I saw Jake, my favorite patrolman, standing on the front lawn of a beige one-story with a clearly broken window. He held up a hand. "Gonna hold you back, Skyler."

I quirked an eyebrow. "What do we have?" I'd already heard on the scanner that there were two males battling it out and a possible hostage situation. The word *hostage* was what had Ty and me exchanging a look and heading right over. If the situation escalated, and we were already in position, we would scoop the other stations.

Jake shook his head. "Can't help you. We're still in progress, and until we secure the scene, I'll need you far across the street. No argument."

I nodded, understanding that we could put everyone in danger if we inserted ourselves, and dutifully followed Jake's instruction. But from across the street, I kept one ear on the action.

"Hey, we're inching closer to the noon broadcast," Ty said fifteen minutes later, phone to his ear. "Tam wants us to go live. They're sending Charlie with the truck."

I turned to him. "What? No. I don't have enough information. There's no story yet. Why would we go live?"

More shouts from the direction of the house. "Get the hell away from me, asshole!"

"It's my lizard, you fucker!"

Ty shook his head. "Slow news day. We got to put together what we can."

I nodded. It was time to step up and deliver. Two more squad cars arrived, and I was able to overhear that this was likely a dispute between a father and a son that stemmed from a borrowed credit card. Also, something about an iguana, who was apparently the hostage in question. Slow news day indeed, but I would work with what I had. I waited until Jake appeared again, and the shouting seemed to have died down. "Can you give me any details? We're apparently going live."

"I can't give you anything official. You know that. You gotta talk to our information officer."

"Off the record. Between friends." I stared at him and watched the exact moment he crumbled. He seemed to have a weak spot for me.

"The son blew a bunch of money on some online poker site and used the father's credit card to do it. Now the father has moved the iguana into his bedroom as collateral, and the son is ready to blow shit up to get his friend back."

"Got it. For the love of a lizard."

"Something like that." He looked behind them. "They have them separated now and are taking statements, but it was fiery."

"You're the best, Jakety-Jake."

"I have no idea how you know my nickname." He headed back to the house with a smile threatening.

Twenty minutes later, we were on air. When the lunchtime anchor tossed it to me, I was ready. "Lisette, police were called to this west side home when neighbors overhead shouting and threats. We're currently in the midst of a father–son showdown with police standing—"

Suddenly there was movement on either side of me. A man raced by, passing between me and the camera. "I will mess you up, old man," came a call from the second man, who followed the first, barreling through.

"As you can see, Lisette, we are in the midst of it here, even now."

"Henry, freeze right there!" It was Jake. I wasn't sure who Henry was, but he wasn't listening. The two men continued to chase each other, until the older one caught the younger one by the collar and threw the first punch, landing it with a sickening thud. That was all it took. The fight was on.

I stepped to the side, speaking over the grunts from the men and shouted orders from police. "The father and son in question are in the midst of a brawl," I said, watching them pummel each other, inches away. The police were intervening, but this was getting too close for my comfort. "In fact, Lisette, it might be wise if we—"

That's the last thing I said before I found myself blinking up at Ty's face peering down at me. Wait. What? The shouting had stopped, and it had gone eerily quiet. How had that happened so quickly? One minute, shouting. The next, nothing. I blinked again. There was Jake, too, speaking into his shoulder calmly. Where was the hubbub? Where was Lisette in my ear? Jake said something about an ambulance, but he still seemed far away, the whole world did.

"Why am I..." I looked around, orienting myself, remembering speaking to Lisette back at the studio. "What happened to my shot?"

Ty's eyes were wide, and he'd gone pale. It took a lot to rattle him, but something had. He peered over me, smoothing my hair. "You just took one hell of a punch, kiddo. Smack dab in the face. You okay, Rocky?"

I moved my jaw back and forth, but it was my left eye that screamed out with pain. He wasn't kidding. "I think so. Face hurts. I'm in the grass?"

"Yep," Ty said. "Assholes got ya, and you went down like a sack of baking potatoes. *Bam*." Ty was nothing if not expressive. "But we got you. You're gonna be okay."

"No, no." Jake held up a hand as I tried to push myself onto my elbows. "Just lie right there, Skyler. Gonna get you checked out."

That's when a god-awful, horrible thought descended like a lightning bolt. "We were live."

"Ah. Yeah," Ty said. "Got it all."

"I got hit in the face on live television?"

He nodded and winced. "Like I said, *bam*."

I shelved the horror, knowing it would be back in full force given time. "Where are the guys now? The ones who were fighting."

Jake gestured behind him as an ambulance pulled up to the curb. "Back of this squad car, and that one."

"Couple of buffoons," Ty said. "Can't believe they did that to you." He was angry and protective. I would have thought it sweet if my head wasn't pounding like something out of a cartoon. There had to be a mouse with a drum somewhere. Instead, there were people looking into my eyes with tiny flashlights. Paramedics. I thought about the people who made tiny flashlights for a living. My brain was being weird.

"I'm okay," I told them. I felt mildly out of it, but it was nice how attentive everyone was. Ooh, and look at the pretty red and blue lights over there. All swirly and festive. "I'm all right." I closed my eyes then because that felt really nice. "Did I tell you I'm okay?" Just a little snooze and I'd be good as new.

❖

I woke up in a dimly lit small room with green walls and a curtain around me. There were some beeps and sighs from some machinery to my left. I had an IV. Huh. Why? I had to take a minute to work out the puzzle. The buzz of something nearby followed by a squeezing of my upper arm told me that something was taking my blood pressure. I glanced down. Yep. An automatic cuff. And there had been an ambulance ride. I'd been in and out for it. They'd given me something, and I'd gone to sleep again. Now, a hospital. But why?

That's when it all came flooding back to me, ending with the realization of the granddaddy of all horrors: I'd been knocked out cold on live television. "Oh no," I whispered.

"You're up."

I knew the voice. I smiled at the sound automatically, a warm and welcome caress. I turned to my right and saw Carrie sitting next to my bed. She didn't fit into the puzzle. Her hair was pulled back into a ponytail. Never seen that before. Her face was devoid of makeup, too. Even lip gloss, which I rarely saw her without. "Hi." A pause. "What are you doing here?"

"Making sure you're alive. Do you know how terrified I was?" I didn't but was learning because her face told the story for me. Her eyes swam with anguish, and she kept clenching her hands into fists. That was also new. Through my head fog, I could tell that this whole thing really had her worked up.

"I'm okay. I promise." I jutted my chin. "You're making fists, though."

She looked down and relaxed her fingers. "I'm serious, Skyler. Don't you ever do anything like that again. Do you hear me?"

"Yes." I pushed myself up in bed, and the ache in my face doubled. "I will not insert my face between two lizard-loving lunatics in the future." A pause. An awful thought. "Did you see it?"

She nodded, a look of distress crossing her features. "I was getting ready for work and had the broadcast on." She placed a hand on her heart. "When I saw you fall, I swear, I wanted to jump through the TV." She was standing, had her hands on her hips, and shook her head, looking at the wall.

I smiled. "You care about me."

She sighed. "Yeah, okay. I do. So there. Very much. So you can't give me any more heart attacks."

"All it took was me getting clocked in the face. Why did I wait so long?" I looked around. "Also why am I in the hospital?" I had a hunch. My head hurt.

"They think you dodged a concussion, but they want to keep you overnight just to make sure you're okay. It's a highly public case, and they want to do everything right." She shook her head. "Not only did you get punched by the idiot, but you hit the ground pretty hard. You're on the good drugs, though, to keep you comfortable."

"Oh." My mind immediately started to play catch up, and a myriad of new considerations entered the picture. "My dog. And Sarah. What if she saw? Can we call her?"

"I already did. She's already been here to see you. She took your key and went to feed Micky and will be back later. Said something about needing to smash your cheeks in."

"It's how she shows love." I smiled to myself. "How's my hair?" It occurred to me that I might look like Frankenstein's bride over here with the woman I'm interested in looking on. Was there such a thing as hospital lip gloss, and could I get a hold of it?

Carried laughed. "It's gorgeous. Thick and dark and beautiful, like always." She smoothed the top, and I closed my eyes, enjoying her touch. I'd missed it in the days prior. She took my hand, and I looked down at our now intertwined fingers. The image was so natural it startled me.

"Speaking of visitors, you do have one more."

"I do?"

Carrie nodded. "He refused to go home until he could talk to you and see with his own eyes that you were okay." Carrie disappeared briefly and returned with a bleary-eyed Ty at her side, hands stuffed in his pockets like a nervous little kid.

"Hospitals have weird food." He offered me a grin. "I've been stalking the cafeteria. You okay?"

"You didn't have to hang out," I said to Ty, while at the same time knowing that if he was hurt, I'd have been here, too. We were partners and friends, and our bond was growing by the day. I didn't know how long I'd been there, but I had a feeling it was hours.

"Couldn't just leave ya, you weirdo. Had to see that you were still, you know, kickin'."

"My face hurts, but I'm gonna be okay."

His smile faded, joking now aside. "You sure? That was pretty scary."

"I'm sure. Tell Sandra I was feeling good enough to tell you that you have ketchup on your face." He swiped at his mouth, and I grinned. "Just kidding."

He smiled for real. "Sending you respect for that one."

Carrie offered his arm a squeeze. "I'll text you any updates. Go home and get some sleep."

He nodded, held his arm up to say good-bye, and took off. My heart squeezed at that gesture, and not just Ty's. When Carrie returned to my bedside, I took her hand and held it. "I'm glad you're here."

She shook her head. "Last week was stupid. I was stupid. I just get in my own head sometimes and…"

"Retreat."

"Yeah. Old habit. And then when you were hurt and they cut away, all I wanted to do was make sure you were okay. Sit right here until you were."

I stared into her eyes. "I'm dead serious about Kacey. Not what it appeared to be."

She scoffed. "We don't have to talk about that now. You're hurt."

"I'll live. Plus, I *want* to talk about it and make sure all cards are on the table, okay?"

"Okay."

"There's nothing there." I raised a shoulder. "We used to hook up before I moved to San Diego. Nothing since. We were never a couple, even if I occasionally thought we could be. Then I met you. The world changed forever."

She nodded, seeming to take it all in. "I should have let you explain."

"Yes. You should have."

She smiled. "So…am I even allowed to sit here? I can camp out in the hall. I probably deserve it."

"I want you right here."

"Good." She took my chin, turned my face to hers, and leaned in for a gentle kiss that, quite simply, made it all better. Pain? What pain?

A thought struck. "Wait. Don't you have a broadcast to anchor?"

"Aww." She shook her head. "You really were hit hard. It's close to one a.m."

I frowned. "You should be in bed, young lady!"

She laughed. I loved the sound of it. "I told you. That's my seat over there." She touched my cheek. "And I meant it. If you'll have me." She swallowed, nervous, which was so crazy to me I couldn't see straight.

"Yeah. Of course." I looked at the less-than-comfortable-looking recliner, warmed. "You're really gonna stay all night, though? You really don't have to. I'm a big girl. I took a punch and everything."

"Your nurse brought me a blanket. I'm looking forward to snuggling beneath it."

Everything squeezed. She was actually planning to stay in the hospital with me. *In a chair.* "Of course they did. You're famous."

"And milking every moment of it today."

The next morning, she wasn't the only famous one. "What is going on?" I said quietly to myself, staring at my phone as the sun came up over the skyline of San Diego. I had hundreds of emails, dozens of text messages, and more notifications on social media than my brain could properly process.

Carrie stirred in her chair next to my bed. "I'm sorry. What did you say?"

"Sorry. I didn't mean to wake you, but for some reason, the world is trying to get in contact with me."

She exhaled. "Right. Did I mention that the video from yesterday has gotten quite a lot of play?"

I frowned. Realization hit. I'd gotten punched in the face on TV. Of course the video was being passed around. "I've gone viral."

"Afraid so. It might have been on *Late Talk* last night. It's also on my Instagram feed. And making the rounds on Twitter."

Late Talk was national. "No."

She winced. "Yes."

"How are we doing today?" I turned at the sound of a very enthusiastic voice entering the room.

Carrie pointed. "Your nurse. Tinky."

"Like Tinker Bell?" I asked. Why was my life so weird?

Tinky brushed a strand of extra-curly blond hair from her forehead and beamed like the magical fairy she was. "Exactly like that. I have medication for you and good news. You're getting out of here." She handed me a paper cup with two pills.

"That's fantastic. Key question. Have you seen me get punched in the face?"

Her eyes went wide. "Oh yes. The whole nurses' station has."

"Wonderful." I popped the Tylenol. "Thank you, Tinky."

"Anything for you. Back with that discharge paperwork shortly." She floated away to medical fairyland once again.

"Cheer up," Carrie said with a smile. "This can't hurt any worse than that eye."

I touched the swollen-feeling skin. "Is it black?"

"Oh yes. But can I have your autograph?"

I sighed. What a week.

CHAPTER ELEVEN

I know you."

"You do?" I squinted at the cashier at the grocery store. She looked like maybe she was in college. Maybe even a broadcast journalism major. I added my bananas to her conveyor belt, wishing they were a little more ripe. "Have we met?"

"No." She tapped her lips with no real interest in ringing me up until this mystery was solved. "Where do I know you from?" She jumped up and down a few times as if the motion would jog her memory.

I decided to help. "Do you watch the news?" Now that I'd been at the station for a decent period of time, my face had become more recognizable, and I was noticed more and more. It was fun, in a way.

Her eyes went wide. "Oh my God. Oh my God. Oh my God. You're the one who took the punch." She covered her mouth with both hands and took a step back.

I sighed and dropped my spinach in front of her. "No."

"Yes, you are." She extended her hand and pointed. "My roommate Timothy loves you. He plays that shit on repeat." She straightened and adopted a more presentational style of speech. "*In fact, Lissette, it might be wise if we*—Boom. Right in the face. Ouch. Are you okay? Like, you've healed?"

I relented. No point in fighting my public. "I'm doing great. Thank you." And you know what? I was. The bruise had all but faded, and after a short break and TLC from my cousins, I was back at work this week. In fact, Carrie had just left me a sweet voice message to make sure I was having a good day. The low, soft quality of her voice had tickled my ear, and I couldn't wait to see her. Hell, maybe I'd even figure out how to cook something with all these groceries, and we could have a nice dinner in.

"Will you say hi to Timothy?" she asked, holding up her phone. "I'm recording. Say hi."

I smiled at the uninvited lens. "Hi, Timothy." I pointed at my eye. "All better, see?"

She dropped her arm. "He's going to die. He's going to lose it. I can't wait."

A few minutes later, I handed her my credit card and got the hell out of there, certain that there would come a time when I would be known for more than viral-victim status. But worse things had happened in the world than one little video.

"Hey, BuzzFeed wants to do a write-up on you," Marilyn from PR said as I arrived at my desk the next morning. "Can you take a call with their staff writer at eleven?"

"Is that a good idea?" I wanted to be taken seriously as a journalist, and this might not be the way to go.

"She'll do it," Carrie said, approaching. "Trust me on this one."

"Really?" I whispered. "Because I don't want to be the punched woman for the rest of my career."

"*Career* being the operative word. Anything that makes people interested in you is good in the world of TV. Especially when you're an up-and-comer. And you are."

"Yeah, okay. I'll do it."

"Perfect," Marilyn said. "Eleven o'clock."

"Am I dating a famous woman?" Carrie whispered. My cheeks went instantly hot because she'd just said we were dating. I loved hearing that. I wanted her to write it in whipped cream across my chest.

"Yes. Very famous." I batted my eyelashes. "The clamoring for me is out of control. You should probably lock me in."

"Do I need to?" She rested her cheek on her hand in the most adorable pose.

"Not when you look at me like that." She grinned and went back to her screen, yet I continued to watch her. A few moments later, her cheeks went pink.

"You're staring, Ms. Ruiz."

"Damn straight I am," I said, grinning around my pen.

A pause as she click-clacked away on her keyboard. "Are you heading out on a story?"

"Not until the Commissioner on Agriculture has his press conference in an hour. Why do you ask?"

"Really cool footage I want to show you. But only if you have time."

"Oh yeah. Of what?" There was no footage. I knew exactly where this was heading based on our last rendezvous and couldn't like the idea more. A tingling sensation moved across my skin at the thought of kissing her, touching her. The editing bays had locks on each door and no windows. Thank God for whoever implemented those design features. Flawless.

"You know. Footage," Carrie reiterated. "Of the really cool thing I was telling you about."

"Hmmm," I said studiously. "You know, I have been wanting to see that cool thing for a while."

"Really?" She nodded sagely. "I've been wanting to show it to you. Follow me."

I did. Happily, like a puppy. The door closed, the lights stayed off, and her warm breath tickled my neck. I was in heaven. When she kissed me expertly on the same spot, my whole body went slack in her arms as I relished the stolen moment.

"I've missed this," I said, wrapping my arms around her. She moved her attention from my neck to my lips, and we were off. In a jumble of kissing, groping, and all-around decadent behavior we left ourselves breathless and longing. Our hips pressed together and moved in subtle rhythm, a nod to what we really wanted to be doing to each other. Soon.

"This is a fun but cruel practice," Carrie whispered in my ear.

"I want to do so much more to you," I said in the darkness, running a slow finger up the inside of her thigh, inching her skirt up and pausing mere inches from where I really longed to go.

Her breathing went noticeably shallow when I reached the edge of her underwear, tracing it from her midthigh down. "Free later tonight?"

"Mm-hmm," I said, placing a kiss under her jaw. I found her lips and sank back in. We danced together. Our lips clung, sexy and perfectly in rhythm. Kissing chemistry was important, and we seemed to have it in surplus. It was intoxicating and addictive, kissing Carrie.

Someone tried the door, and we went still. Caught.

She took a step back. "Come over tonight."

I nodded my agreement as she flipped the lights on. With one last wink, she exited the room, leaving me alone. I sighed. Back to real life and sitting next to the most beautiful woman on Earth and pretending I wasn't in the land of lust. How many hours until the ten o'clock ended?

Now if only I could get through the day without exploding into a hot and bothered ball of flames. A flash of Carrie's lips pressed to my neck hit. I went immediately warm and wet. The odds were not in my favor.

❖

Carrie's street was quiet when I killed my engine in her darkened driveway. The world had gone to sleep, leaving just those of us who worked odd hours awake to see the midnight sky. I'd driven along the beach on my way to her place, taking in the sounds of the waves rolling in, my windows down and my senses firing.

Carrie opened the door and handed me a glass of wine, wearing a baby-blue T-shirt and light gray cotton shorts. My brain stumbled. She had the best legs, a hint of a tan and sculpted. The curves of her breasts were outlined nicely under the fabric of the T-shirt. It was clear she'd ditched the bra upon arriving home, and I applauded the decision. "Hi," she said, grinning at me.

I took a sip of the white. Dry. Crisp. "Sav blanc?"

"You're good." She turned and led me through the entryway. Tension clung. We both knew why I was there, and the anticipation was palpable.

"I'm not, but I'm learning. Great job tonight." I meant it. She was on.

"You watched?" She turned and faced me, sitting on the arm of the couch.

"Damn straight, I did." I'd submitted my last story by eight and made my way home to freshen up, get Micky a walk, and drop him to hang out with Grace, who was thrilled to have a cuddle buddy for the night. In between, I'd watched Carrie anchor the ten, taking notes on how effortlessly she transitioned, how naturally she engaged with the other anchors, and most importantly, how she connected with the lens, making me feel as if I was the only person watching. Her gift, and why she'd done so well in the field. The best in the business as far as I was concerned. And okay, the sexiest, too. By far. She didn't even have to try. A pair of cotton shorts and I was gone.

"And? What was the verdict?" she asked around her glass.

"That you're incredibly smart and poised and—" I exhaled. "Confession. I've missed your lips. More than I can even believe."

"Then come here, Skyler Ruiz, and say hello to me." Those lips curled into a smile as I moved to them, hovering just shy, enjoying the slight height advantage I finally had with her sitting on the edge of that couch arm. Finally, I captured her mouth with mine, and our connection lit up the room with startling intensity. Everything in me hummed when I kissed this woman, and in seconds I was drunk with lust and a need for more of her mouth, her body. It was only a moment before she stood in the midst of our kissing and angled her mouth for better access, parting her lips and allowing my tongue entrance. How did she know just the perfect way to kiss me so that I felt it everywhere? My skin prickled fantastically, my breasts longed to be touched, and my center ached for her alone. I'd only been in her house for four minutes, and we weren't wasting any of them. She slipped her hands beneath the hem of my black T-shirt, her palms flat against my ribcage. She eased them upward until they covered my breasts entirely through my red bra, the one I picked out in hopes she'd like it. I closed my eyes, saw bright light, and tried to steady myself. Good God, she wasn't shy.

"Coming off," she whispered against my mouth and lifted my shirt easily over my head. Her fingertips descended on exactly what she wanted, across the tops of my breasts, as I pulled in air. She cradled them as I struggled for strength. I shifted to relieve some of the sensitivity between my legs. I was so turned-on that I trembled but tried hard to play it cool.

"Sorry," I said. Surely she'd noticed. "You do this to me."

"Then we're even." She reached around and unclasped my bra, setting it on the couch. God, her confidence astounded. "Your breasts are so beautiful." She took her time, taking in their visual as I stood before her—topless, hers, waiting.

I watched as she lowered her mouth, lifting a breast to her lips and taking in the nipple. Slow. Everything was measured with Caroline. *God.* She took her time, which was maddening and wonderful. With the gentle suck, a shot of something overwhelming hit between my legs, leaving me unsteady and no longer playing it cool at all. I'd murmured something. No clue what, but I felt her grin against my skin. I bit the inside of my cheek and threaded my fingers through her hair. "Carrie," I said quietly, savoring the feel of her name on my lips. My new favorite word.

"I want you in my bed," she said, lifting her head and meeting my gaze. Her eyes were dark and determined. I nodded and allowed her to lead me by my hand down the hall to her room. She dimmed the lights, laid me down, and while I watched, slipped out of her top and shorts and climbed on top. It was everything, the feeling of her skin on mine.

I sat up and pulled her mouth down to mine for a crushing kiss. This left her straddling me in her panties alone. My hands itched to touch her breasts, explore them, really look at them. I pulled my mouth away and let my eyes feast on the reality of her lit dimly by the lamp across the room. Her breasts were round and perfect. I cradled them softly and watched her eyes darken and her lips part. I kissed her right breast softly, reverently. Ran my tongue across her nipple and back again, encouraged by the quiet sounds of pleasure she made. "I've dreamt of this. You touching me." I pulled her into my mouth, sucked softly as her hips matched my rhythm. My cheeks were hot and my center throbbed from just that little bit of friction. I lifted my hips to press against hers and the ride became a dizzy one.

She scooted to the side and slid my leggings down my legs. My underwear followed, and to my utter shock, Carrie reversed course. Instead of slow and methodical, her hand was immediately between my legs. I hissed in a breath, totally engulfed in sensations I'd never felt before, coming from somewhere deep within me. Like a tidal wave approaching from miles away, slow and intentional. I moaned, and I wasn't someone who did that. I rocked against her hand, and she didn't hold back. She pushed inside, shattering me, inching me closer to the edge with each moment. "Baby, let go," she whispered from alongside me. I felt the heat from her body and opened my eyes to the sight of her, exposed and gorgeous.

I palmed her breast and opened my legs, granting her more access. "Touch me," I said. It was a request. A plea. That tidal wave was close, and my body shook in anticipation. The lack of control was thrilling and terrifying. I saw her grin and move down the bed. When she took me into her mouth and did wonderfully torturous things to me with her tongue, I called out, maybe too loudly. My hips were moving quickly, drunk on the tension, and seeking the ultimate release. It was only a matter of seconds before I received it. White-hot pleasure flooded my system like a bolt of lighting.

Carrie continued to work me over with her tongue as the shockwaves took their turns, an electric current. Sometime later, I floated back to Earth, forever changed by the knowledge that *my body* could feel *those things*. The intimacy of what we'd just done together consumed me. I'd had sex before, sure, but the deep tug I felt to Carrie was in another league. Our connection was. She stroked my hair. Ran a hand down my body as if in awe of it, circling the curve of my breast, learning it. I smiled, loving every second of her touch.

I longed to explore her, too. With my fingertips, I traced the top of her shoulder, down her arm. She closed her eyes as if savoring each sensation. I watched her lips, entranced by their heart-like shape. She'd sometimes bite the lower one, like when I ran my finger along the outside of her thigh. When I paid the same attention to the inside, she swore out loud, her eyes fluttering closed. My cue. I gently eased her onto her back and settled my body entirely on top. "Hi," I said, capturing her mouth for a hungry kiss. I pulled my mouth away and impressed the moment upon my memory. With our breasts pressed together and me looking down into those blue eyes I couldn't get enough of, I was in heaven. Carrie still wore her panties, and now that I was settled between her legs, I could feel how damp she was through the fabric. It turned me the hell on. I circled my hips against her, and she gasped, molding her body to mine. We moved together, and it was literally the sexiest thing I'd known.

"I might…I don't know if I can wait," she said, quietly arching her back. "I can't help it. You drive me crazy."

"Good," I said back, sliding her panties off with one hand between us. She kicked them to the floor and sucked in air when I parted her legs and kissed her center with an open mouth. Cupping her ass, I slowly ran my tongue along every inch of her, eager to taste her everywhere. I traced her most sensitive spot with the flat of my tongue, moving circles around it in time to Carrie's rhythmic breathing. Or were they whimpers? I dipped a finger inside, into wetness and warmth, and closed my eyes. I'd fantasized about this moment, touching Carrie so intimately. The intensity of her response was a sheer bonus. Her desperate sounds overwhelmed me. I entered her fully and took my time, my tongue offering light touches of attention. My fingers pushing in and out were less gentle. The sounds she made were sensual, guiding me each step of the way until suddenly her body went taut, her back arched, and she shuddered. Absolutely beautiful. I watched as she still rode my hand. Her form engulfed in pleasure was a sight I would never forget. I climbed on top, lifted her breast, and kissed it passionately, sucking in a nipple, swirling it with my tongue. I paid the same attention on the other breast, worshipping it with my mouth. Never enough.

After a couple of moments, I noticed her respond. Her breathing went shallow, and she rocked against my thigh. *Yes.* I slid my hand between us and stroked her ever so gently, featherlight, until she jerked and cried out a second time. "Skyler Ruiz," she whispered in mock-chastise, shaking her head. She tossed an arm over her eyes.

"I had to," I said. "No choice."

An hour later, we'd yet to take our eyes off each other. We'd turned on some music, decompressed, still naked in bed. She'd played with my hair. I'd studied her face.

"We do that really well." We'd been talking about other things, but I knew immediately she meant sex.

"I have to agree."

"We should do it more." She eased her hand between my legs and played. "Would you agree now?"

I didn't answer. I couldn't. Instead, I nodded and surrendered to the wonder of this night. This woman. Would I recognize myself in the morning? Did I want to? As the orgasm claimed me, and I found her lips for a toe-curling kiss, I knew without a doubt that I was right where I was supposed to be. We fit, she and I, and this journey was going to be different than anything I'd ever known.

I was ready.

I woke up in a bed that was not mine with a woman's arm tossed over my midsection and her blond hair splayed across the pillow next to mine. My body was warm. Happy. Tired in the best sense. The night before came rushing back to me in a jumble of unabashed heat. We'd slept together, Carrie and I, and it had been the most intimate and amazing night of my life. What I wanted more than anything was to revisit all of it with Carrie this morning. There was just one problem. If I wasn't in the shower in the next five minutes, I wouldn't just be late for work, but woefully late. As the newest reporter on the team, it wouldn't be the best look.

I placed a soft kiss on her lips as she slept before beginning to slip out of her bed. She stirred, and I paused and watched as awareness slowly descended on her features. Her eyes opened and found mine. "Hi," she said as a slow smile blossomed. "Oh my. It's all coming back to me now."

"Right? I know the feeling. It was a…night. But I'm late," I said with a smile-wince combo. It wasn't the best opening sentence. I'd have to work on those. I needed to be sexier in the morning, maybe stretch like a cat and pout a little. So not me, but this was all new.

"Oh no." She pushed herself up onto her elbow. She had the sexiest bedhead. Her lips were swollen, which I took immense pride in. "We can't have you late." But she was kissing my breast, so her commitment to helping me get to work was severely in question.

"Oh. Um, okay," was all my mouth was willing to say, because *stop* would end the amazing wash of pleasure that had just collapsed over me, and I was now wondering if unemployment mattered in the least. This was too important a moment. She sucked on that particular nipple with abandon, which had me wet and my hips rocking slowly. I was fully back in bed, on my back, and at her mercy.

"Oh, look at that," she said, now aware of my arousal, her hand between my legs. "We can't let that go to waste."

My eyes slammed shut at her intimate touch. I moved my hips automatically because it felt too damn good to not participate.

"Yep. Just like that," she said, pushing her fingers inside me, circling me with her thumb. My hips moved faster, riding her hand, head back, eyes closed, until she gently stroked my cheek. "Look at me."

I did, and the connection was like a wildfire, catching and spreading, until I came like a shot, much faster than I should have, in an intense surge that left me shaken and trembling.

"I couldn't let you go to work without one last good-bye," she said, stroking my hair. "God, you're gorgeous, Skyler."

I shook my head. "Totally worth the time I'm going to have to make up. May I borrow your shower to get ready for work?"

A proud grin. "After last night, you can borrow anything you want. My car keys are over there. Need a plant? There's a few in the kitchen."

"Do you know what I really want?" I said, drinking in the sight of her topless and lounging. "To stay here and return that favor. News be damned. The people will figure it out for themselves, right?"

"I don't know," she said, lying back on the bed, the sheet falling just a little bit more to show off her stomach. This was a painting, I swear. "I kind of like the idea of having you owe me."

"Well, when you say it *that* way, me, too." It also answered my next question. The concept of next time. Now, I knew there would be one. Everything in me knew that this was not just a hookup, but hearing her indicate more to come certainly helped my confidence.

"Go get yourself camera-ready, though I kind of feel like the people are missing out on this version."

I was standing next to the bed naked and had just been owned in the best way possible. "No, no. This is just for you."

Something behind her eyes softened. "Good. I like that."

I made myself at home in her bathroom, hurrying on one hand, and taking the time to experience Carrie's space on the other. The incredibly soft dusty-blue towels. The little chair with the rounded back and white cushion that sat in front of her vanity station. The perfume that immediately reminded me of every interaction I'd had with her. I'd found the culprit. I was surrounded by everything Carrie, and it made me happy. Lighter.

When I emerged all blow-dried and dressed in the work clothes I'd brought over, Carrie was waiting for me in the kitchen, wearing a satin floral robe that came to mid thigh. She held a travel mug of coffee and a warm pastry on a plate. "I made these yesterday. Blueberry scones."

I stared at the amazing-looking scone, warm from a reheat in her oven. "Yesterday? No. You worked all day."

"The gap before work. I exist outside of the station, too."

I took a bite and melted into a joyful puddle. "This is what you produce in your short time off." I shook my head. "I just watch Bravo and stuff my face with processed food, literally as much as I can get in my mouth."

"Well, your mouth is one of your best qualities. I now know."

The scone died on its way to its destination. I'd need to notify its next of kin, because Carrie just said *that*, and from the look on her face, she meant it. "Well, now I don't have words."

"None required. Kiss me and get outta here." She placed a hand on her hip and smiled.

That I could do. With my hands full, I leaned in and kissed her softly. "See you soon?"

"I should be there for the story meeting."

"And I'm supposed to just pretend it's any other morning?" I mused on my way to the door. "How am I supposed to do that? We were just naked."

"I have confidence in you."

I opened her front door and made my way through. "I have none!"

"Bye, Skyler."

"Bye, Caroline McNamara." I grinned, popped on my shades, and made sure to drive along the ocean as the sun climbed in the morning sky. San Diegans made their way to their various places of work alongside me on the highway. My morning music played, upbeat and cheerful. My coffee had never tasted better, and my blueberry scone was outta this world. I had very few complaints.

CHAPTER TWELVE

I liked having a sexy little secret.
It kept the day tension-filled and a hell of a lot more exciting. The best kind of drug. I surveyed the busy newsroom and turned to my right where Carrie was lost in her notes, with that look of intense concentration as she bit the inside of her lip. I grinned. I'd be leaving for a live shot from the scene of an overnight hotel fire shortly, and she'd be heading to the studio for the five p.m., and no one would know when we spoke to each other across the airwaves that we'd been naked and devouring each other just sixteen hours earlier. There was something special about that, and I enjoyed having it tucked away for just us. Not nearly as much as I enjoyed every second we spent together. I liked my apartment, but I'd only spent two nights there this week, and she and I had talked on the phone both nights until we'd fallen asleep.

"What was the first story you went out on?" she asked earlier that week. I loved the way her voice tickled my ear. It was part of the reason people tuned in to the broadcast. She had a great one.

I scratched Micky's head and his eyes closed in surrender. We were snuggled up in my bed, he and I, enjoying the getting-to-know-more-about-each-other conversation that Carrie and I had going. "That's easy. A local car dealership was giving away a free hundred-dollar gift card to the person who showed up in the best costume."

"Halloween?"

"Not at all. That's just small-town entertainment for you."

"And who won?"

I squinted. "I feel like it was a roller-skating cow."

"The roller skates are a nice touch. Allows for creative movement. It's those details that matter in the snagging of gift certificates."

"What was yours?" I asked.

"You mean all those years ago? Let's see if I can remember." She was teasing, of course. "Carjacking. A two-year-old was in the back seat when the guy took off in it."

"Wait. That was your first story? I get roller-skating cows, and you're already Ms. Cutting Edge News? How is that possible?"

"I got lucky, I guess. So did the two-year-old. Safe and sound."

"Glad for that part. Still in awe of your career path."

"Oh, I'm not sure you should be jealous. It was almost like being thrown to the wolves to see who survives. I think I got pulled into my news director's office and screamed at at least once a week back then. Learned very quickly not to let her see me cry."

"Still. It worked."

"Eventually. I learned on the job. I screwed up a lot but always got back up. I watched the other reporters, learned their tricks and the things that got them praise."

"I try to do that. It's possible I've been watching you, too. For reasons other than the obvious flat-out lust factor."

"That goes both ways, that factor."

I grinned. "But seriously, you're so damn good at your job. The best I've ever seen. I'd be an idiot not to take notes."

A pause. "I'm glad someone thinks so." There was a shift in the timbre of her voice. She'd alluded to criticisms from the station higher-ups in the past.

I wondered what her face was doing. I longed to touch her cheek. "Why would anyone not think so?" I asked.

I heard her exhale. "According to them, I've been around a while, which means I'm old."

I frowned. She was anything but that. "That's the most insane thing I've ever heard you say."

"Well, think about it. The other stations in town have younger anchors, and when the ratings take any kind of a dip, I'm called in as the culprit and my image is revamped."

"Like the racier top."

"Or how they want me to lose ten pounds."

"From where? Seriously." I thought about her trim frame. It would be impossible.

"Thank you for saying that. I don't really see it ending, so it's part of my life now. Unless I eventually lose my job."

"No, no, no. Your job would never be in question."

"Just my soul. I'm going to be in lace-up boots and a halter top before this thing is over."

A pause. I hated that sex appeal had anything to do with reporting news. "This business can be brutal. I haven't been in it as long, but I know that much."

She exhaled. "Why do we do it again?"

"The thrill of the story. Is there anything like it?"

"Nope. I can't argue."

"Now tell me your favorite movie. No. Your top three."

We went on like that each night that we were apart and tore each other's clothes off each night we were together. I kept waiting for her body to become something I was used to, but it had yet to happen. Being with Carrie was just as exciting as the first time. The bonus was now I knew how to touch her, what made her come alive, and what each of her sounds meant.

"What am I going to do with you?" she asked late one night as I lay in her arms, against her chest. She stroked my hair in that unique way that was all her, soft, relaxed, and perfect. Like she'd practiced it. At the same time, I knew neither one of us had practiced for the other. I could see as much in the way she often looked at me, like this wasn't real. Like I might break to pieces in her hands. "You came on the scene and changed everything."

I lifted my chin and looked up at her. "Change can be good." I narrowed my gaze playfully. "It's good change, right? Not like when the garbage goes bad?"

She shook her head, mirth tugging at her mouth. "I can't believe your reverse simile involves garbage. Only you, Skyler."

I squeak-gasped. "Caroline McNamara of news fame. I'm a hard-hitting reporter, hell-bent on facts, and want to make sure that my presence is longed for, wanted. Can you confirm?"

She softened and cradled my face. "I can. Your breasts and presence are longed for daily. Please don't go anywhere. What would I do without this skin? That smile?"

I took out my imaginary microphone. "Is it also a fact that you enjoyed tonight and the things we did to each other?"

"It is, Skyler." Her voice took on the energy of an excited witness at a scene. "I have to say that tonight was a new level." She wasn't wrong. God in heaven. When she'd taken me from behind, I was pretty sure I'd met him, and Santa Claus, too.

"Care to elaborate?"

"Always, Skyler. It seems the way you used your mouth is extra-compatible with the kinds of things that turn me on. Then again, everything you do with your mouth is. Have you seen yourself eat ice cream? It's something to cherish."

"I haven't, Caroline," I said with my best news voice. "But I will purchase a mirror and get back to you. From Carrie's sexy love bed, this is Skyler Ruiz."

"Damn right it is," she said and captured my mouth, sliding on top. I allowed her hips to settle between my legs, my body wonderfully wide-awake again.

"You're wet," I whispered, pressing up against her.

Her eyes closed and her lips parted as I held our contact. "It just so happens that your reporting does that to me." She rocked her hips against me. So sexy. "Think about this the next time you're on a live shot."

I gulped. "How am I going to get through those now?"

"Hopefully, with grace and confidence, as always. I'll be waiting for you after. Like this." She stared down at me. "Now kiss me like you mean it."

"Not hard to do." I kissed her mouth, her breasts, her thighs, and her center until her back arched and she lifted off the bed with pleasure, her body still the most gorgeous I'd ever seen.

"Back to you, Caroline," I said, falling exhausted onto the bed with her laughter not far behind.

❖

It felt like a sexy little oasis from the world, Carrie's place. We met there late each night after stealing moments together throughout the day in the form of quiet, flirty conversations, stolen glances, and veiled emails. There was no policy against intra-office dating, but we decided to take our time before making any kind of obvious gestures.

Ty was onto us. But he was probably the most observant person I'd ever met, something I'd discovered over time. "Did you notice when you were interviewing that woman who bought the winning ticket that she was checking in with her husband about every fourth sentence?" Ty asked as we walked away from the home. "Gave me the willies." Two weeks later and the same guy was jailed for domestic battery, and we were covering *that* story. Not only that, but when we were out in the field together, I noticed him offering subtle suggestions or nudges in directions I might take the story, never overbearing or overt. His suggestions were good ones.

I hopped back in the SUV after following up on another suspicion of his, this time about our current subject. "You were right. The doctor we interviewed is the same guy from the nightclub. He DJs on the weekends, and it's totally going in the story." We fist-bumped, and I once again owed my buddy, Ty.

"You can pay me in green Slurpees. Better be extra-large, too. I don't want you showing up with miniature Slurpees, trying to get the same kinda credit."

"Your requests are specific. Do you lie in bed thinking of these things, adamantly swearing off small Slurpees as you drift off? Does your wife know?"

"I know what I like." He bopped my head as we drove back to the station to record my voice-over. "You in love with her?" he asked a few minutes later. Nope. He didn't miss much.

I decided there was no use trying to hide or deny that I'd been seeing Carrie. "Um…I don't know that we're there. Yet."

"Damn. You just said *yet*. This is serious."

I shook my head slowly, pondering. "I think it could be."

"Damn again."

"It's entirely new territory for me." I turned to him. "You're long-term married. What's the secret to doing it right?"

"Don't ask me. Pretty much just hurled myself onto Sandra's front porch each morning and begged her to notice me. Still do that, only it's my front porch now, too."

"So I should not only figuratively throw myself at Carrie, but literally. Good tip."

He paused, scratched the back of his head, and turned in total shock. "Did you say *Carrie*? Wait. We're talking about *our* Carrie? McNamara. From the station?"

"Shut up. You know we were." A feeling of dread hit. Had I just let the cat out of its extremely comfortable bag unnecessarily? "Didn't you?"

He grinned. "I one hundred did. You're just too easy."

Relief struck. "Ty, one of these days I'm going to see you coming."

"No, you won't. My charm prevents it." He did a shoulder dance, and I calmed the hell down.

In the meantime, my viral video continued to blow up. The clip recycled itself on Instagram and Twitter, and TikTok now had a reenactment duet happening, where the user could go back and forth with a clip of Lisette, playing the role of me. My horror had slowly shifted to acceptance and, finally, mild amusement. Let them have their fun. I could laugh along with them. And when I was recognized these days? It was by name. A very odd way to arrive on the map, via punching, but I was certainly there now, posing for selfies all over town, and still fielding interview requests at the national level.

"Hey, Skyler," Kristin said, falling in step with me as I walked down the hall. "We're trying to arrange a one-on-one with the mayor's office about the new beach regulations. Get his responses to all the criticism on the record. His people have requested you, and we're on board."

I quirked an eyebrow and let that information settle. "Me? You just said they requested me?"

She laughed. "Do you think you're up for it? It would be a big score. We can talk through strategy first."

"Um, yeah. Of course I am, and I welcome all strategic talk." This would be the most high-profile story of my career, and I didn't want to screw it up. My head began to swim with not only questions, but the order in which to ask them, which I'd learned was just as important.

"Great," Kristin said. "Come by my office in an hour, and we can have a work session. I'll set the interview time for just after lunch. We're hoping to have it for the ten, so a tight turnaround. I don't want Channel Five scooping us. I'll let Ty know."

"Perfect." I stared at her, wanting to spin down the hallway like Maria von Trapp on a mountain, but held on to my professionalism and instead nodded curtly at Rory, who I passed in the hallway. We were conservative colleagues, dammit, who were very serious. Not mountain-spinners. I slid into my desk chair with perhaps some extra energy, which pulled Carrie's focus.

"Okay, what's going on over *there*?" she asked, dragging the last word out.

I batted a strand of hair off my shoulder with a flourish. "Oh, nothing, except a sit-down with our very own mayor is teed up for air at ten. Today."

"Get out. You're on it?"

I nodded in exaggerated fashion. "They requested me. Face-Punch McGee over here. Why didn't I get punched sooner? I really dropped the ball."

"No one calls you that."

"I do. In the mirror."

She laughed. "This is amazing, though. Congratulations on the score." She was beaming, which made this all the better. "I look forward to getting to toss to the piece. *Your* piece. I will try not to exude overt pride and scream and stomp like a cheerleader."

"Definitely don't applaud."

"I'm considering it. I might need to." She went back to her keyboard, paused, and turned back. "Yeah, I'm gonna." Her blue eyes sparkled with amusement, and my heart filled with intense emotion from having her in my corner, the person who was quickly coming to mean more to me than anyone I'd ever been with, dated, or been attracted to. And yet, it was early. That was the scary part, trying to imagine what my feelings would be as time went on. Was there even room? I trembled a little through my smiling. Everything would be just fine, I told myself. *Enjoy the journey and today's victory.*

With Kristin's help, I prepped for the meeting with the mayor. I was shocked later when he told me that the face-punching only bolstered his appreciation for my work, and that it had been the story on the police cruisers that first snagged his attention. I was ten feet tall about it.

I watched the story Ty and I edited in record time from the back wall of the chilly studio as it aired. "What are you doing with your hands on your head like that?" Davonte asked, squinting from his spot between cameras one and two. "Do you have horns?"

"I'm nervous," I whispered. "So I'm being a moose. And they're antlers, not horns. It's a thing I do. You should try it sometime."

"Gotcha," he said slowly.

The antlers were something I'd relied on since I was a kid, and I wasn't embarrassed to trot them out when I needed them. They never let me down, though they did pull some strange looks. In fact, I'd received one from Carrie just moments before when she'd caught sight of my hand-antlers in her eye line. She still hadn't missed a beat while on camera, and that polish made me want to do naked things with her, and soon.

"You had no reason for antlers. The story killed," she said as we walked to the parking lot after the ten. "You did a great job."

"All Kristin. I just showed up."

"I didn't see her anywhere on that footage."

"Huh. Strange."

"Nope. That was you sitting with our mayor. You were appropriate, warm but hard-hitting. That's the kind of journalism people are interested in. No one wants a jerk, or someone too afraid to ask the uncomfortable stuff." She opened her car door and paused. "You were neither. You held him to the fire with respect and even some humor. See? No antlers required."

"Thank you for saying that. It helps a lot." I exhaled. "I'll keep the antlers on standby. Send them home for the night."

"Perfect. Grab Micky and come over? We can veg out and stare at the wall."

"That's my favorite. I'm sick of myself."

She perked up. "*I'm* sick of *myself*! So we'll focus on each other."

"And the wall."

"Don't I know it. See you in twenty."

I grinned. "I'll be there. With antlers on."

I didn't knock anymore upon arrival at her place and liked the informality we'd established. I found her staring at a legal pad when I followed Micky's jaunty trot into the kitchen.

"That's not a wall," I said, my brow furrowed. "We had a wall pact, and you're working. Flag on the play. I will storm the hell out of here."

She turned. "You better not. I just didn't want to start without you."

"Oh." I relaxed. "Well, that's much better."

She dropped the pad. "Just making some notes for a presentation I'm giving at the PSJ conference."

Ah, yes. The Professional Society of Journalists was hosting their annual conference later that month in Denver. I'd seen photos from the conference each year but had never attended. It was a big deal, and my little station had never been willing to fork over the money. "I didn't know you were speaking."

"Giving a talk for aspiring anchors on breaking into the business." She raised a finger. "And before you say anything, I'm aware of the irony, given how I treated you on your arrival. But you're different. You were under my skin and taking me wildly out of my comfort zone in under sixty seconds."

"You crushed on me." I rocked back on my proud heels.

She closed her eyes and held it. "So hard. And then your personality and talent lived up, and I was in trouble. Still am."

"Good," I said, leaning in for a slow kiss and luxuriating in its unravel. "Let's stay in trouble. Say yes. We do trouble real well."

She nodded. "For someone who plays it safe, that says a lot." She scooped up my dog and peppered his head with kisses while he wagged his whole body in adoration. He knew he got tons of attention when Carrie was around and was clearly milking it. I was beginning to feel he liked her more than me, which was outlandish given our bond.

"Stop the lovefest. I'm standing right here." A pause as I reflected on her statement. "I don't think I would have guessed that you played it safe before meeting you."

"I'm working on my reckless side, but it's slow going." She winked at me and placed Micky in the extra dog bed she'd picked up for when he came over. It looked expensive and chic, and he seemed to know it, sitting there proudly likely a newly crowned Prince of the Mutts.

"Give me the speech." I folded my arms and grinned.

Her brows dipped. "No."

"Yes. I want to hear it. Stand on the counter."

"Absolutely not."

"I'll ply you with moonshine until your inhibitions take their leave."

"You sound like you're on *Little House on the Prairie*."

"What?"

She sighed. "I forget how young you are. It's a show. Look it up one day for family-friendly viewing."

"Say the speech."

She sighed. "I guess it couldn't hurt to practice."

I rubbed my hands together. "Now we're talkin'. I'm getting a speech."

Carrie gave her hair the most subtle of tosses. I'd seen her do that very action seconds before her broadcasts went live and swallowed a smile at its appearance now. Cute. Her gaze settled on me and then imaginary people to my right and left. "Good morning, everyone, and thank you for having me."

"Let's not get crazy. Define have. I've had you, but have *they*? All of them. Really?"

She paused. "Stop harassing the speaker. It's a formality. Shall I go on?"

I gestured to give her the floor. "Please."

"The road to the anchor chair is not an easy one, but it does come with some magnificent sightseeing along the way."

"I can agree with that." I slipped off my shoes, hopped on the counter, and crisscrossed my legs.

Carrie smiled with serenity. "I was twenty-two when I was offered my first reporting job in Bossier City, Louisiana. I packed up everything I owned from my college apartment and got on the road to what I just knew would be the most exciting, glamorous job anyone could ever hope for." I grinned, enjoying the show. "It's safe to say that I was more than a little bit green."

"You're also very pretty."

"Thank you, random woman in the audience."

"You're welcome, speech lady. Please go on."

She settled back in. "I learned a lot in that first year and had more than a few rude awakenings. Some I plan to tell you about this morning."

"I can hardly wait."

"Excuse me, ma'am. Are you planning to heckle me from a countertop throughout this whole presentation?"

"I'm just so riveted."

Caroline laughed and dropped her pad to her side. "You realize, when I give this thing, all I'm going to hear in my head are these comments as I remember how adorable and sexy you look right now."

"That sounds like a win-win. I should pop popcorn for the rest. Do you have those microwave bags?"

"You should get over here is what you should do."

"Ooh la la." I didn't have to be asked twice, especially since I'd been undressing her with my eyes as she spoke. I hopped down and closed the short distance between us, taking off my top as I walked, tossing it to the floor, and watching her eyes feast. I loved that part. My cheeks went hot, right on cue. My nipples tingled as her gaze settled on them. We didn't have sex every time I slept over, but damn near it. Our physical connection was certainly undeniable. When we kissed, it was effortless, satisfyingly off the charts of comparison to kissing any other woman. We were in sync in so many ways, it was frightening. And the aspects of life we differed on—cultural upbringing, stations in our careers, and how one should properly eat a slice of pizza—brought the necessary tension, tossing gasoline on our fire. We'd not had *the talk* about what it was that was happening between us, but I already knew. I wasn't just in lust. And this was no longer someone that I simply looked up to and crushed on. I was starting to fall, and it had my head spinning in a wonderful, terrifying, grateful jumble. I thought she might be feeling the same. I hoped she was. The alternative was too much to consider, which meant I put everything I was feeling into my everyday actions, holding nothing back.

Except the words, of course. Those were held back.

No time to dwell on what was still unsaid. Her hands landed on my breasts, and we were off in a flutter of urgent longing. The rest would have to wait.

Lord, help me.

CHAPTER THIRTEEN

"Y ou interviewed the mayor of San Diego!" Aunt Yolanda yelled. "Little Skyler is sitting with my mayor."

I shrugged like it was no big deal, meanwhile enjoying every last bit of this praise as she pampered me with fresh tamales and that hibiscus tea I'm addicted to. No one made iced tea like Yolanda Matamoros. "We're old pals now."

"What did your mama say?" she asked.

I shifted. Honestly, she hadn't said much. We'd touched on it briefly before she moved our conversation on to all that she'd been up to at the law firm. My mother meant well, but she'd never been one to dwell on my successes. Success was expected if you worked hard enough, and she worked harder than anyone I knew, a price I paid growing up. Before my mother started law school, Sarah had frequently spent nights at our place, babysitting me to earn extra money while my mother worked and studied. When my mother moved away for law school, I'd been left in Yolanda's care. "She's very proud of me," I told my aunt, exaggerating.

"Of course she is. I bet she's telling everyone."

I nodded, my heart dipping a little, because I wasn't so convinced. I nodded vehemently anyway and tried to look excited. "She really, really is." I decided to change the subject. "I heard Emory is doing better with her treatment. Getting used to it."

She shook her head. "Yes, but the light is not there in her eyes. I think this diagnosis is hitting her harder than she anticipated."

I covered my aunt's hand. "She'll get it back. She lives with Sarah and Grace. They'll take care of her."

"Sarah says they've been arguing. She's been helicoptering around Emory and feels like Emory is shutting her out."

"Oh no."

Yolanda sighed. "My heart hurts for both of them."

Mine did, too. I loved my cousin, but a part of me had always identified more strongly with Emory. We had similar upbringings, setting aside the large amounts of money she'd been born into. I knew what it was like to have a parent who kept me at arm's length. But Emory Owen, to me, was invincible, which was why this whole thing reminded me of my own vulnerable place in this world. Bad things happened. And if they could happen to Emory, they could happen to any of us.

"I didn't mean to bring down the mood," Yolanda said. "Not when you have so much to celebrate. Oh, I bought you a toilet seat cover. Fuchsia. Do you like fuchsia? I can take it back if you don't. They have blue."

I laughed. "What? Why?"

"When I visited last, you didn't have one, and it's a nice thing. Not a necessary thing. Those are the kind of gifts I like to give. What about the color?"

My heart warmed. I leaned in and kissed her cheek. "Thank you, Aunt Yolanda." I reminded myself that I didn't have just one mother, and I needed to remember that. "I love fuchsia, and I love you."

❖

"Why do you think Rory always wiggles his hips when he's waiting for his coffee to brew?" I asked Carrie, whose head rested on my shoulder. I needed to get up for work shortly, but there were pressing questions to address first.

"I know what you're talking about. It's his coffee dance, and it's in rhythm with the machine's sputter."

"Yes!"

She laughed. "I'm not sure he even knows that he does it. It's like he's celebrating the coffee's impending arrival in his cup."

"Aww. Rory can be a lot, but that's actually kind of sweet. He loves his coffee that much."

Beneath the covers, Carrie moved her hips side-to-side and did her Rory impersonation. "Coffee. Coffee. Coffee. Coffee."

"Oh my God, that actually sounds like him."

"It should. I've spent close to a decade next to that guy."

"When is it that you're leaving for your trip? The conference."

"Two weeks. I'll miss you. It's a shame you can't come with me." A pause. "Well…now that I'm thinking about it, can you?"

I thought on it. "Really? I might be able to put in for the conference. Or take time off on my own." I pushed up onto my elbows and frowned. "Are you sure you mean it?" I didn't want to overstep if she was just talking out loud, but taking a trip together and getting to be there for Carrie's big speech would be nothing short of amazing.

"Of course I mean it." She looked at me, really looked at me, and I understood. "I always want you around. Don't you know that?"

My swollen heart felt ready to burst. "I do now. And yes, I want to go!"

"Settled, then. You're coming." She smiled and her eyes danced with happiness. "Look out, Denver."

"They're not gonna know what hit 'em."

It shouldn't have been too difficult to convince Kristin to give me a couple of days off, or better yet, let me attend the conference on behalf of the station. But I was aware that I'd waited pretty late to put in my request.

"So, how would you feel about me attending the PSJ conference this year?" I asked her. We'd been chatting casually in her office that morning before the day took off and we'd not have time to connect again. It had become our new informal routine, a checking in with each other.

She shifted her lips to the side, taking in my query. "Does this have anything to do with Carrie's speech?"

We had too many people in common for me to try and sidestep the implication. She had to know we were seeing each other. Emory and Lucy were best friends. I grinned, acquiescing. "Sure. It definitely motivates me to want to be there. It's also a great opportunity to learn, mingle, rub elbows."

She pursed her lips in thought. "I want you to talk to Tam about it." Apparently, this was a bigger ask than I'd realized, and I'd have to go up the ladder. "In fact, let's talk to him together right now."

She stood and walked past me down the hall to Tam's office. I followed, curious and now a little intimidated. We found him making strides on his new treadmill desk. He raised a hand when we entered and slowed his pace. "Hey."

Kristin walked all the way into the office and closed the door behind us. "Skyler is interested in attending the PSJ conference in Denver this year. Interesting, huh?"

That had his attention. In fact, he stopped the treadmill function altogether. His brow furrowed. "No, no, no. You can't do that."

My heart sank. "Well, if you don't want me to attend on behalf of the station, could I request those days off and go on my own time?"

Tam tented his fingers on his desk and Kristin looked on. "You could. That's one option."

Okay, good. This could still work out.

"Another is you stay here and anchor the five and ten while Carrie's away."

Silence. Holy hell and a half. "You want me to anchor. Why?" My brain was struggling to stay in the race and hadn't caught up to my mouth or the room.

Kristin stepped in. "We're always looking to groom new talent, and our audiences have taken a liking to you. It's a great chance for some anchor experience, too."

"You test well," Tam said and took a giant bite of a full-sized carrot like Bugs Bunny himself. "Really well. And you're new and fresh. What do you say?"

I grappled. This was a chance that didn't come around every day. Ever, actually. "Well, there's no way I can say no to that." I looked from Kristin to Tam. "Is there?"

Tam looked confused. "It would surprise me if you did."

"It's a pretty big deal," Kristin added.

Excitement bubbled and overtook every other plan I had. I'd miss going on the trip with Carrie, but she was someone who would understand the gravity of this opportunity. Plus, we would have more trips ahead of us. I'd happily plan one myself.

"I'd love to fill in," I said decisively.

"Great." Tam turned his treadmill back on and got to walking. "We'll get you a few rehearsals and talk about camerawork. Nothing too difficult. You're a pro."

I nodded from my spot somewhere in the stratosphere. "Okay, thank you." I paused. "Is this because I got punched?"

Kristin laughed. "No. Definitely not."

Tam looked thoughtful. "It probably didn't hurt. Any attention is good attention, right? I mean, as long as you're not a criminal. Don't do crime."

His dry delivery left me unsure of how serious he was being. "Not forecasted for any, so…"

"That's what I want to hear." He looked to Kristin. "You got this?"

"I do."

"Great." We were excused. He went back to his TVs, carrots, and treadmill. I was confident he never slept. Or cried.

Once we were alone in the hallway, Kristin turned to me with a warm smile. "Proud of the work you're doing, Skyler. Keep it up, okay?"

I surely grew two inches in that moment. This was my boss, and she thought I was doing okay. She was *proud* of me. But it didn't stop there. I called Carrie from my desk minutes later. She wasn't due to the station for another couple of hours, but there was no way I was going to be able to wait that long with this news leaping up and down from within like an impatient kid at the candy counter.

"Skyler, wow. They're putting you in the big chair?"

"The big chair."

"Do you know how huge a deal that is? We have reporters who've been with us for years, decades, who've not seen the anchor seat."

I shook my head and smacked a hand across my forehead. "I wish I knew why they're taking the leap. They said I test well."

"Well, everyone loves you. It's true." She got quiet. "I guess this means no weekend away together."

"That's the sad part."

"You know what? That's okay. This is important for you, and you should do it. You are, right?"

"As long as you're in agreement, I planned to."

"Are you kidding? I'm dating the hot new substitute anchor of the nightly news. Let me fan myself."

I laughed. "Now you know how I feel daily."

"We have to celebrate."

"No."

"Yes. I'm taking you out this weekend." We both had it off and, other than Jack's, had not done any formal nights out. Mainly just the two of us at her place or mine. This felt like a new, exciting step. "Alejandro's?"

"Oh, you really want to be fancy. We're going to eat nice food among the friendly people of San Diego."

"I really feel like we should. I want to spoil you and stare at you in dim lighting while the world looks on."

I laughed. "Pick me up at eight. Let the wooing begin."

❖

"What about a little extra eyeliner?" Grace asked. She'd come by the apartment earlier for a little cousin movie-watching date and stayed to help get me ready for my night out. She'd been dabbling with makeup tutorials and watching them online. I indulged her to an extent, but mainly when I was staying in. Tonight, I had a date.

I shook my head. "Less is more for me."

"Well, you do have beautiful brown eyes and TV glamour. Not that I'm jealous." She glared.

I stood and hugged her. "What do you have to be jealous of, Miss Super Achiever?"

She shrugged and plopped onto the bed where Micky was asleep on my pillow. He lifted his head, took Grace in, and went right back to the land of slumber. "Truth. I think I like someone, so I'm experimenting a little bit with stuff like makeup." Aha, now I understood the tutorials. She held up a hand and her brown eyes went wide. "Don't say anything to my mom, or she will go completely crazy and blow it out of proportion. Usually, I let her embarrass me, but this is different. I'll die."

I scoffed. "Um, excuse me. That's what you have a cousin for. To *not* tell your mom when you like someone. Who is it?"

"Their name is Bobby and they have the sweetest smile. A little quiet. Very smart. And everyone likes them. Like, *everyone*."

"And those are their pronouns? They/them?"

She nodded and I gave her a squeeze, thrilled to see her so excited about someone. It still blew my mind that she was old enough to date, but here we were. "And does Bobby have similar feelings?"

She threw up her hands. "How is a person supposed to know? That's the infuriating part."

"Infuriating, huh?" I was enjoying this and her blossoming vocabulary.

"Well, do they pay attention to you?"

She nodded. "And they bring me things. Like, when they go to the vending machine, they come back with two of whatever they get. One for me."

"Oh, this sounds like hard-core love. Vending machines are telling."

"They are?" She lit up and then went pensive, probably planning her next move. Grace was ambitious, always had been. She wasn't a dedicated member of the chess club for no reason.

There was a knock on my door, and I checked the clock on my nightstand in accusation. "Oh no." Carrie was five minutes early, and

Grace and I had lost track of time to begin with, which wasn't unusual when we hung out.

Grace stood calmly. "I'll get the door. You put on the cute dress. Make an entrance. I hear that works." She paused. "Does it? Sometimes I make things up."

"It can." I offered a salute, dashed into the bathroom, and slipped into the turquoise number with the cap sleeves that went perfectly with my silver strappy heels. From down the hall I heard the front door open.

"Hi, Carrie. I recognize you from Instagram. And the news, of course. Come on in."

"I am. Are you…Grace?"

"Pleased to meet you. Sky is finishing up and will be out soon."

I was hesitant to interrupt this meeting, amused at the way Grace held the room like a forty-year-old. Then again, she'd always been an old soul. "She's told me a lot about you. You play chess, right?"

"I do. I'm the captain of my team and a big fan of the fianchetto attack." She raised a shoulder, like it was a casual reference. "From the Dutch Defense, the Leningrad Variation."

"Oh. Of course," Carrie said confidently.

"Where will you two be dining tonight?" This kid.

I covered my mouth because here we went. I caught sight of Carrie nodding astutely at the question. "There's a great little bistro not far from here. Alejandro's. Do you know it? You're welcome to join us."

Oh no, she wasn't.

"No, but thank you. And this is a date? A real one? Of the romantic variety."

My cheeks flamed. We were off script. Grace was suddenly my concerned father.

"Um, yes. Is that okay?"

Grace nodded. "Definitely. Just checking in. So, you must like my cousin a lot?"

"I do. She's pretty great."

"I think so, too," Grace said. "I especially like her kind heart. What about you? What are your favorite qualities of hers?" She folded her arms and waited.

Oh, man. She was a bulldog, and I needed to get in there before it went further. I made my entrance into the living room, intent on saving Carrie from what was inches from an interrogation.

"Hey, you," I said.

Carrie looked up happily, her eyes dancing. Seeing me had done that, and my heart squeezed pleasantly. "Hi."

"I see you've met Grace. She's…inquisitive."

She nodded. "In the best way. We're getting to know each other."

"Do you get to know a lot of people? When was your last relationship?" Grace asked, eyes narrowed.

I stared. "Grace."

She rolled her lips in and relaxed. "Too much?"

"Probably so."

"Just trying something new." She held up her phone. "But would you look at that? Emory's outside to pick me up." She stood. "You two have fun. Don't stay out too late."

I smiled, hands clasped in front of me. "You got it."

She looked from one of us to the other. "Safe sex is best."

I covered my eyes. "Grace. Just…no."

"Sorry." She held up a hand in apology, tossed in a smile, and waved before slipping out the door.

"She can be a whirlwind," I told Carrie once we were alone. "And she's growing up incredibly fast."

"Well, she seems pretty great to me. She loves you. Also, can we pause just for a moment? Because the way you look tonight is…" She exhaled slowly. "Yeah. Just…yeah."

Oh, I was enjoying this. "Carrie. I do believe you're blushing a little."

"You do that to me." She shook her head, and I admired the manner in which her sleek black cocktail dress hugged each subtle curve. The dip in the front offered only a conservative glimpse of cleavage, but I knew innately that I'd be preoccupied with the hint all night, as well as the way that blond hair, partially swept up, fell softly as if she'd meant for it to tickle her neck and shoulders. I hoped I'd be kissing those later.

For now, I took her in, pure elegance. And not only that, but she was *my* date. I still couldn't wrap my mind around that. Pride and happiness mingled.

"What?" she asked, angling her head with a smile, her eyes never leaving mine in that flirty, lighthearted way. Anticipation pinged.

"Just admiring my view."

She held out her hand. "Shall we continue this appreciation session over some sinful wine and food? This place has a spinach dumpling appetizer that you have to try. I want to watch your face when you do."

I placed my hand in hers. "I'm all yours." I meant it as a casual, fun reference to the evening ahead of us, but we both heard the words and their gravity.

Something shifted behind her eyes, and she softened. "Yeah?" The question came with unmistakable vulnerability that I didn't often see from her.

"Yeah," I said, attempting to communicate the depth of my feelings through that one little word. She seemed to understand. For a moment, we just lost ourselves in each other until she lifted her hand to my cheek and cradled it. We exchanged an important smile and headed out for the night.

Over dinner, I fell for her even more.

The soft lighting, gentle music, and amazing food didn't hold a candle to the company. Carrie enchanted. I adored her witty quips just as much as her sage advice. My favorite, though, was the way she flirted, sometimes overtly, but mostly she fell on the subtle side. A soft squeeze to my knee as we waited on our food. A wink when the conversation hit a lull. Or sometimes when she'd catch my eye and just say, "Hi," in that quiet little voice she'd adopt, the one that said we were the only two people in the world. I'd never adored that word so much.

"How's your dinner?" I asked. She'd ordered the pasta in white wine asiago sauce, and the little noises she made upon first tasting it told me it had been a good selection.

She gestured to her plate, still piled high with pasta. "I'm sad because I can't eat it all and want to."

"Well, your pout is admirable, so I bet the pasta understands. You can take it home with you. Bonus pasta. In an unfortunate turn of events, I don't have the same option."

My plate was clean, my food long gone. I'd ordered the medallions of filet and hadn't been more pleased with a meal in years. It was definitely the perfect spot to celebrate.

"I'll share my leftovers with you tomorrow. I get to see you tomorrow, right?"

"I was planning on it. What if we went down to the beach? Just us and the water and a long afternoon."

"I can't think of anything better. Plus, you in a swimsuit alone would have sold your idea."

"Excuse me." We looked up at the smiling, middle-aged woman I'd seen dining a few tables away. "I know you're having a nice dinner, but would you mind if I got a photo with you. Big fan."

"Not at all," Carrie said with a serene smile.

When the woman handed Carrie her phone and raced around the table to pose with me, I think we both took a moment to absorb her intentions. "Oh," I said, turning to her. She was already smiling for the camera, so I did as well.

Once the photo was taken, the woman turned to me. "My kids are gonna flip. Keep up the good work."

"Thank you so much," I said, caught off guard but also touched. The photo seeker dashed away, and I turned back to Carrie, wide-eyed. "I thought for sure she was here for you."

She shrugged. "I'd want my photo with you, too. I get it." Her smile was still in place, but a few watts had slid off.

I leaned in, grappling to fix it. Our relationship had been built on her being the more successful one, and in my opinion that would never change. However, I was also aware of her recent insecurities at work and wanted to help. "It's our night off. Why don't we take dessert to go?"

That seemed to perk her up. "We don't need the wall tonight. We could pick up Micky, maybe watch a movie? Forget the world?"

I could tell that she seemed to need it, and I was more than willing to be her respite. "I'd love that."

"Thank you."

"But first, we need that to-go dessert. I think it would be wrong to leave here without it."

"How about we have them box up one of everything?"

I blinked. "I've never been more in love." The words were automatic, which had to mean something. My mouth and my heart seemed to have a thing going tonight, and they didn't want my brain involved in any way. I froze for a beat, understanding that I'd voiced the words out loud. To her credit, Carrie didn't so much as miss a beat.

"Then I should spoil you with food more often."

A deep internal sigh of relief hit. Nothing was lost or over-confessed, jeopardized or made awkward. Just two people out for dinner. Two people who very much enjoyed each other's company. And hopping into bed together. And kissing with the fire of the sun. And maybe love was part of that in the larger scheme. It wasn't an easy emotion to shy away from once it was upon you, and I felt its presence unmistakably.

Love.

As we fell asleep that night, our limbs intertwined in her bed, our breathing slowly ushering us to sleep, I felt it with every fiber of my being. I *loved* this woman. Deeply and without question. I wasn't sure what appropriate amount of time was supposed to go by before an official proclamation, but for me, it was a done deal. I was in love and, frankly, a little drunk on it. I lifted my head from where it rested on her pillow and placed a soft kiss on her cheek. I watched a brief smile play in the light of the moon before she was out again.

Beautiful. Peaceful. Loved.

Everything was as it should be. The universe had smiled on me and granted me the gift of this wonderful and unexpected connection to another person. I was blessed and knew it.

CHAPTER FOURTEEN

W e're live in five," Devante called out to the room as he made a lap around the studio, following his last minute checklist prior to air. As for me, my heart was pounding with such vigor that I wondered if others could see it beneath my shirt.

Focus. Just another day on air from a different location. No big deal. No life-changing moment about to take place in front of hundreds of thousands of people. Carrie had left for the conference the night before, and with a kiss in the studio parking lot beneath the stars, she'd offered me encouragement. "You take care of my spot, okay?"

I winced. "What if I screw up? Go silent and wither away and die a slow on-air death. Because that's kinda what I'm afraid is going to happen."

"That's the most ridiculous statement I've heard you make. You're calm as a cucumber in the face of chaos. I've seen you continue reporting with two grown men beating each other, feet from you."

"That's true." I raised a finger. "I also had to report on an ice-cream eating competition once and did not get offered so much as a taste. I kept my cool."

"See? A seasoned pro already." She slid her attaché into her car. "I plan to watch online and will be cheering for you. Can't wait." She cradled my face lovingly and exhaled as if memorizing my image. We'd be apart for the next four days, a record. "Now kiss me again before I fly away. I want to relive it in the air. Taste your lip gloss."

"Your wish." I wrapped my arms around her waist, sinking my lips against hers. "I will miss you," I whispered. The parking lot was relatively dead at the late hour, but it didn't matter. We'd stopped hiding what was happening between us, and yes, the whispers had certainly picked up. And policy-wise, as long as we kept things professional, there should be no trouble with the higher-ups. I didn't report to Carrie in any capacity.

"Skyler, you good?" Kristin asked, moments before the broadcast went live. "Anything?"

I shook my head, ordering my nerves to stand the hell down. "I'm just ready."

I looked over at Rory, who nodded to me with an encouraging smile. I pictured him doing his coffee dance and then imagined Carrie imitating it to perfection. That certainly helped untangle some of my tension.

I consulted the iPad in front of me with an outline of the broadcast and a script I'd need should the teleprompter fail. It was funny that they called it the big chair, given that there actually was no chair at all. I'd be standing behind a glass desk as I anchored the five and ten, and thereby made sure my blouse was smoothed and my skirt on straight.

"And five, four, three." Eduardo, the stage manager, mouthed the two and the one and tossed it to me with an underhanded point. I was live from the anchor desk and ready to drive this thing home. "Good evening, San Diego. I'm Skyler Ruiz in for Caroline McNamara, and there's lots to get to tonight. A fire in North Park this afternoon had crews scrambling to contain the blaze that threatened to spread to neighboring homes. As families struggled to evacuate in time, the image of the raging fire no doubt ignited fear in their hearts."

Rory picked it up from there, and we were off. Headlines, a live shot from Carlos, weather, cheerful banter, sports, community interest, more banter, and we were out. It was a marathon that, at the same time, zipped by in a stressful, exhilarating flash.

"And we're clear," Eduardo said.

I looked to Rory. "Thank you." He might love himself a whole lot, but Rory had been kind to me and made the experience a good one.

"No, thank you. You were a champ." He offered me a high five, which I accepted, loosened his tie, and was out of there. Just another Thursday for Rory Summerton. For me, I felt like I'd taken a round trip to the moon. I stood, still on uneven footing, and absorbed the quiet bustle in the studio as cameras were reset, lights were dimmed, and the place put back in order for the start of the ten. That's right! I got to do it all over again in a few hours. I rolled my shoulders, now extra smiley.

"Fantastic job. How do you feel?" Kristin asked, emerging from the booth.

"Good. I think." I squinted. "I suppose that depends on how it went."

"Couldn't have been happier. My only note would be to let yourself loosen up a little on the in-between chatter, and tighten up those transitions. Too many beats before."

I nodded, absorbing the helpful criticism. "Got it. Not a problem at all."

"You have some time now. Get something to eat and take a look at the stories we have working for the ten. Familiarize yourself. Let me know if you have any questions about anything, and we'll go from there."

I'd seen Carrie make this turnaround a million times. A big chef's salad at her desk and her laptop open as she read through the copy as soon as the producers uploaded it. She'd furrow her brow and nod along, likely saying the words in her head, flagging the copy with questions.

When I returned to my desk and retrieved my phone, it was ringing. Carrie. "I saw. You killed it. I'm so proud of you I could leap through the phone."

I could hear every ounce of genuine excitement in her voice, and it was contagious. I beamed. "Please leap. I would love to see you right now." I blew out a breath. "It's a little nerve-racking, your job. So many moving parts."

"There's a lot of choreography that most people don't know about."

"You can say that again. I've seen it done a million times, but it's a whole different animal when you're the one with the reins."

"Everyone there knows what they're doing, including you. Remember that. Nothing to worry about."

"I will. Good tip."

The ten o'clock went even better than the five, and I felt like I'd found a little bit of traction. I smiled more during the handoffs and let myself breathe deeply whenever I had a short break. I ended the night on a high, strolling to my car, and angling for a celebratory glass of champagne when I got home. The only downside was that my favorite person wasn't there to celebrate with. I went home to Micky and snuggled into my bed, happy the day had gone so well and gearing up for my second and final day as temporary anchor. If someone had told me a year ago that I'd be anchoring at KTMW while waiting for Caroline McNamara, who I was sleeping with, to return home from a conference, I would have laughed them off the planet. Yet, here I was, basking, luxuriating, and enjoying every damn minute.

❖

I was sitting on the trunk of my car when the cab carrying Carrie from the airport pulled alongside her home. I couldn't contain my smile as she emerged, having been counting the minutes until I could talk to her, stare at her, and kiss her properly.

She walked directly to me, even letting Micky jump all over her until she'd greeted me. "Hi, you," she said, immediately pulling me into a kiss. "God, I missed you a lot. Let's not do this again ever."

I still hadn't said anything, my smile dialed to constant and probably hyperbolic. Couldn't help it. That's how I felt, like I was finally back in the arms in which I belonged, and that required my happy display. "Agreed. Don't leave anymore. I'll pay you."

"How about I just take you with me?" Were her blue eyes even more blue now? I stared into them dreamily, lost. I adored them.

"Or that."

She smoothed a strand of my hair with affection. "Unfortunately, you couldn't cover for me at the station if I did that, and you're the best fill-in."

"Too bad. They'll just have to find some other moose. I'm with you."

She kissed me, pleased. "Yeah, you are." Then, she sat down on the damn driveway in her designer jeans and entered into a ten-minute lovefest with my dog, who had lost his damned mind at her return. I thought he was about to wag himself into space with the intensity of his celebration. "Did you miss me, you little furry nugget?" She cradled his cheeks for several of her signature puppy kisses, quick little pecks on his face that he seemed to enjoy every second of. It was the one time he'd gone still since the cab had pulled up.

"He wrote you letters each day. Howled sad songs at the base of my bed. Ran his tin can along my headboard."

"Is that true?" she asked Micky, sympathy in full gear. "Oh no."

"I joined him. A duet."

She laughed and touched my chin. "Well, howl no more, you two. I'm home. You're still beyond beautiful. Let's go inside, order in, and you can tell me everything I missed at the station, and leave no gossip behind."

"Deal." I grabbed her bag, she grabbed my dog, and we wandered our way through the greenery-lined sidewalk to her home, which was beginning to feel awfully comfortable to me. I liked that I knew where things like the good scissors lived. I could find my way in the dark for a drink of water and knew how to work each and every remote. Things were getting serious. We were domestic.

"You've given me the conference headlines, but how was it?" I took a seat on the couch and Micky hopped into my lap. "Was your talk well received? Did they love you?"

"They really did." She took a moment and looked skyward as if piecing together her thoughts. "It went better than I thought it would, and Skyler, I really think I needed that."

"Yeah?" I grinned, happy to hear it. "Tell me more."

She sat on the couch and swiveled so she faced me, full of energy. "I don't think I'd realized it, but my confidence at work has taken a bigger hit than even I knew. But being in that environment, exchanging ideas, meeting people who were excited to hear what I had to say was… so encouraging. Like the best kind of pep talk. I left the conference feeling bolstered and renewed, ready to get back to work."

She was right. There was a new lightness and an elevated energy to the way she carried herself, like she was ready to conquer the world rather than stare at a blank wall. "It sounds like it served as a reset button."

She beamed. "That's exactly what it was like." She paused and placed a hand on my leg. "And at the same time, all I wanted in the world was to rush back here and tell you all about it."

My body went warm and soft as I let the words wash over me. "Really?"

She nodded, and that's when I saw it. Her eyes were filled with tears. "I have enjoyed every moment we've spent together, Skyler. And I want more. Lots more."

"Me, too," I said, sitting taller, thrilled with the moment, my feelings, and this connection. "I had this fantastic experience and left work so excited, and it lost something because you weren't there to share it with me." I took a deep breath. "That means something, right? We should maybe pay attention."

She nodded. "I think so."

"This is different for me. Us. I've never had this before."

She didn't miss a beat. "I haven't either." The exciting energy between us bounced back and forth, highlighting the fact that we were on the same damn page, and how amazing was that?

I smiled. "Not even that Audra woman? She's beautiful, you know."

"She's not you," she said, smile gone. "No one is you."

I felt every word of that sentence and pulled her hands to me, staring at them, tracing each vein, allowing myself to tap into every part of her. And, oh, did the floodgates open. My heart grew, and I got this unusual lump in my throat. "I want to be good at this. At us. In fact, I'm terrified not to be."

She nodded and intertwined our fingers. "I happen to think you're doing a great job. Are you afraid of me?"

I considered the question. I wasn't afraid of Carrie or what I was feeling, but I was afraid that my feelings would surpass hers. After all, I had a history in life. I'd always been the chaser rather than the chasee and just didn't want to have to watch another uneven relationship in my life play out. That was my fear. I wanted someone to want me every bit as much as I longed for them. I rolled my lips in and exhaled a short breath. "My mom worked really hard, but she wasn't around much as a result. I don't blame her, but she wound up with her own life, friends, and interests. For a while, when I was young, she lived in another city entirely. It was for a noble cause, but I was always aware she made the choice to be far away from me." I closed my eyes, embarrassed. "And I have zero idea why I'm telling you this now."

"I do."

"Yeah?"

She kissed the back of my hand. "It sounds like from early on, you've been seeking out love from other people who weren't always there for you."

Well, she'd just gone and summed up my entire existence in one sentence. Because it hadn't stopped there. I'd seen it in even my short-term relationships. Kacey, no less. "Yes. That would be accurate. I don't think I've ever heard it out loud before." I laughed sardonically. "Has a nice ring to it."

"I think it's perfectly natural to want love."

I held my breath because the word was right there, introduced into the conversation by Carrie, and the perfect opening. It played on my tongue as I waited to see what direction she'd go. I wanted to tell her how deeply in love I had already fallen, but I'd be first. Terrifying. What if I was met with silence? What would I do then?

"That's the thing." I met her beautiful blue eyes that now searched mine with white hot intensity. "I'm already gone on you." It wasn't quite the word love, but surely she understood. "And maybe you're still early, maybe you're—"

"Gone, too?"

"Oh." I inhaled. My heart skipped pleasantly. "Maybe that."

"Then let me show you, so you're sure." She tilted her head and leaned in, brushing her lips across mine softly, slowly, reverently, before deepening the kiss. My lips parted, and her tongue made entrance as every part of me craved her. I came alive beneath the brush of those lips. She climbed onto my lap, and nothing had ever been as satisfying as the welcome weight of her body on mine. She sat back and met my gaze. "More than a little bit gone." She let the words hang in the air a moment before leaning in and picking up where she left off, kissing my neck sensually, pulling soft murmurings from me until I insisted we move things to the bedroom. I needed her skin on mine. Her chest pressed to my heart.

Everything felt different between us that night. Part of it was the time we'd spent apart, but there was so much more behind it. We were moving toward something wonderful and long-lasting. We shared sustained eye contact, a slower pace, softer touches. We were expressing ourselves in a way we never had before and nothing had ever felt more ordained. I wrapped myself up in her before releasing myself to sleep, excited to see what the next day had in store for us. The both of us. Together.

CHAPTER FIFTEEN

This bed was what heaven must have felt like. I woke up the next morning naked beneath a big fluffy white duvet with four little paws on my chest. I blinked up at my enthusiastic pup who very much wanted his breakfast. "Good morning, Michelangelo," I said and received a tiny tongue swipe on my nose. "Are you hoping for kibble?"

"He's had breakfast. A lot of it. Don't let him lie to you," a voice from the kitchen advised. I grinned because Carrie was up early. I checked the window rather than the clock. The sun was on its way up, which meant I needed to abandon this warm, wonderful bed and get a move on.

"I hear you're pulling a fast one," I told Micky with a squint. "You have bacon breath to prove it." He licked his lips proudly.

Carrie appeared to my right, carrying an oversized white mug full of piping-hot coffee. "For you." She winked. "I kept you up a little late. Least I could do."

"You're the most wonderful human I've seen today." I emerged from bed and gave the belt on her robe a gentle tug, helping the knot tumble free. Hot pink panties and nothing else. "So sexy," I said, giving her a kiss. I slipped my hands inside the robe and around her waist to feel the warmth of her skin.

"If you greet me like this every morning, there's more coffee to come. I kind of love it when you ogle my body."

"Done." I quirked my head. "But you don't have to be up yet."

"I have some work to do on that piece about domestic violence in teen relationships. Tam wants it to hit air by midweek, and we're not quite there. Something is missing, and I'm not sure what." She tapped her lips. "I'm consulting with a psychologist who specializes. I want to do this thing right."

"I get that. It's an important topic." I kissed her. "Wanna shower first, or me?"

She looked behind her toward the bathroom in contemplation. "I know a way we could save time."

"I'm always amazed at your ingenuity."

She dropped the robe altogether and led the way. So I'd be a little late today, it turned out.

From there, the day took off and never quite slowed down. I had a million messages in my voice mail that had piled up over the weekend. Tips. Requests. Offers. I still hadn't quite gotten used to the new faster pace, and the attention only seemed to be increasing.

"Do you think he would be willing to say so on camera?" I asked the tipster. She'd called in, claiming her husband, one of the guards from the county jail, had witnessed his superior deleting surveillance video of an inmate who'd died while in their custody. It was an interesting story, but without someone with firsthand knowledge on record, the story was incomplete. Kristin had taught me that much.

"No, he doesn't want anything to do with the news. But it's not right," she exclaimed. "Someone needs to look into what's going on at that place. It's out of control."

"I hear you, but without a source, things get a little more difficult."

Out of the corner of my eye, I saw Carrie arrive at her desk. I tossed her a smile, but it didn't seem to register. The expression on her face was quite simply nonexistent, blank. Odd. I wrapped up the tipster with a promise to look into things and ended the call.

"You in there?" I said it lightheartedly and added another smile.

When she lifted her gaze to mine, I knew instantly that something was dead wrong. She was pale, shocked, sad. "I'm out," she said simply.

I tilted my head, processing. "What do you mean *out*? The domestic violence story?" Oh no. She'd been working so hard on that one. Why would they kill it?

"Altogether. My last broadcast is next week. I was just informed."

I looked behind me, stupefied, trying to assemble meaning. As it settled, I went still. Then I tried to undo it. "No. Did you and Tam have a disagreement?" Those things could be fixed. "Maybe he just—"

"Skyler. They fired me. It's done. I'm sure the plan has been in the works for a while now. Luckily, my agent was smart enough to build in a golden parachute, which means they're buying out my contract and then some. Not that any of that matters." Her blue eyes had lost their light, and I wanted it back.

"Well, it's the most outrageous thing I've ever heard. I don't understand what they're trying to do." I was numb. Upset. Then angry. I stood with utter determination, ready to throw something across the room. "In fact, I'm going to walk down to those offices and tell them." I meant it, too. My temper flared hot and ready.

"Stop that," Carrie said, her voice low and even. "You are not. That is not how I choose to walk out of here after over a decade. It will be with my head held high. No drama."

I clenched and unclenched my fists, feeling helpless. This couldn't be happening. I looked around the newsroom to see everyone in it continuing on with their days as if it was business as usual. Rory making his way to his desk with a fresh cup while tossing a quip behind him to Chase, one of the camera ops. Mila answered the phone. Kristin leaned over Carlos's desk. Didn't they understand?

"Well, what am I supposed to do? I can't just sit here and work."

She shook her head and stared at the surface of her desk, not in a position to answer, which made perfect sense. This wasn't a moment for her to be there for me. It was the opposite. Time to shelve my own feelings and concentrate on hers. "Let's take a walk. We need air. Come on."

Probably because she wasn't sure what else to do, she stood wordlessly and followed me through the newsroom and out the side door, which dumped us onto a downtown sidewalk that was less than clean. A touristy family of four, wearing shorts and carrying shopping bags, stepped around us. For a few minutes, we just walked, passing gift shops, office buildings, restaurants in the midst of lunch-to-dinner transition, and even a Segway tour of the city.

"You realize they're idiots, right?" I finally said.

I heard her take a deep breath as she walked beside me. "I guess they're just doing what they think is right for the station. Ratings have taken a dip."

"That's not your fault."

She shrugged. "Maybe it is. I'm no longer who the viewers are interested in. It happens." She gave her head a sad shake. "It just hurts when it happens to you."

"No. That's not it. We're dealing with a few nameless executives putting pressure on Tam to solve a problem. But they know nothing about what we do." I turned to her and squeezed her hand. "You're the best in the business. You need to hear me on this."

She nodded, a look of determination on her face. "Thanks. Just trying to work through what all of this will mean. What now? I'm just still in shock. I should have known this was coming. I'm so mad that I didn't."

What now? That part hadn't even occurred to me. If Carrie wanted to continue on as an anchor, she'd have to seek out another market, a concept that had my brain screaming. "You know what? Everything is going to work out. You're going to have so many exciting opportunities now. You're famous in this town, and the phone is going to start ringing." I was convinced of that part. Too many people adored her. Right on cue, a couple approached.

"Love you on the five o'clock, Caroline," the woman said. "Been watching you for years. You have dinner with us every night."

"Thank you for watching," she said back with a gracious smile. "And for the dinner."

The couple continued on, beaming from having run into Caroline McNamara.

I winced. "Well, they're not going to take this well." That pulled a laugh, which was something.

She nodded. "I'm going to be okay. I am, right?" She was asking the cosmos.

"You are. I know that with every fiber of my being. But I'll still scream my head off at the suits if you'll let me. I swear to God. They will regret this."

"Probably not the best for your career." She gave my hand a tug and paused our walk. "But thank you for wanting to, and for getting me out of there before I imploded."

"Anything you need." I squeezed back. "Can I ask a question?"

"Of course."

"You really didn't see this coming?" Because I sure as hell didn't.

She shook her head. "No. Can't say I did." I hated that answer because it meant she'd truly been blindsided, and she didn't deserve that. Not after all the years she'd given them. My heart hurt even more. "Thank you for the walk, but we better head back. I need to be present. Let everyone know everything is fine."

Another credit to her. She still cared about the station that just turned its back on her.

I wondered if the shake-up would continue. Would Rory be next? No. Rory had been signed for three more years and was practically dancing through the newsroom at whatever they'd offered him. Another example of the way women went underappreciated and were held to unfair standards. I seethed. Word of Carrie's firing slowly made its way through the newsroom that afternoon. The mood dramatically shifted, and everyone kept their voices low and their heads down. They'd lost a valued leader. Morale had taken a definite hit, and just before going on air for the five, Carrie took matters into her own hands and climbed on top of her goddamned desk. My jaw hit the floor.

"Can I steal a moment of your time?" she called out to the newsroom.

The precious minutes before the broadcast were ticking by, and deadlines were looming. That didn't stop the place from going quiet as all eyes turned to Carrie. "I know this is a weird day, and the changes coming down have us all a little on edge. But I wanted to reassure you that everything is all right. We're still family, and we still have a ton of news to bring to the people of San Diego over the next week. So let's set aside everything that we're feeling and come together to make that happen."

She was met with nods and smiles and even a shouted, "Love you, Carrie!" Her words seemed to work, and I felt the room collectively relax over the next two hours and then wake the hell up. I was amazed.

But that's who Caroline McNamara was, a leader and the glue that held us all together. She would exit her role at the station with every ounce of respect and grace she came in with.

In the midst of my own broken heart, I couldn't have been more proud of her.

❖

The week from hell played on while I watched in horror, willing it all away. Carrie put out a heartfelt statement on her social media, announcing her departure from the station after over a decade on air. Her goal was to get ahead of what would surely be a sensationalized version of her firing that would hit the rumor mill soon. Once word was out, calls from her loyal viewers flooded in for a day or two before the world forgot and moved on.

I hadn't.

We had three days left as colleagues when I got a dreaded call from Tam, too. "Skyler, can you come down to my office when you have a sec?"

"Oh. Of course," I said, closing my eyes, my palm to my forehead. I hung up and stared, numb and nervous. My stomach turned over, and

I wished I'd eaten a lighter lunch. Surely, just a check-in of sorts. I'd been with the station a few months now, and he probably wanted to work in an impromptu performance review. I'd had a couple of stories go to air that, honestly, could have been fleshed out more. I knew that. I'd been distracted this week and would be ready to own up to that in the meeting. I considered texting Carrie before walking down the hall. She was in the editing bay, consulting on her domestic violence cut. Something told me to let her be. Why send her into a similar panic?

Ty's eyes went wide when he saw me approach Tam's door. I passed him a silly look, which was every bit aimed at putting me at ease as it was at him. I couldn't come up with any reason for Tam to fire me. In fact, I was well aware that they were more than happy with the attention I'd brought to the station with my viral video. Ratings had gone up after I'd been punched, and I'd scored points with the viewership. Tests had determined all of it. So what was it?

"Yeah, come on in," Tam called, following my knock. He wasn't on an overly intense multitasking mission today. In fact, the busy monitors were all off, the treadmill was silent, and a very calm version of my news director sat in front of me. He wore a tie and smiled the smile one offered before the kill. Fantastic. "Skyler. Let's move to the conference room. Have a talk."

"Okay, sure," I said and followed him down the hall. Something big was happening. My brain made a list. "The conference room."

I wondered if Kristin would be joining us as she usually did. Instead, sitting at the rectangular table was a redheaded gentleman with a folder, a silver thermos of coffee, and a pleasant enough smile. "Who is this?" I quietly asked Tam.

"Ted Bellows from Human Resources. He's going to sit in with us today." HR. That had my attention. Flashes of make-out sessions with Carrie all around the station bounced through my memory. I thought we'd been discreet enough, but now I had my doubts. This was a TV station. Maybe they had cameras everywhere. But no. Caroline was leaving. If they'd seen us kissing, it wouldn't involve this level of intervention.

I raised a hand in greeting, my adrenaline already firing. "Skyler Ruiz. Hi."

He smiled. "I've caught you on air. Sorry about that punch."

I pretended to check on my jaw. I was getting good at fielding these comments. "Me, too."

A knock on the door. What in the hell? I looked behind me as a woman I'd never seen before entered. She was pristinely put together—jet-black hair pulled back to a knot, a green starched business suit—and carrying a folder in one hand and a Starbucks venti in the other. I was popular today.

Tam folded his arms and sat on the corner of the table. "Skyler, this is Evelyn Ramirez from Sylvan."

I blinked. The Sylvan Broadcast Group owned the station. I began to understand what was happening. There was an anchor slot available. I'd recently filled in. Was it possible they wanted me to apply? Audition? There weren't currently any Latina anchors in the San Diego market. Only reporters. This could be a big chance for me. Was it really in the realm?

"Nice to meet you. Skyler."

I nodded. Evelyn accepted my handshake with a warm smile and quietly took a seat.

Tam didn't delay. "You're aware of the changes we're making to the five and the ten?"

"Yes," I nodded, my left leg bouncing beneath the table. I hadn't been wrong. This was about the big chair.

"I know you and Carrie are…close." That was code. He knew everything—that little pause he'd taken said so. Now what?

I eyed him. "Also true. I don't think that breaks any rules that I know of. I'm not a direct report of hers." I looked from Tam to Ted to Evelyn for some sort of reaction or confirmation.

HR Ted shook his head and slipped his coffee. Another weekday for him. "No policy violation there."

"Good." My curiosity could no longer contain itself in the name of good manners. "Okay, so what's going on? Can you just tell me?" The room felt too cold, and I wondered distantly who had cranked up the air-conditioning and had it been on purpose to torture me? I watched Ted scribble a note and frown. About what? We'd been in the room three minutes.

"Fair enough." Tam leaped in. "You may have already guessed this." I had. "We want to give you a shot in the studio. Move you up to anchor for the five and ten."

"Really?" I played it cool, unsure how to feel. Part of me wanted to leap from the chair and dance on the table. It was all I'd ever dreamed of. The other half of me knew the larger implications of stepping into a job that the person I cared about still very much wanted.

Tam pressed on. "You're still green. And it's a risk, but I'm good at picking the right risks. I think you might be exactly what those broadcasts need right now. New blood, but familiar to our viewers. It's a great combination."

My eyes shifted to Evelyn, who beamed at me like I'd just been crowned Miss America. I wondered if there was a bouquet of roses under her seat. "You're saying you want *me* to anchor?" I had to be sure we were all on the same page. There were so many choices out there that made more sense. They could do a nationwide search. In fact, they should. "Me?"

Tam nodded. "Here's the thing. The viewers really responded to you when you filled in for Carrie, and that's the kind of engagement we're looking to recapture."

"It's a leap, but one we're ready to take," Evelyn supplied.

"We'd be offering you a three-year contract," Tam said. "There are conditions, of course. We do have an out if it doesn't go well."

Evelyn opened her folder and slid me an already designed ad with me behind the news desk, taken during the days I'd filled in. "Welcome, Skyler Ruiz," I said, reading the caption out loud. "The Sky's the Limit."

I thought about the billboards along the highway of Carrie and Rory, and how they'd have to come down now. That made me sad. And now they wanted my face to go up in her place? At any other juncture, I wouldn't have hesitated. But the Carrie factor was real. The particular circumstances made all this feel...off. Garish. Exaggerated. This was Carrie's job, and I wanted *her* behind the desk, as much as I wanted it for myself.

"I'm sorry. I just...am trying to work through the implications." I slid the ad back, trying to process. Tam and Evelyn exchanged a look that said this wasn't going the way they'd anticipated.

"Why don't we go over the offer?" Tam asked with a knowing smile. He signaled Ted, and the presentation began. The money was insanely good, a large leap from what I'd been making and enough to change my entire lifestyle. The vacation package was generous, the benefits impressive. They'd even included a nice stipend for clothes, hair, and nails. I was overwhelmed, and my head swam.

"Would I be done with reporting?" I actually liked being out in the field, ear to the ground, hunting down stories with Ty. It's what made me get out of bed in the morning.

"There's no reason you couldn't still contribute features here and there. Just like Carrie."

It wasn't the same, but hadn't the anchor spot always been my ultimate goal?

An hour later, Kristin found me pensive in the break room, sitting with an untouched cup of coffee. "I wondered how you'd take today's news. Doing okay? You look a little less excited than I'd hoped."

"No, I am. Trust me. A little part of me wondered when I filled in if I'd have a future behind the desk at KTMW. I let myself dream a little." We were alone, and I felt like I could speak freely. "But now it's here, and it feels so different than I imagined it would. Mainly because there's Carrie to consider, and this is not the way I wanted it all to go down. It was one thing when she lost her spot, but it's another now that it's been offered to me. That's Carrie's chair. *Her job.*"

"I get that it's not easy. But here's the thing. Don't for a second feel guilty about this," Kristin said. "Whether or not you go into that chair doesn't change the fact that the station is moving on from Carrie. Do you want it to go to someone else, on principle? That doesn't make anything better, and you'd regret it one day when your career isn't where it could have been." She shrugged, sad but professional in her demeanor. "It's just part of this business, unfortunately."

"The part I hate."

Kristin sighed. "We all do. But Caroline McNamara is a damn pro in this industry. She will see this for what it is. Trust me." I'd avoided Carrie and our area of the newsroom since talking to Tam. I wasn't ready to tell her until I had a firm grasp of the situation, and I was nowhere close.

Kristin was right, of course, but as professional as Carrie was, she was also hurt and mourning the loss of her job and identity. I'd been sleeping over most every night and had witnessed the changes in her firsthand. She was quieter, pensive, and would stare off into space for long stretches until she noticed I was watching and then—caught—forced herself to brighten.

"You doing okay?" I'd asked a few nights earlier. "You seem extra quiet."

She shrugged. "Just feeling sad. Off. But nothing I can't handle." Her eyes had filled, and it hurt to watch. My face must have shown it. "Oh, stop. I'm gonna be fine. I just have to get through these last few days with my head up, try not to be fucking embarrassed when I read about myself online."

"You will accomplish both."

She softened. "I'm happy you're here with me, though. This would be so much harder if I didn't have you."

I wrapped my arms around her on the couch, nuzzled her hair, letting it tickle my nose, and inhaled the wonderful scent of her lilac soap. "Well, you do, and you're stuck with me."

"A sentence I'm really quite good with."

I was already at her place when she got home from the ten o'clock. I had to tell her about the offer. Putting it off was not an option. I made us a couple of spiced rum and Cokes and waited.

"For me?" she asked when she arrived home. "Bless you and your beautiful face. I could get used to this." She accepted the glass and held it high in the air in thanks. "And hi." She placed a kiss on my lips and exhaled. "Another day down. They found that little boy that went missing yesterday. He wanted to go camping, so he took himself."

"I watched. Ambitious. And terrifying."

"Crazy news day, though." She leaned back against the kitchen counter, decompressing the way one does when they're finally home and allowed to just breathe. "One change after the next, right up until air tonight. I'm exhausted, and my brain is more than scrambled."

We clinked glasses. "You'll be living the life of a woman with her evenings free in no time. Wild and fancy-free. Can you believe it? Think of all the late-night gardening you could get in."

A small smile hit. "That part I'm actually looking forward to. Being home at night. At least in the temporary."

We hadn't talked about what she planned to do next with any sort of specificity, but maybe it was time. "Do you think you'll want something with more of a nine-to-five schedule now? Or maybe just take some time off?"

She paused. "I've never really known a life like that. Sounds crazy to me. Daytime hours." A pause. A thought must have hit. "It might be nice, though. I could cook dinner for us. Scallops and pasta. Watch sunsets together on occasion. Take walks down to the beach."

"Do you know how nice that sounds?" I asked, melting. Like heaven on earth. Then I remembered my own news, which would derail all those plans, and my smile dimmed. I needed to tell her. I wasn't sure how. At the thought, I felt my blood pressure rise. My palms itched.

Carrie quirked her head. "What's that look? What's on your mind?"

"Okay. I have something to discuss."

"Okay. We can talk about anything."

I paused, rolled my lips in. "Remember the other night when we were wondering who they would bring in to replace you?"

"Yes. Why, did you hear something? Oh my God, is it that young blonde from San Fran? Stacey Press? Something like that." She shook her head in an I-knew-it fashion. "I told you she visited the station a few months before you were hired. I just had this feeling about her. That they had their eye on her already." She paused. Swallowed. "Not Stacey, huh?"

She knew. Or at least suspected.

"The station offered the anchor spot to me." Ripped off like a Band-Aid. The words were out of my mouth, and I waited, my heart thudding hard and fast. Time felt like it had adopted a slower speed.

"They did? I wondered if they'd go that route." Carrie went quiet. Her lips were still parted as if she was about to speak but had been pulled up short while her mind worked it all out. "When was this?"

"Today." I exhaled and searched her eyes. "What do I do?"

She set her glass down and shook her head, clearly as surprised as I had been. "Well, first of all, Sky, that's great. Congratulations." She passed me a smile, and I could tell that she was choosing to focus on my success in this moment. She blinked a few times. "Wow. This is… wow. This is huge for you." She held up a hand. "I just thought they'd go with—"

"More experience. Me, too. That's why this feels like it came out of nowhere. It's like when I filled in, this train left the station and hasn't stopped since." I was talking fast, probably to express my shared surprise. We were in this together.

She tapped her lips in thought. "But it didn't. They brought you in for a reason. The second I saw you walk in that door, I said to myself, *Now there's a potential replacement.* Then you were all over the national news. People learned who you were, paid attention, and now they love you." She nodded. "A natural progression. It honestly makes sense. I imagine they've been putting you in front of test audiences behind the scenes, and when I was at the conference, it was the perfect opportunity to audition you." The smile slid off her face. "Looking back, the writing was on the wall. I knew it, too. Just didn't want to face it."

"What? No. None of us did."

"I'll tell you what you do," she said. "You take the job. How can you not? If I can't have it, you're my next choice. I'm happy for you."

I covered my face with both hands. "It all feels all wrong. This isn't how any of this was supposed to go. In fact, I hate it when I should be thrilled."

Her arms were around me in an unexpected show of warmth and unselfish support. "Hey, hey. Stop that." She held me and rocked sideways from one foot to the other. "You need to focus on how ridiculously exciting this is. Did you call your mom?"

"No." It hadn't occurred to me. None of this felt real. "I wanted to talk to you before anyone."

"And now you have." She pulled back and met my gaze. "You're gonna knock this out of the park, you hear me?" Carrie was beaming, which was so incredibly big of her. She was cheerleading. For me. In the midst of what had to be a difficult moment, learning who they'd picked to replace her.

"Thank you, but how do you feel about it? You haven't said." That was my focus right now. Was she secretly upset, rattled, or sad and just putting on a brave face for my benefit? She had to be.

She blew out a breath. "I guess I just regret that I won't be there with you every day. I won't get to see you in action anymore."

I let the sentiment linger because this really was the end of what had been a short and amazing era, working alongside each other. I wouldn't see her daily at work. "You're not going to be at the desk next to me. This is the worst." It was really hitting me now. I leaned back against the counter and shook my head, my gaze on the ceiling. "I won't be able to just turn to you and ask a question. See your gorgeous face. Tease you. Undress you with my mind."

"I'm just a phone call away. And you'll see me after. Just maybe not for that dinner I imagined making you. Easy come, easy go." She tried to laugh. This was hard. We both knew it.

"Is it weird? Imagining me in your spot."

"Yes. I'm still wrapping my mind around it, but that doesn't change how great it is for you."

"Still." I bit my lip, trying to examine it from every angle.

"You're taking it," she said definitively. "Decided. So stop it."

I nodded. "Only if you think it's the right move."

She placed a kiss on my lips and reached for her drink. "I know it is, and I've never been prouder of you." She moved a strand of hair from my shoulder to my back. "You're a rare find in this industry, and they know it. You have the *it* factor. That's not something you can teach, and Tam knows it. Hell, I saw it from the first staff meeting. I should have packed my desk then."

Hearing those words from her in particular made me feel like I could take on the world. "I can do this if I know I have you behind me. If not, well, they should find somebody else."

"Skyler. Look at me." In spite of what had to be decidedly weird news, her blue eyes sparkled with pride. "You most definitely do. I'm right here."

"That helps more than you know." A pause. "And do I still get to have sex with you?"

She relaxed into a lazy smile. "You better. Did I mention you're really good at it?"

"No. Never," I said seriously. "Say it a bunch more times. Write it down. Frame it. Make it art."

"You're like my drug in bed, okay?" She leaned in and hovered just shy of my mouth before going in for a slow kiss. "See what I mean? Little drunk now because your lips are so close." She came back in for more, and I relaxed, hanging out in happiness and relief. We were going to be okay. She was, which meant I could continue undressing her with my eyes at home, at least. I had plans for her body tonight. And then I wanted to hold her close afterward. Kiss her temple and talk quietly in the dark.

"Can we also still eat junk food and stare at walls?" I asked around the kiss. "I could go for that popcorn you drizzle with chocolate."

Her eyes dipped to my chest. "So many things are fun to drizzle with chocolate."

My lower half clenched. "Please say that's an invitation." The already sexy movie in my mind just graduated. "Let there be chocolate."

"You know I'm adventurous."

"And I thank heavens for that daily."

She laughed, and we eased into our late night, which had very much become *our* time. Tucked away beneath the stars while the rest of the world slept, tired and spent from a night of passion, laughter, and finally, talking quietly before sleep, my favorite, I began to drift. Tonight had been good and put my fears at ease. Maybe all of this would bring us closer in the end. We seemed to need each other now more than ever.

I pulled Carrie's arms tighter around me, ever secure in their embrace. She was mine and I was hers, and I could luxuriate in the happiness that brought. I never slept better than in her arms, a place that felt safe, exciting, and wonderful. I wasn't sure what I did to deserve her, but I definitely wanted to keep doing it. It felt like I'd finally found the place where I belonged.

CHAPTER SIXTEEN

Carrie didn't want a station good-bye party. She also didn't want a lot of fanfare to see her on her way. In fact, the embarrassment of her ordered departure was something she seemed to be trying to get through quietly, which still tugged at my heart. Her last broadcast for KTMW was like any other except for her final moment. "It's been a pleasure to bring you the news, San Diego." She looked directly into the lens and smiled warmly, only a hint of emotion bleeding through. "You take care of yourself, and I hope to see you soon. Good night."

There were tears in my eyes when she said it, and they weren't just for my girlfriend. Caroline McNamara, the newswoman, had meant a lot to me as someone coming up in the industry, and this was the end of a much-loved era.

"Want to grab a drink?" I asked as we left the newsroom right after. She'd already cleaned out her desk earlier in the day, making the broadcast her last official act. She turned back to the newsroom, giving it one last look and nodding her farewell. "Nah. If it's okay with you, let's just have a quiet evening."

Her spark had dimmed, and I wasn't sure how to help her get it back.

Things only got worse. She'd watch me leave for work in the morning with a faraway look in her eye. She'd smile and kiss me good-bye, but her heart wasn't in it. For the first time since I'd known her, she seemed adrift, lost.

"Plans today?" I asked one morning.

"Lunch with Monica. A friend from college." She shrugged. "Nothing scheduled after that. Maybe I'll learn to knit."

"I'm all in favor. Think of the scarf potential around here." She didn't say anything. "Well. Enjoy your lunch," I said, stealing another kiss. I hesitated, wanting to help but unsure if my words were welcome. After all, I was heading off to her job. "Has there been another time in your life when you've had this much freedom to do whatever the hell you wanted?" Maybe a look at the bright side would help. Maybe she'd murder me in her mind.

She wrapped her arms around herself. "No. But I'm not sure I'm cut out for a life of leisure."

"Temporary," I reminded her.

"Yeah. I know." She didn't sound at all convinced. I was worried she was depressed.

The next two weeks were full of prep work for me to take over the nightly news. Rather than just popping me into the job, the station wanted to make a big deal out of my debut, ramp up the fanfare, and get people excited. They'd launched an entire PR campaign announcing my start date.

"Do we know how Rory is feeling about all this?" I asked Kristin before the photoshoot, the first time I'd be working alongside him officially. He was a veteran and Carrie's partner. I wasn't sure how he'd feel about me, given her firing. They were a duo, after all.

"Rory is Rory. If it gets him attention, he's in."

I blinked. That part made me a little sad. Where did his loyalty go?

Kristin hadn't been wrong. When Rory arrived to the shoot, he was easy-breezy and ready to put me on the map. No hard feelings involved. Now that we'd be working together, I noticed him more. Saw him in a new, more personal light. Rory was tall. He was graying at the temples and looked very distinguished in his brown plaid jacket and expensive-looking shoes. I squinted. He'd likely had Botox days before.

"Where are you from?" I asked him between publicity shots. A little get-to-know-you chatter couldn't hurt.

"Columbus."

"Cool. What else should I know about you?"

"Ten brothers and sisters, a fiancée, and a new baby on the way."

It was a lot. I'd imagined Rory had a personal life, but the specifics were new. "You don't mess around."

"Life's too short. What about you?"

"No kids. Just a girlfriend who was fired from the anchor chair in a top-thirty market."

"Over here, guys," the photographer said. We posed and smiled as he *click-click-click*ed his shutter. "Perfect. And another. Skyler, chin in your hand, and…got it. Throw me sass. Look at each other. Sky, look at me. Rory, hold on her. Can I get laughter from you, Sky? Got it."

Rory relaxed and turned to me, his voice hushed. "Holy shit. You're dating Carrie?" How did he not know? His jaw dropped. "And stepping into her job at the same time?"

I deadpanned. "I am."

"That takes balls." He didn't hide his horrified-intrigued combo, and I appreciated the honesty.

"It's complicated."

"Hell, I bet." He nodded a lot, absorbing. "Hey, I'm sure you'll work that out." He offered a fist bump as if it would help. He likely believed it would. He was Rory.

That afternoon, we shot the commercial that would run for the next week before I started my new job. Lisette was handling the five and ten in the meantime. After that, I met with the consultants, who asked me to take three inches off my hair, add a subtle highlight to soften my look, and work on incorporating more jewel tones into my wardrobe. According to them, they were my best colors. I took note of all the little tips and requests, including nixing two of my favorite lip colors because they—quote—didn't pop on air. Who knew? On my drive home that night, my head swam with all the details, the expectations, and the pressure of arriving on scene as the only Latina anchor currently in the San Diego market. I wasn't the first, but I damn well had to make sure I wasn't the last. Taking my torturous heels off and relaxing with Carrie and Michelangelo were all I wanted in the world.

"So, what was it like working with Rory on the photoshoot?" Carrie asked with her feet in my lap and a cocktail glass of spiced rum in her hands. She'd found a little-known distillery that made killer stuff. She knew all the secret places. "Let me guess. He missed me desperately. Did he recite a grief-laced poem?"

"Yes. It rhymed." She laughed and I gave her ankle a shake. "He seemed a little skeptical of us."

"Well, we're certainly more complicated now. You stole my job." She said it with humor, but there was an underlying truth there that we were both aware of. It never left the room and seemed to fill up space between us. More and more with each passing day. I wondered when that would end. I prayed for soon. She shook her head with a smile. "Quite the story. Ousted anchor and her replacement shack up." I laughed, and she tugged my sleeve. "Your boobs look awesome in that top, by the way. I keep staring at them."

"Simple is boring, and the boobs missed you today." I stole her rum and savored a sip.

"Shall I get you a glass?"

"No. I much prefer to steal from yours."

Carrie raised her shoulders. "It kinda makes me feel sexy, this rum."

I sat taller because she seemed to be in better spirits today. "Well, you're definitely that. I've been objectifying you since you started swirling your glass like a boss."

She smiled. "Good. But before you do any more of that, I have news."

I frowned. "And I don't know it yet? How am I wildly behind? I've been here half an hour. Share with the class already, McNamara."

She set her rum on the coffee table and scooted closer, wrapping her legs around my waist so we were face-to-face. Oh, I liked the intimacy of this moment very much, and as soon as the news was out of the way, I planned to use the boobs she was eyeing to my advantage. The electricity between us was already bouncing back and forth.

"Well, Sherry Tuplo called. Remember her?"

I frowned, unfamiliar and making duck lips as I searched my brain.

"You know, that producer woman with the hair and the eyelashes and the overt effervescence? Kind of a socialite."

"Yes!" I said, pointing. We'd met her at Jack's at a work gathering. Lots of red hair, likely extensions, and eyelashes you couldn't help but stare at as they reached for the stars in desperation. "What did she want?"

"She's producing a new show, kind of a San Diego food and wine weekly feature with a touch of home and gardening tossed in. A lifestyle show. An hour long. Big budget. She offered it to me outright. I'd host the whole thing and be credited as an executive producer, choosing the segments and molding the direction of the show entirely." Her eyes were wide as she waited for my response.

I could barely breathe. Not only was this perfect for someone like Carrie, who knew all there was to know about food, gardening, decor, and all the amazing restaurants in town, but it was *local*. I found air for the first time in weeks. This meant she didn't have to pick up and move to another news market to keep working. I just about burst into a ball of confetti right there on the couch.

"You haven't said a word." Carrie studied me.

"It's too amazing to speak about. It sounds like a show designed for you. I'm gonna lose it and kiss all over your face like a lunatic."

She laughed. "To hear Sherry talk, it almost sounds like it *was* designed for me. She'd wanted to run with a show like this for a while, and when she heard I'd been freed up, she got the investors on the phone and got the ball rolling immediately. They don't want to wait. It'll run locally on the network every Saturday with a replay on Sundays. Lots of on-location shooting, but it's mostly in-town stuff."

"You said yes, right? You sent a messenger pigeon and a smoke signal as backup?"

She smiled, serene and in control. "I told her I wanted to think about it. Skyler, it's a big decision."

"What's there to think about? There's no thinking required. This is dream-come-true material." I almost screamed that one. Her response did not compute. This offer was golden. They didn't come any better. "Is it a money issue? Are you holding out to get them to come up?"

"No. What they're offering is actually quite generous."

"Call her right now," I said, laughing.

"Here's the thing. It sounds fun, but this kind of show is not really what I do. I'm a newswoman. I like the hard-hitting stuff. It's in my blood."

"You're also an expert when it comes to pairing a great glass of wine with any and every dish while on your break from nursing a shrub back to life and picking out a stellar paint color. You'd be the perfect guide for a show like this."

She tapped her chin. "It would certainly take me down a new path. I just have to figure out if it's the right one."

I wanted to leap onto the kitchen counter and explain via impassioned speech that this offer was the answer to everything I'd been afraid of. The perfect fix. It meant she didn't have to leave San Diego and seek out another market. She'd have a job she enjoyed and get to use her platform for something meaningful and relevant to the viewers who had watched and loved her for years. Instead of giving said speech or, better yet, performing a musical number of all the ways this was great, I instructed myself to exercise patience and let her explore the option on her own. "Well, I'm thrilled for you and hope that you'll seriously consider it."

"I will give it some careful thought. I promise."

"That's all I'm asking."

She sighed and stared into my eyes. "You're so beautiful and smart. How did I get so lucky?"

"Speaking of lucky. How long till I can take these off?" I asked, touching the fabric of her leggings and cupping her ass. She wasn't wearing a bra, and I watched her nipples harden against the fabric of her shirt. She rocked her hips, and I descended on her lips. "Does that mean we can have couch sex? I'll show you my boobs," I said around the kiss. "Say yes." She nodded and slid onto my lap.

Moments later, we were off.

I'd thank the stars, but I was already seeing them.

I woke up the next morning to freshly baked biscuits and a gorgeous woman with a spatula plating one for me. There was also homemade jelly, which was probably the most flavorful I'd ever eaten. I gestured to the air around me as I stared down at my plate. "I am spoiled rotten and don't deserve the outpouring of amazing food. I need to pick up more charity work or something. I'll call around if you give me a biscuit."

"Ever been to the Willamette Valley?" she asked.

"No. Is that where I should volunteer to pay the universe?" I asked, my mouth already full.

"Maybe," Carrie said. "There's this little town in wine country I want to take you to someday with the best little spot for biscuits. All kinds. There's a line to the door each morning. I've been trying to duplicate them ever since, but haven't been successful."

In that moment, my feelings for her swelled. I wanted trips to wine country every bit as much as I wanted everyday life with her. I couldn't take my eyes off Carrie and couldn't imagine my morning without her right there in front of me. I knew I had to communicate, let her know. "I'm going to say this, and you can take it for what it's worth." She quirked an eyebrow. "I don't want you to leave for some other city because you're a newshound. My feelings are a little out of control for you, and I don't think that's a bad thing. So please, take this lifestyle show job, and stay right here in San Diego, so we can have more nights like last night and more wonderful mornings like this one."

She blinked at me, jelly knife in midair. Perhaps she hadn't seen this coming.

I held up a calming hand. "Not to freak you out or anything."

She lowered the knife. No one spoke until, "Okay."

I leaned in. "I'm sorry. What did you say, and what does it mean?"

She grinned. "Okay. I'll take the job. Decided."

"No!"

"Yes!"

I jumped from my seat, ran around the counter, grabbed her by the waist, and hauled her in. I kissed her neck. Her face. Her shoulders. "Did you just say *okay* like it was no big deal because I will tackle you to the floor and kiss you senseless!" I continued my kissing fest.

She laughed, allowing me to shake her by the shoulders while I jumped up and down. "What can I say? You convinced me. I was almost there, but your speech gave me an extra amount of perspective because you're right."

"You're gonna love it. You're about to be the food and wine guru of San Diego, and the people are going to eat it up. And I am, too. I want to go to all the restaurants and try all the food." A thought struck. "Oh! Maybe you can redecorate my apartment. You're hired. I pay in favors. Put me on the show."

"I just keep raking in the offers." She exhaled. "Now kiss me properly this time, and go to work. Only one more day as a story-hungry reporter. Soak it in."

That part made me a little sad. I did enjoy my time out in the world, Ty by my side. As I drove through downtown, I wondered about the new reporter he'd be paired with now and felt a twinge of jealousy at their partnership.

I'd chilled at his place for dinner the week before while Carrie had been out with a friend. His wife, Sandra, was an amazing chef who'd whipped up some gourmet burgers that I was sad Carrie had missed. The last time I'd been over, I'd managed to pick up her lasagna recipe because it was so good that it had to reach more people and their stomachs.

Though both Ty and I had offered to do the dishes, Sandra had refused and shooed us out of the kitchen. "No, no, no, no, no. Get outta here. I can work faster on my own. You'd be doing me a favor."

"You sure?" Ty said, grabbing the last plate from the table and rushing it to the sink like a bank robber on his getaway.

"Time me," Sandra said, swatting his ass. "I'll join you for an after-dinner drink when I'm through. I'll even let you do the mixing."

"You're on." I watched them share a kiss, smiled, and looked away, giving them their moment. Ty was such a ball of mush around Sandra. It was really sweet to see.

We went and sat together on the back patio, watching the night and shooting the breeze.

"You think you're in the news business for life?" I asked Ty after a few minutes of settling in. I'd eaten way too much.

"Nah." He took a pull from his beer bottle.

"Really?" I hadn't expected his answer. "What will you do instead?"

"I always thought I'd set up my own production company. Nothing big." He shrugged but had a really cool gleam in his eye. I'd just stumbled upon a dream of Ty's, one he was very much capable of bringing to fruition. He not only knew everything there was to know about cameras, lighting, and overall production, but he was creative and had a great eye. "We'd shoot small commercials. Sell muffins. Insurance. Things like that." He scratched the back of his head. "Maybe a few high-octane sports videos. *Vrooom*," he said, impersonating a motorcycle whizzing past. "I love that kinda stuff, man. Gets my blood going." He glanced over at me, grinning like Christmas morning. It made me want it for him all the more.

"What's stopping you? Do it now."

"Gotta save a little more dough. But I'm close. Maybe in a couple of years." He ran a hand through his hair and gave it three back-and-forth rubs. "Sure is fun to think about, though."

"Well, I believe in you and know you can do it."

He looked over at me, beer hanging to the side of his chair. "Yeah? You mean it?" He didn't get too sentimental on me often, so I placed a high value on the moment. He cared about my opinion. That was clear.

I smiled. "I very much do. Not that I wouldn't miss you around the station."

"You wouldn't have a chance to miss me. We'd still hang like this. Eat too much food together."

"We better."

We clinked our bottles, sealing the pact, and stared off into the night some more. We'd come a long way, he and I. It was nice to have a friend to share silences with without the need to cover them. That's when you knew you had a valuable bond on your hands.

"You're a good guy, you know that?" I said.

He shrugged, his cheeks turning red. Just that kind of night. "You're okay, too. Kinda chatty."

My mouth fell open. "Shut up."

"You shut up." A long pause. "Which was my whole point."

I laughed. Ty did, too, because he was by far the more talkative one. Yep. This was the stuff I lived for. A much-needed good night all around.

❖

"You ready?" Ty asked later that day as we drove to the nearby elementary school that had been vandalized overnight. We had our game faces on, set for a day of rounding up the news.

"For spray paint and angry principals? Bring them on. The more fired up we get that woman, the better the bite."

"For the big time, bonehead. I'm talking globally. Taking over the news world, one high heel at a time."

"Don't call me bonehead, lug nut. And I think so?" I scrunched up an eye. "I never realized how much scrutiny these anchors faced. There are people in boardrooms evaluating my style of banter and debating the direction I part my hair. Feels like a lot of pressure."

Ty didn't hesitate. "It is that. They will chew you up and spit you out if you let 'em." He looked over at me, sincere. "Don't. You hear me, numbskull?"

"I hear you, birdbrain. I appreciate your looking out for me." I was feeling all kinds of sentimental as we got to the end of our time working side by side. How often would I get to work with a true best friend? "And don't you go forgetting about me and our adventures."

He lowered his sunglasses. "What's your name again?" I slugged him as he put the car in park. He looked across his dash at the school in front of us. "This is it. Likely the last one. Better make it count."

I grinned. "I owe you a Slurpee after to commemorate the occasion. A green one."

"Yep. I knew it." He slapped his steering wheel. "You're the best damn reporter ever."

"You know it."

He grabbed his camera and tripod from the back, and we headed to the front of the school, off to nab another story for the people of San Diego like the newshound duo that we were.

CHAPTER SEVENTEEN

The weekend always had a way of slowing the world down and reminding me of all the important things in life, especially when it came after a whirlwind few days like mine. Seeing my family exaggerated the effect and worked like the best kind of salve. Carrie and I sat around the table at Sarah and Emory's place, stuffed from a magnificent roasted chicken dinner, and grinning from fantastic conversation. The sun was down and dessert plates sat half empty, leaving the kind of satisfaction that only came when you were fully fed, a little buzzed, and relaxing with people you loved.

"I need this mousse recipe," Carrie called to Sarah, who headed to the kitchen with a stack of plates and silverware. "I'm going to wake up thinking about this chocolate."

"She does that on purpose," Emory informed her. "Makes you bring Skyler back here more often if we feed you wonderful food. All part of the master plan."

I tossed my napkin onto the table. "You don't have to lure me with chocolate."

Carrie shot me an admonishing look.

"Sorry. Yes. There better be more freakin' chocolate, or I'm never returning." We laughed, except for Carrie, who we'd lost to a notification on her phone. "Everything okay?" I asked, touching her arm.

"I think so. Do you mind if I step out and take a call?" she asked us, holding up her cell.

"By all means," Emory said. "You can use the deck if you want privacy."

"Perfect. Thank you." She moved quickly from the room and flashed us the *just one minute* sign.

When we were alone, I turned to Emory. "How are you feeling? I didn't want to put you on the spot in front of the others, but you've been on my mind. Be honest."

She nodded and slid a strand of blond hair behind her ear. "Coming to the end of my treatment. The fatigue they promised was no joke, but my stamina should be back soon."

"That's fantastic."

"Well, hopefully. We won't know for a while if we got it all, but my doctors are optimistic."

"The waiting," I shook my head, imaging that kind of stress. "I don't know how you do it."

"No choice. That and, well, I've learned that I'm not superwoman, and all I can do is surrender myself. That was news that certainly hurt." Emory smiled ruefully. "But I've also learned that it's okay to let myself be vulnerable." She stared off in the direction of the kitchen, of Sarah. "Lean on that one in there. But that lesson hasn't come easy."

"No?"

She laughed. "We've never fought more in our lives, but she's in the right. It's time for me to accept her help, give her the wheel, and stop trying to act like I got this." That's when I saw the tears. I swallowed, stunned. I'd never seen Emory cry before. What was happening? What should I do?

"It's okay," I said automatically, just in case she was embarrassed. I felt an uncomfortable lump in my throat, too.

"No, no. That's just it. I'm just fine letting you see this." She laughed, grabbed a napkin, and wiped her tears. "I never would have allowed this to happen just a few months ago. The new me. It feels… really nice."

Sarah arrived back and slid into the chair next to Emory. She looked at me and then Emory and nodded. "It got serious in here, huh?"

I smiled at Emory when I said, "We were talking about Emory's journey."

A similar smile slowly took shape on Sarah's face. "I'm so proud of her, Skyler." She reached over and squeezed Em's hand. "And her doctor thinks things are going really well."

I exhaled. "I'm relieved to hear that."

"Moral of the story," Emory said. "I've learned to take nothing for granted because no one is guaranteed a tomorrow. Put all your cards on the table. We don't have the luxury of holding back from the people we love."

I absorbed the advice, the words carrying that much more power after seeing the two of them battling something bigger. I'd been honest with Carrie about my growing feelings, but I *had* held back the one word that felt ridiculously scary. But I loved her, plain and simple. Things were going really well between us, and that should give me the encouragement I needed to put myself out there on that lonely platform and take the ultimate leap. She was everything I wanted, and I shouldn't leave it unsaid.

I'd never told anyone I was in love with them before.

But Carrie was the one. I knew that as plainly as I knew my shirt was blue. I wanted to be with her forever and wondered what she'd think about that.

"Sorry about that, everyone," Carrie said, giving her head a shake. But there was a new energy about her now. She seemed charged up, wired.

"What was that about?" I asked.

"Long story. But everything is fine." She placed her hand on top of mine. "Can I update you later? It's boring work stuff."

"Of course." But she was distracted, and it showed. She partially checked out of the group conversation after that, her gaze roaming the room as if her thoughts had hold of her. We'd had a great night, but things had shifted noticeably after that call.

Once we were alone together in the car, I turned to her as she drove. "So, what's going on? Something has you preoccupied."

"You think so?" She watched the road. "No. No. Nothing major. Just Corey with some interesting gossip."

Her agent. "What was it?"

"WBAA in Seattle is looking for an anchor, and he wondered if I'd be interested."

I frowned. "What happened to theirs?"

"Pregnant and choosing to not come back."

"Oh. Well, good for her, then." A pause. A cold shiver moved through me. "Are you considering it?" No. Surely not. But I could hear my own heartbeat as I waited for the answer.

"Not actively, no. But you know what? It is an interesting turn of events. Isn't it?" She tapped the beat of the music on her steering wheel. "It's an excellent market. Seattle."

She wasn't wrong. San Diego was a top-thirty market. But Seattle was a top-twenty, a step up. I didn't like the way this felt. My throat constricted. Uncomfortable, I rolled down the window. The newly autumnal air was chilly, and the burst of it across my face helped me breathe easier. I gulped it in. "You just seem, I don't know, happy to hear about it."

She looked over at me and seemed to understand that I was upset, on high alert. She turned down the radio. "I'm not trying to leave you, Skyler. In fact, that's the last thing I want to do. God, I can't imagine that."

"Yeah?" I exhaled in more ways than one. "It's really good to hear that because for a moment I was worried you had one foot on the road to Seattle, and we'd be battling it out on the nightly news each night." I added a laugh I didn't really feel.

"No. I'm simply enjoying that my name came up during a time when it feels like the industry has put me out to pasture. A top-notch station has expressed interest. In *me*. It's…nice. I guess I'm reveling for a few minutes."

"Well, of course they have. You're amazing and at the top of the list of badass anchors." I could easily celebrate with her now, knowing that I wouldn't be losing her to this opportunity. "I would seek you out if I had an opening. They'd be idiots not to."

She reached over and touched my cheek. "Thank you for saying that. There are moments where I sit confidently, happy as I look back over my career, and others when I'm terrified about moving on from it."

"You don't have anything to be terrified about. Really cool things are happening for you. For us."

"They are, aren't they?" She smiled big.

We drove on, enjoying the chilly ocean breeze and the stars twinkling over us like a blessing. Doing my best to make out the darkened waves as we drove along the shoreline, I ruminated on Emory's words about making myself vulnerable to the people that mattered because nothing was ever guaranteed. I looked over at Carrie, her beautiful profile, as she studied the road, and my heart swelled and squeezed with love for her.

It was time to say the words. Three little utterances, but they seemed so terrifying. I just had to summon the courage and manifest the perfect moment. Carrie was my future, and every last part of me knew it.

"Carrie, I have to say something." Everything in me hummed with anticipation, the fear-laced kind. But there was excitement there, too. I focused on that.

Her brows dropped and she glanced over at me. "Okay, what would you like to say?"

"This isn't the perfect moment. I know that much. But I feel like I can't wait another second to tell you that I love you. I really, really do. I'm in love with you. There. Said."

She didn't speak, and I wondered briefly if I'd just gone and freaked her the hell out, ruining that perfectly wonderful thing we had going by saying the words too soon. No. Uh-uh. I didn't believe that. I didn't ruin anything because my feelings were real and present already. Announced or unannounced, they'd informed every moment we spent together, and it was time to acknowledge that, once and for all.

"Oh, Skyler," she said, her eyes still on the road. "I think I fell in love with you long before I even knew it." She glanced over at me, her eyes crinkling at the sides slightly, a slice of moonlight illuminating her face. "Sometimes I can be a little slow."

"You love me?" I heard myself ask. My heart was reaching with everything it had.

"I'm very much in love with you, yes."

"We love each other," I said, quietly celebrating. "Us."

"I'm glad you said it."

"I had to." There was going to be no waking up in the morning and living normal life until I did. "You're my reason for most everything these days."

"Then we're in the same boat." She picked up my hand and kissed the back of it. "My place tonight? You and Micky?" she asked with the sweetest smile. "Say yes."

My spirits flew somewhere into the stratosphere, and my heart squeezed wonderfully. There was a lot to celebrate. "Nowhere else I'd rather be."

❖

I'd been on the air as anchor of KTMW for two short weeks. I was still nervous, excited, and felt like I was living in a dream. Kristin assured me that the feeling would pass and I would make this job my own, and I did look forward to a time when I was at home in the anchor seat. For now, it still felt like a mountain I needed to climb. I'd already had screwups, times when my mouth didn't work right or when a transition I'd attempted came out clunky. The billboards along the highway were also surreal with their plays on my name. *Blue Skies Ahead* followed by a shot with me with my arms folded. *The Sky Is the Limit* with a shot of me looking up. Little me. Up there.

Meanwhile, I couldn't help but wonder if my mother had pulled up any of my broadcasts. I was curious what she thought of the job I was doing but was almost hesitant to ask, fearful that the answer would be that she'd—quote—heard great things and would pull one up soon. That would be the standard.

But my heart soared when she called just a few days later, exuberant. "Querida, I just watched yesterday's five o'clock broadcast online, and you've taken my breath away. What poise! What command of that desk. My heart is full of pride."

I grinned like a kid who'd just won the spelling bee, sliding my hair behind my ear. "Really? You don't know how happy I am to hear that. I was wondering what you thought." Literally, every day. I hated to admit that even to myself.

"What I thought? I thought you were stunning. The only thing is to remember to smile at the fun parts. Puts us all at ease."

My smile faltered a tad, absorbing the likely valid tip. "Yes, of course. I will do that. Thank you."

"I'm also calling because I'll be in town tomorrow and want to see my baby girl. Are you free?"

I hadn't seen my mother since moving full-time to San Diego and was more than a little excited. "Of course I'm free. I can't wait."

"Fantastic. I'll make us a reservation. You just show up."

The next day, I got up extra early to make sure the apartment was clean and touched up, trying to envision the space through her eyes. Catch any flaws. I'd taken Micky to the groomer's the afternoon before and had him smelling fantastic and sporting a smart bandana that he could wear for the visit. My mother had high standards for me, and I wanted to impress.

Wearing a smart turquoise skirt, white blouse, and heels, Carla Ruiz stood next to her chair at the fancy steak house she'd picked out for us. I grinned as I approached, and she extended her arms. "My baby is here." Her brown eyes, not unlike mine, sparkled.

"Hi, Mama," I said, hugging her and accepting the kiss she placed on my cheek. I was also in my work clothes and thought we must look like a couple of colleagues out for a business lunch. That part made me grin, feel important. I was proud of my mother and the success she'd found. She'd worked so hard.

I settled in across from her, and she grinned. "Well, don't you look smart and put together." Like me, she sounded like a native Californian, after so many years Stateside. Maybe it was silly, but I sometimes missed her accented English. It reminded me of my childhood, snuggling on the couch and talking about the life we'd have someday. And here we were.

I glanced down at the plum jacket I wore, perfectly tailored to my shape. I had to admit, I felt like a million bucks when I wore it. "The station has given me a sizable budget for some nicer clothes. Well beyond anything I'd pay for on my own. I've been trying to stay within the lines they've given me. Certain colors. Certain cuts. Things to avoid for camera."

"Of course they gave you a budget and advice. They know what they have in you and are the lucky ones." She nodded her thanks to the server who placed a glass of sparkling water with precisely two squeezes of lime and not too much ice in front of her. "How are you feeling? Do you have your footing? Is there anything that you need? Tell me." She studied me seriously.

I took in the series of questions, knowing she was ready to hand over her debit card if I needed it. "I'm getting better at the job each day, but there's a lot of scrutiny. More than I accounted for, coming into this large of a market. Everyone from the viewer at home to the news director has an opinion, and they want me to hear it. It's been... overwhelming."

"Well, when you feel overwhelmed, you just think of the end goal. You put your focus there and you hang on." She pointed at me with her butter knife. "That's what I did, working my way through law school, when my professors wouldn't give me the time of day. And it's what you'll do."

My mother cared about me a lot, but high achieving had always been the highest ranking attribute on her checklist for me. She wanted me to find success because it was a reflection on her and how she'd raised me. Yes, the pressure had served me well, but at the same time, once in a while, I just wished she'd hug me and tell me everything was going to be all right. I smiled at her. "It's good advice. How's LA?"

She shook her head. "Full of pretty people with attitude problems, but I'm making my way. I have a big case going to trial next week, and we're going after everything the guy has."

"Well, I wouldn't want to be on the other side of that divorce."

She laughed. "Nor would I."

We ordered our lunch, my mother raising an eyebrow when I chose the pasta with the white wine sauce. "Not just a salad?" The implication was clear. She was so different from tía Yolanda. I had trouble imagining them growing up together under the same roof. Neither was unkind, but they had wildly different outlooks on life.

"Oh, I have a long day ahead of me," I said, embarrassed now. I had been looking at this lunch as a little splurge, finally seeing my mom in person. "I just felt like I needed sustenance."

She smiled serenely. "Well, you know best."

We ate and chatted, mainly about her workload at the firm and family gossip. She asked a few questions about my short-term career goals at the station. I gave her the quick version, imagining we could delve into more later.

As lunch wound down, I moved us forward. "I have some time before I need to be at the station today, so I thought we could swing by my place. You can finally see where I live and say hi to Micky."

She dabbed the corners of her mouth with the cloth napkin. "I would simply adore that, but my schedule is tight. I'm meeting with a witness who is being deposed tomorrow, and let me tell you, they have a lot to say about this divorce." She leaned in, a gleam in her eye. "This woman has everything documented, too. Every incident in which she witnessed the husband's mentally abusive ways. She's a true score for our side."

"Oh." I nodded and attempted an understanding smile. "I can imagine. Well. Another time, then? I'd really love for you to see where I live and meet my girlfriend." I grinned. "She's pretty great."

She folded her napkin and placed it on the table. "Oh, I googled her. Have no fear. She seems accomplished and beautiful. We'll set something up soon when I'm back in town." She signaled for the check, and I downshifted. She'd used that term on me my whole life. *Soon.* I'd learned to despise the word.

"Just let me get through this semester. *Soon* we'll have more time together."

"*Soon* I'll bring you to LA for a long weekend. We'll go on a tour of a real movie studio."

"I know I couldn't come to your school play this time, but *soon* I'll be able to do things like that."

She'd meant it, too. At least at the time. Those things just hadn't ever manifested, and she'd never circled back to apologize. I couldn't seem to let go of that, like something uncomfortable stuck in my throat.

My mother wasn't a bad person, but on her list of priorities I ranked somewhere in the middle. I couldn't complain. So many people had it worse. I was lucky enough to have my aunt and uncle and cousins to prop me up when I was feeling like an afterthought.

Yet here I was. A grown woman, thirty years old, sitting across from my mother, and feeling the same way all over again.

"I would like that very much. She's becoming important to me. Carrie." I wanted my mother to hear her name, this woman who was my all.

She beamed. "I can see it written all over your face, and that's all any parent wants. Happiness for their child." She covered her heart. "I'm just thrilled for you, mi vida."

"Thanks, Mom."

But after a hug and the short wait for a cab, she was off into the world again, and I was alone on the curb watching after her car, feeling empty. In fact, for the rest of the day, I was a lesser version of myself, rejected in a sense, when I'd been so excited for her visit. I kept my head down at the station, buried myself in notes so not many people would talk to me, and tried hard not to dwell. My mom was a busy woman. That was all. She cared about me, I told myself over and over. She truly did. It didn't change the way I felt, though.

Maybe one day I would have enough confidence in myself to enjoy what she was able to give. Wrap it up, hold it tight, and be grateful for who I'd grown to be.

One day. Just not today.

The following week on air came with even more hiccups. The teleprompter, something I'd worked with in the past, could be my best friend or my mortal enemy, depending on who was operating it. I'd lost my place more than once on air, saved only by a moment of light banter with Rory. While there were some viewers still angry over Carrie's firing, our test numbers were decent and expected to grow with time. People were still getting used to my partnership with Rory. We didn't have the same steady rapport he and Carrie had. "You're either his kid sister or the younger woman in his life, depending on the broadcast," Carlos told me in the break room one night. "I can't seem to decide which is better for you."

"Both seem awkward," I said. "We have to iron that part out."

"Oh, I think Tam will do that for you," he said with a knowing grin and turned the corner. My heart sank at what the chatter might be behind the scenes.

"Now that you're so much more at ease, I want you to work on your connection with the camera," Kristin told me one night after the ten. "It's not a flirt, but it's not *not* a flirt."

I blinked, trying to make sense of that note. "So what is it?"

"It's a connection between you and that lens. You hint at it, but you don't fully go there."

"Ha. I can identify," I said, as we walked the hall together.

She turned. "Things with Carrie good? Because from where I'm sitting, they look good." She leaned in with wide eyes. "*Really* good. Like, get-a-room good, and I say that as a compliment."

I sighed. "Yes. It's been amazing." In reality, I think the moment I went on air as anchor, things got harder for her. She watched from her couch as I performed the job she'd loved, and with each passing day she got a little quieter.

"Hey, beautiful girl. How was work today?" she'd asked a few nights earlier.

I slid out of my blazer, kissed my dog, who pranced at my feet like a jaunty fellow, and joined her on the couch.

"Devonte was on comm tonight and was constantly in my ear until the second we went live. I never got a minute to compose or organize once I arrived at the desk."

"Yeah, you have to tell him to chill out. When he fills in, he's sometimes a little too present. Better yet, have Kristin talk to him about those last few moments before air. They're important for you. Claim them. You have that power now. People will do as you say."

"Great advice." I kissed her cheek. "How was your day?"

She shrugged. "You're kinda looking at it. Micky and I had lots of snuggle time. He's a blanket hog, by the way, but we're working it out." Right on cue, he leaped onto the couch, turned in four circles and collapsed. All of his people were now accounted for, and he could tap out. "Sherry called for a work session. We touched base briefly on some first episode content, and she's batting around some titles for the show."

"I have a feeling they all feature your name."

"I guess. I don't know." She wasn't herself. Where was the joy? I missed it. "Am I a food and wine personality? I'm just trying to imagine the fit. The day-to-day. And it's hard."

"It's new, and that's probably why it feels weird."

She exhaled. "That's a good word for it, weird. And who knows if it will even happen? They could scrap the whole idea. Maybe I'll be stuck in this house forever until I spend every last dime I have and get a job as a bartender somewhere and listen to other people's troubles."

"Somehow I don't see that as your path," I said with a laugh, trying to keep things light.

"You never know. I'm just warning you of a possible detour now."

The night after that one, I came home to find her irate at a tray of chicken breasts. She'd told me not to eat a full meal, so I'd abstained from anything more than a bag of chips. I stared at the series of bowls and pans that lined the countertops. It looked like a late-night flour bomb had hit the room with aggression.

"Don't eat those," she said, pointing at what looked to be perfectly cooked chicken breasts along with some sort of brown sauce. "They're horrible and don't represent me. I was trying a new recipe, and it's an epic loss." She sighed loudly, a defeated hand to her hip. "I wanted to pamper you with a nice dinner when you got home, but I can't seem to do that right, either." She tossed a pan into the sink with a clang.

I winced. "Either?"

"Just not a ton of life successes these days," she said and wiped her forehead with the back of her hand, signaling that she'd had a time of it tonight. She gestured to me. "You look great, though. I hope your day was good. Was it?"

"It was. And thank you." I glanced down at my on-air attire. A dark green dress, silver necklace, and heels. "One of my new outfits. The consultants like the color on me."

"Because it's gorgeous. *You* are. Hi." She came to me and kissed me hello, and I went to warm putty. Best part of my day so far, and it had already been a good one. "I'm sorry I don't look half as good."

"What are you talking about? You're beyond attractive." How could she not know that? Even in this moment, she amazed me with her God-given beauty. "And don't worry about the chicken."

"Trying not to, but what are you going to eat?"

I pulled out a pot and deposited it on the stove. "Hot, buttery popcorn with a side of spiced rum. Solved."

She smiled but her eyes were watery. "Good. Yes. I just want you to be happy." She stared at the floor in pause. "I'll be right back." She held up one finger and disappeared into the bedroom. I had a nagging feeling she'd taken a moment to gather herself. When she returned, she was smiling, noticeably lighter on her feet, and eager to hear all about my day. While admirable, I didn't want her to bypass her own feelings.

"Carrie. It's okay to have a hard day and let yourself feel that."

"Yeah, I'm not sure that's the best course of action to right my tilting ship." She squeezed my hand as she passed, grabbing the oil, clearly intent on making the popcorn for me. "You, however, do the opposite, Sky, and make everything better."

I came up behind her as she poured the kernels into the pot with a rat-a-tat and wrapped my arms around her, savoring the connection I'd missed all day. "It's crazy, and you're literally not going to believe this, but I feel the same about you. I missed you today. We're twins." I'd give anything to have her back at work with me. Things weren't the same, regardless of my newfound status. I kissed a path up her neck, prompting her to pause what she was doing and lean back against me, allowing me to hold her in silence. We stayed like that for a little while, and the world seemed to settle and slow.

But when Kristin asked, I decided to level about how things had been going outside work. She had become a fantastic sounding board. "I think Carrie's floundering. Trying to find her new place in the world, and it's not clicking."

"Huh." Her brow furrowed, and she pursed her lips. "I was hopeful she'd take this new freedom and run with it. She's going to land on her feet. We all know that."

I smiled ruefully. "Everyone but her, it seems."

"Give her time."

"I definitely will."

Carrie and I made love that night and it was absolute perfection. I held her close, tight, in awe once again at how perfectly we fit together in the bedroom. I traced her skin, kissed her fingertips, luxuriated in her. It was after three before we drifted off with me stroking her hair softly, lifting it, and letting it drop. When I heard the heavy, rhythmic breaths of sleep, I allowed myself to drift as well.

CHAPTER EIGHTEEN

It was late in the day on Saturday when my phone buzzed with a text. I was standing on a stepladder in my kitchen changing out a light bulb like the responsible renter that I was. Carrie. I smiled to myself. *Something's come up. Do you have time to talk?* I stared at the message. I'd stayed at her place the night before but was home for laundry, cleaning, and reorganization for the upcoming week.

I immediately called her back. "Hey. What's up?"

"So, here goes." She didn't delay and launched in, talking fast. "It's the Seattle thing. They called Corey and they want to make it happen. Officially."

I frowned and began walking the length of my small living room. "Who is they? What do you mean?"

"WBAA in Seattle wants me to anchor evenings, and they're extending an official offer. We've glimpsed the details, Skyler, and they're…impressive." She laughed nervously. "I don't even know what to say about it. I just didn't expect them to actually follow through. Those things are so often just a lot of talk, and then they hire the new fresh face, you know? That's what I expected. Probably Corey, too."

She was animated. The excitement in her voice inspired both happiness and terror in mine. "Okay, well, let's think this through." I was being conservatively supportive but didn't want to think anything through. Seattle could find someone else, and she should tell them that. Now. But at the same time, if this was something Carrie wanted, could I live with myself if I stood in her way. "What are the pros and cons?" How was this real?

"Well, we'd be apart if I took it. That's a definite con. I can't even imagine that." She was actually considering this. Leaving me. It was like being hit with a two-by-four. "A pro would be a second chance in a more prestigious market. I'd feel like myself again and get back to doing what I love. Erase the failure." I didn't say anything. Her voice got soft. "It's been hard, Skyler. You know that."

"I know." I'd seen it firsthand and would love to see her happy again, thriving. This job seemed to be what she wanted. I wanted her to want me, though. I stared at the ceiling and said the one thing I knew to be true. "I love you Carrie. I love us."

"Me, too. So much." A pause. "They would want me in Seattle tomorrow."

"God. Tomorrow? That gives us no time to think or react. Can we just slow down? Please, please, please."

"I hate it, too, but they're ready to move. It's a contingency of the offer. I'd start right away. They don't want a gap."

I couldn't find air. My lungs felt shallow. Balloons with holes in them. "I'm coming over."

"I'll be here. Maybe we can talk it through."

I left the ladder right where it was and grabbed my keys. My mind raced, and I did my best to figure out how to respond to what felt like quicksand. I wanted to support her—in fact, I had to—but I selfishly wanted her here with me. More than that, I wanted *her* to want to be.

When I arrived at Carrie's place, I found her in the bedroom, suitcase open on the bed. I felt the blood drain from my face and I paused in the doorway. The world slowed down to a sickening pace. "So that's it? You've made up your mind." I blinked at the offending suitcase. I'd never hated an object so much in my life. I wanted to kick the thing. Hurl it out the window. Instead, I sagged.

Her face had apology written all over it. "I don't know. I just... There's a flight tonight that would have me there in enough time. I don't know that I can make myself get on it, though. Not if you're not there with me."

"I want to be, but—"

"Your dream job is at your feet."

I nodded, lost, unsure what to do.

"And I was there for you at your side, supporting you every step of the way."

"That's true. You were."

"Please do that for me now. Please."

This was a horrible situation. "Then I guess the only thing for me to say is get on that plane. Find your happiness." God, the words gutted me. I didn't mean them. I wanted to *be* that happiness, and learning that I wasn't enough was information I'd have to set aside for later.

She picked up a blouse and placed it inside the suitcase, and it took everything I had not to take it out again.

Desperate now, I was ready to put it all on the line. "We love each other. We both said so. We can make it work, right?" But inside, I was no longer sure. I was wildly off balance and hurting.

Her features softened. "Yes. Of course we can."

In a last attempt to keep her with me, I needed to put myself out there, be vulnerable, because then she'd see that I was all in. "I love you. With all I am and with all I have. If this is what you want, then I want it for you. But it hurts to see you go." I swallowed. It was up to her now. I'd said how I felt. I'd given her all the pieces, everything I had.

She paused, set down the handful of hanging clothes, and looked me straight in the eye. "I love you, too, Skyler. I do." My heart squeezed, and I exhaled. My fingernails had been digging into my palms. They stopped. "Trust me. I get how big of an ask this is. And I will find a way to make it up to you. I will go out of my way to make us work, because I know that we can."

As much as I wanted to put myself out there and say *Choose me*, it wasn't fair to Carrie. But that's not to say I didn't will it to happen. *Choose me, Carrie. I choose you. Choose me.*

Silence hung between us.

"I love you and I support you," I said again simply. "And if we're in love, then that should matter most."

"It does," she said, but inexplicably, she was continuing to pack. Why was she doing that?

"When will I see you?" I asked, wrapping my arms around myself.

"I'll be back in a week. Two at the most, depending on how heavily they schedule me at first."

"And then what? You'll be living in Seattle."

"I'll still have my place here. We can go back and forth. Just think how amazing those weekends will be."

The problem was that I was already having flashbacks to early Monday morning drop-offs at Aunt Yolanda's when my mom would head out for the week. She had every intention of being a good parent just as soon as she could get ahead in work or school. But she'd never fully come back to me. Even to this day, I was still waiting. Watching Carrie pack now had me sick to my stomach. It didn't have to be this way. There was a perfectly good job waiting for her here. It wasn't enough for her. I wasn't either.

"What if I came with you? They can find someone else to anchor here, and maybe I can get picked up as a reporter in Seattle." I heard the panic in my voice and couldn't stand it. I was that little kid again, desperate not to be left. I hated myself, and part of me hated her for putting me here.

She came around the bed and took my hands. "And walk away from this opportunity? Skyler, no. You can't do that. And I won't let you. I won't be the cause. You'd end up resenting the hell out of me for it. This is too big of a chance for you."

"Right." I pulled my hands back. It was clear now.

Carrie didn't want us as much as I did. It was that simple.

What I had just offered required nothing on her part. The fact of the matter was that if she had said yes, I would have walked away from it all. For her. That's how much I loved her, with every fiber of my being. She couldn't do the same. "So, you should go."

"Until *next week*."

"Until next week," I said, watching my whole world crumble around me. Something inside me had shifted, walling off the acute emotion, and allowed me to see this situation for what it was. Likely the end. People made promises. They just had a hard time keeping them. A week would turn into three, and then a month between visits, until we'd finally drifted so far from each other that the idea of the real us became only a far-off memory. I was familiar.

Her blue eyes held mine, tearful and sad. "Skyler. I'll stay if that's what you want. I will."

"You supported me. I'll do the same for you."

She hesitated. "For the record, I'm not choosing a job over you, and I hope with a little time you will see that."

"Me, too." I heard the little bit of fire behind my voice.

Her eyes carried sorrow. "Do you know what kind of person I'll turn into if I don't go? Hell, you wouldn't even recognize me. You wouldn't want me."

I blinked. "I've always wanted you." It was the reverse I was afraid of.

There were tears in her eyes as she returned to her suitcase and zipped it up, the last of her packing for the week complete. "I knew this would be hard for us, but this feels like I can't breathe." She met my gaze and held it, and I wondered if maybe, just maybe, she was reconsidering. Hell, she had the lifestyle show in the palm of her hand. It was a job most people would kill for, and it was perfect for her. There should be no question.

I waited, feeling like I was in the midst of a standoff where the stakes were incredibly high.

Her phone buzzed, and she glanced down at it and sighed. "My Uber is here."

I nodded and watched, nervous to see just what she was going to do. Carrie walked to me, leaned in, kissed my lips softly, and picked up her bag. "I absolutely hate this."

"This job will be good for you." I took a deep breath and found what I'd forgotten to say. "I'm really proud of you."

"Thank you, Skyler."

They were the last words we said. I stood strong until she was out the door, but my heart had been slashed. She called that night and then again the next day. She had tons to report about the apartment they had her set up in, the private office and dressing room at the station, all for her. I didn't say a whole lot back, but Carrie didn't seem to notice. I couldn't help but notice that we didn't feel like us anymore, and I wasn't sure what to do about that.

As for me, everything in my life following that moment dimmed considerably. I went about my week, camera-ready in a brand new wardrobe, smiling at the lens in my brand-new job—but underneath, still just the girl that everyone could either take or leave. The familiar feeling landed even harder because the blow was coupled with how much I missed Carrie. She had become my something to look forward to. Even now, I got off work on a high because parts of me still seemed to think I'd get to spend the evening with her, talking or not talking. Kissing or grinning or eating or laughing. I'd have to break the news to myself all over again, and it was the worst kind of pain. It didn't end there. They'd given me her vacated desk in the newsroom, which made me miss our private glances, the whispered words of affection in a hallway, or the quick back-and-forth before one of us headed off on an assignment. The loss consumed me, yet I couldn't seem to do something as simple as pick up the phone and call her, see how her day was going.

She finally left me a message at the end of the second week to make plans for our weekend together. "The only catch is that I can't make it until Saturday morning because I'm on the ten o'clock on Friday. But we'd still have all day Saturday and the night together, right? Okay, talk soon. I love you." Everything in me wanted to try it her way. But then I remembered where that would put me. Forever chasing after the person I wanted to love me.

I sent a simple text: *You've got your hands full and I have an event anyway. Let's do it another time.*

I didn't have an event, unless you counted sitting on my couch, feeling sorry for myself.

I received a voice mail back within half an hour. "Skyler, are you sure? I was looking forward to seeing your face, but if you're booked, I get it. Maybe the week after. I love you. Did I mention that?"

Maybe. Soon. Next time.

No thank you.

She was gone.

So was my light.

After that, my sense of doubt began to fester. My self-esteem when it came to Carrie was nonexistent. As a result, a coping mechanism, I picked up fewer of her calls. I placed even fewer of my own. It wasn't easy. My heart ached beyond measure, but for the first time, I had to choose myself and find a way to breathe again.

Teenagers had a way of taking over a room, and that was exactly what I needed that weekend. Let other people do the peopling, while I played the role of supporting character.

"So, I told Bobby that you're my cousin and they said that their *whole family* watches you on the news and even saw the video of you getting punched."

I nodded and handed Grace the flash cards we'd been using for her chemistry test preparation. It was Saturday, my day off, and I was damn sure going to fill it to distraction. Even if that meant chemistry homework, my sworn nemesis. "Yeah, the punching seems to stand out for a lot of people."

She quirked her head. "Isn't life weird in that way? Something awful that happened to you winds up being one of the most helpful things ever."

She had a point. "And something you thought was the best thing that ever happened to you winds up being the most painful."

"Well, that's a dark take." She sat back. "You're talking about Carrie, huh? Now I'm depressed. Things aren't going well, huh?"

They weren't going at all. After offering less and less of myself, Carrie was on to me, and she wasn't at all happy about it. In fact, I'd never heard her so upset, angry, and hurt.

The messages were piling up in my voice mail. "Skyler, stop it. What is going on with us? When we do talk, you're overly polite and say a total of eight words. This week, you're not even picking up. I know you're alive because I see you on air. Call me. Even if it's to have it out. Let's do it. But it does require your participation." The *I love you* had been dropped from the ends of messages. I couldn't say I blamed her.

I'd cued up a return call about ten times, but never pressed send.

The voice mail that came two days later said it all. "Well, I'm sorry you're unable to pick up your phone for the eighteenth time this week. I think I will finally take this as my signal that you have little interest in speaking to me. You have my number. Use it if you're so inclined. If you want to talk about things like adults do. If not, well, that's fine, too. I won't be calling again."

She'd had it.

I'd left her frustrated, worn out, and starved for attention. She'd left me hurt, doubting, and a shell of myself. Talk about doing a number on each other. It didn't mean that I didn't love Carrie anymore, but after everything, I could no longer see myself as the equal in the relationship I once was. Her equal. Because I never would have left her.

Maybe all of this was on me. My own personal baggage sabotaging one of the greatest things to ever happen to me. Yet I didn't see a way to fix it. So I picked up the burdensome bags, like bricks on my back, and walked on.

We were through. She knew it. I knew it.

I looked up at Grace's knitted brows and shook my head, chastising myself for going there in front of the innocent child who knew nothing yet of heartbreak and misery. "Yeah. I'm sorry about that. I'm a ball of joy, aren't I? It sucks when things don't work out. Want to talk about carbon again before you go?" I snatched the flash cards and held them up in offering.

"You're dealing with what sounds like a loss," Grace said, taking over. "It's going to take time for that little heart of yours to find its way." She retrieved the flash cards and began to pack up.

"Stop being the wise one in the room. Sixteen going on forty. It's freaking me out."

"Hey, I'm here for you at any age," she said sincerely. "Know that."

And now I felt the wallop of unrequested emotion right on cue. I pretty much hovered two steps from tears at all times now and caved with the smallest nudge. Like now.

"Plans tonight?" I asked, blinking back tears. *Think of something else and quick.*

She got that starry-eyed look, and I remembered what that brand of excitement felt like. When your stomach did a little happy dance and you got goose bumps just thinking about seeing your person. I'd seen mine on the internet anchoring the Seattle evening news the night before, as much as I tried to avoid pulling it up. Apparently, I was a glutton for punishment, and watching Carrie speak to me and thousands of others through a camera lens was right up my alley. I wondered about a lot after that. How she liked the new station, what she thought of Seattle, and if she thought about me much. I fell asleep with tears falling sideways onto my pillow, leaving a wet spot, a heartbroken cliché I wasn't proud of. But that's who I was now.

"I do have plans." Grace pulled me back from the memory. "I have a date with Bobby, as a matter of fact. We're going to an escape room, just the two of us. They're good at big picture problem solving, and I'm meticulous about puzzles. If we don't make it out in time, we only have ourselves to blame."

I sat back. "How are you guys this cute? I will need all the details of how you escape next time we chill."

"Done." She offered me a fist bump and slung her ridiculously overfilled backpack onto her shoulder, a reminder of her scholarly dedication. Grace was going to take over the world and make it better one day, all while playing the tuba. I loved that about her. She turned back. "If you ever want to talk or vent, just text, okay?"

I placed a hand on the back of her head and smoothed her beautiful dark hair with a new pink streak in front. "You are the sweetest kid. I will." I followed her to the door of my apartment just as Sarah opened it.

"There they are. My two favorite cute people. Shower me with love, immediately." Well, someone was in a cheerful mood today. I had a feeling this was her way of trying to prop me up. Sarah opened her arms, and we easily moved into them, one on each side. It sounded cheesy and strange, but in the midst of that group hug on a Saturday afternoon, I found a little bit of strength. The woman I loved was gone by choice, my mother was my mother, but there *were* people in my life who would lift me up, make me laugh, and see me through this thing.

Regardless of my broken heart and shattered expectations, time marched on, and the weeks rolled by until it had been many months since Carrie left. While the distance helped a little, not a lot changed. I tried not to think about her until I did. I focused on work until I forgot to. I wondered about dating again in the future until I realized I honestly had no interest.

"Did you see the write-up about Carrie in the trades," Ty said as we shared lunch at a small sandwich shop a block from the station. Even though we weren't out chasing stories together anymore, we made a point to hang out whenever we could, which was a lot.

I tossed my napkin onto the table, stuffed from my chicken salad sandwich with the killer pickles. "Nope. I don't let myself think about her too much. That's my new trick."

"Oh, then I won't go there either." He held up his hands.

I squinted. "But you were going to say something about her."

"Nope. I was gonna tell you about the mayo on your face, though. It's a great look. You should keep it."

I dabbed my face with a new napkin but couldn't let go of the hint he'd dropped. "No. Say what you were going to say a minute ago. What was in the trades?"

"Just that her station has received a kick-ass ratings boost since she went on air. A real nice uptick." He nodded around a bite of pastrami. "Not that it matters. Doesn't. How's your doggo?"

I exhaled slowly, absorbing the information. Carrie's mission to Seattle had been a successful one after all. Well, good. I knew from our early calls that she'd been nervous about how she'd be received in the new market. Now she could relax and celebrate. I swallowed the predictable desire to celebrate with her, imagining what that would feel like. A couple of glasses of bubbly, some kissing, and a nice night out, during which we'd toast her. As for me, the ratings at KTMW had actually dipped when I'd taken over but had since rallied a little. Tam said it was all normal for a transition and to be patient as the viewers got to know me.

"Micky is a rascal who's got a new stuffed celery stalk." A pause. I could be big about this. "And I'm incredibly happy for Carrie. She's a pro. We always knew that part."

"It's okay if you're not. Doesn't make you a bad person. You might just need extra Slurpees for a while, and that's not so terrible."

I shook my head. "I just hate the way it all happened. I still cry like an idiot, but I don't wish anything bad for her." I blinked, understanding how true the words were. "I just don't know how we work anymore." I scrunched up my nose. "That's the hard part to accept. But slowly, I'm doing it." I decided a topic shift was in order because Ty had his I'm-not-great-at-emotions look on his face. He had just offered me Slurpees to soothe my broken heart, after all. He was doing his best. I should let him off the hook. "And how's your new reporter working out? What's her name again? Tammy?" I full well knew her name. She'd started the week I'd made the big move, and from what I'd seen, she knew her stuff.

He nodded as he wolfed down the last bite of his huge sandwich. "She doesn't sing with me in the car. Doesn't dance in the car either. Kinda like you on your first day, but she hasn't loosened up any. She's okay, I guess."

"Give her time. Maybe she just wants to get to know you before busting out car moves, you know?"

"I hope you're right. If not, you gotta come back. Plain and simple."

I laughed and gave his shoulder a slug as we exited the shop. "I miss you, too. Let's do a dinner with Sandra some night. I won't have a date because I'm woefully single and alone in life, but third-wheel status is good."

"Sold. But it's gotta be noodles, and I'm not kidding around about that," he said with a level of excitement too large for its subject. "I've been thinking about noodles a lot."

"Noodles it is, you weird person."

"I'm not weird, turnip head. You are."

"All right, meatball."

So, I'd embrace the life I had in front of me, report the news, snuggle my dog, chat with my cousins, and look forward to noodles. So many people had it worse. I missed it, though, the blissful squeeze of my heart when I saw her or the way my breath caught when her eyes landed on mine. Since she'd been gone, I'd let my thumb hover over the call button more times than I should have, wanting to just hear her voice for a few moments. I never actually went through with it.

I'd deleted the voice mails she'd left. I'd listened to the last message four times through tears before erasing it. In a lot of ways, it felt like I was growing up, taking control, and asking for the things that I needed. While I was proud of myself in some ways, I also hated the way I'd handled it. I owed her a call, and that knowledge hung over me like a bad headache.

I knew one thing for sure. I was operating at a loss.

Caroline McNamara was a force who'd burst into my life and changed me forever. So maybe I'd never truly get over her. While a crippling thought, it was a possibility I would have to learn to live with.

CHAPTER NINETEEN

Fuck my life. We were six minutes from going live at five, and they'd just swapped the order of my first three stories, tossing one to Rory and leaving me with the leadoff. It was fine, just another last-minute shuffle to organize. I hated those. I studied the electronic tablet in front of me to get my bearings. Four stories in, we'd toss it to Tammy live in the field for a stand-up about the crumbling overpass along the highway and the dangers it posed to cars passing by. But the weather was dicey, and they were having communication troubles with the live truck, so they'd asked me to be flexible if we couldn't get Tammy up. Yet another possible swerve ahead.

"Okay, got it," I told Kristin. "So if we don't have Tammy, we'll pivot to the lottery winner?"

"Exactly. Then that will bump us to sports. Cue Kip with the new pro hockey team rumor."

I nodded, organizing my brain as I went, hoping it got easier with time. Two minutes. I gave my hair a slight toss and relaxed my facial muscles, opening and closing my jaw.

And we were off.

The broadcast started off without a hitch, a short greeting and a toss to our lead story, a shooting across town just hours before. Rory fielded the next segment, and when it came back to me for the live shot, I was immediately told by the control room to pivot. No Tammy. Just as promised, I turned to Kip in sports as the energy in the room shifted noticeably. People who were normally focused on our group task now exchanged looks and whispered in each other's ears. I wondered what had gone wrong but worked to stay focused on my role. Had I done something? Said the wrong thing? Had someone else?

"We'll be right back," Kip said with a smile after wrapping sports.

I exhaled and looked immediately to Devante for answers. He was busy, speaking animatedly into his headset on the studio floor. I raised my hand to him. He shoved his headset to the side to address me. "Hey. The live truck couldn't get a signal up and we're working to understand why. Nothing to worry about."

I turned to Rory as Devante walked away from the news desk. This felt like more than a live shot failure. "Is it just me, or are they being weird? I feel like there's a bomb threat or something at hand."

He took in the room, happy-go-lucky Rory as always. "Just you, I think."

No. The room became eerily still after that. I wasn't a fool. But the commotion went away just as quickly as it had fluttered in. The on-air team maneuvered our way through the next seventeen minutes of the broadcast, said our good-byes, and were given the all clear by the studio stage manager.

"Okay, that one felt off," I said to Devante, who graciously handed me a bottle of water as I came off set. "For some reason, I was in my head and super cognizant of what was going on in studio. It was weird."

He nodded but hadn't really said anything. He seemed to be standing with me, holding me there for some reason, though. Then that reason presented itself.

Kristin took my hand. "You were great. Let's walk."

"Uh-oh." My stomach dropped. I recreated the past thirty minutes and went over my performance for any kind of misstep, but came up short. "Did I screw up somehow?"

Kristin stopped once we'd reached her office and shut the door behind us. She swallowed, not looking at all like herself. Something had rattled her. "Nothing like that. I have unfortunate news. The kind no one wants to hear."

"Oh." My body went numb. "Okay."

"It was the live shot. Tammy was positioned for her stand-up well off the highway in a grassy area, using the overpass as a backdrop. The rain kicked up."

I nodded, trying to skip ahead and see what was coming.

"A car skidded on the slick pavement."

"Oh no." It was the unthinkable. Reporting in the field was always a risk, and you heard about accidents happening all the time. The idea that it easily could have been me was not far from my brain. "She was hit? Is she okay?"

"She was. Cuts and bruises. Her left leg was injured pretty badly, and she was transported."

I placed a hand over my heart. "Thank God. Do you know how lucky she is? It really could have been so much worse." I exhaled slowly, relieved.

"But Skyler, It's Ty. He took the brunt of the impact and was airlifted." She shook her head. "I just want to prepare you. It sounds bad."

Ty? No. I blinked at her, willing the words away. "Are you sure it was him?" She nodded. "How bad?"

She sent me a sympathetic look. "That's all I know for now."

The walls were advancing on me. My fingernails dug painfully into my palms. Words were spinning in my head but not making their way out of my mouth. I'd never felt more helpless in my life. I held out my hand to Kristin to signal as much. She watched me in concern.

"Just take a breath. You're okay," she said.

But I felt nauseous. My stomach had always been nervous, and it proved itself once again as I barely made it to the restroom down the hall before throwing up. It felt like the world was in motion even though my vision was clear.

Not my *friend*.

I grabbed Kristin's arm. She'd followed me to the bathroom and we stood at the sink. "Sandra."

"She's on her way to the hospital. We called her."

I gripped the edge of the marble countertop and squeezed. "All while I was on air." During that short span of time when I was doing my damnedest to smile, but not too much, keep my transitions relevant and seamless, and make sure I was forming a connection with the viewer, my friend was hurt.

Kristin nodded. "It's one of those freak accidents you hear about from some station you'd never heard of. Not your own."

"Yeah, but what do I do?" I asked, walking aimlessly through the small space. I wasn't even sure where to put my hands. This level of idleness was maddening. "Should I go to the hospital? His family is probably gathering there, and I don't want to be in the way. But I'm not sure where else to be."

Kristin took both my hands in hers. She met my eyes warmly, the picture of a good leader and friend. "You're going to stay here with us, his other family, and wait for an update."

As if the universe had been listening, her phone rang. I listened to her end of the call, which didn't offer me much. When she closed her eyes and scrunched them together, I knew with everything in me.

"He didn't make it," I said.

"No." She dropped the hand holding the phone to her side. Tears filled her eyes. "They lost him in transport."

"I can go to the hospital," I said. The sentence was nonsensical, but those were the only words that came into my brain because everything else had stuttered to a halt. There had to be a rewind button where I could reclaim the spot I'd been in just an hour earlier. I faced the mirror, then away. Then Kristin, then away.

"Skyler."

I shook my head. No more talking because then it would be legitimate. I felt trapped, and a great big shove against my current reality would surely knock me free of it.

"Look at me."

I backed away from Kristin until I ran into the far wall of the bathroom. I held a finger up. "No," I said, as if Kristin was an offending intruder. If I could keep her and the rest of the world away, maybe this moment would evaporate.

She opened her arms as she moved toward me, unwavering. I cowered from her until the moment her arms went around me. The personal contact lifted the spell, and I let myself relax against her, clinging to her even. There were no tears because I couldn't quite fathom that Ty wasn't going to walk in the back door of the station from the parking lot, twirling his key ring on his forefinger. "What are we going to do?" I asked.

"I don't know," she said. My shoulder was wet, and I realized Kristin was crying. That would be the normal response to losing a friend. But I was all out of normal responses.

"We were going out for noodles this Saturday." I blinked. "And he's supposed to start his own production company. What about that?"

She released me. "I want you to go home. We'll have Lisette cover the ten."

I nodded, numb and directionless. I walked blindly to the door that would lead me to the hallway and the newsroom I now hated. But something grabbed me by the throat. I paused. My feet didn't want to go any farther, and I was compelled to turn back. "I'll do the ten."

"What? No, no, no. You go home."

"We're going to have to report this story, right? We are the news."

Through her tears, she nodded. She was battling being a leader and her own feelings, and I needed to do the same. Not only that, it felt like the news *should* come from me. I wanted to be the one to speak on his behalf. I was his reporter, and I could hear him now: *You do it, bonehead. Don't be chicken.*

"I'm doing it. Okay?"

"Are you sure this is what you want?" Kristin asked, still skeptical.

I nodded, more sure than I had been of anything. It was something I could do for Ty, and I was determined to give him this. "It should be me up there. It's what's right."

"Only if you're up for it."

From somewhere unseen, strength descended. "I am."

Three hours later, I did one of the hardest things I've ever had to do. I looked into the lens and told the world what had happened to a great person. "This next story hits home for all of us," I said, as Rory squeezed my hand. "We lost a member of our KTMW family today when Tyler Murphy, a cameraman and friend to all here, was struck by a car while working to bring us a story. Ty was a personal friend, a goofball, and the best dang cameraman you'd ever hope to meet. He will be sorely missed. No charges have been brought against the driver."

"He will be sorely missed," Rory said and took the reins to take us out. When the hot studio lights were replaced by the fluorescents, I calmly got my bag, found my car, and drove myself straight to a 7-Eleven for an extra-large green Slurpee.

Alone, beneath the stars, I sat in my car, held the drink in my lap, and cried.

It was surreal when something monumental happened that should rip the universe in half, but the rest of the world simply marched on, unaffected. There were people walking through downtown, laughing with their friends. Others went to movies or out to dinner. Didn't they know that everything had changed?

From the moment I'd moved back to San Diego, Ty had been my ride or die. He'd been the most welcoming and instrumental in teaching me the culture at KTMW. Our friendship had extended into real life, and now there was this gaping hole.

I wasn't sleeping much.

I ate to keep my energy up, but that was about all I could manage. Going to work just reminded me of Ty and his glaring absence.

Emory and Sarah checked in on me daily that next week, but I stopped getting back to them, vowing to make it up when I could muster the energy. I walked through each day like an automaton, feeling very much alone, and yet couldn't bring myself to do anything about it.

The higher-ups had cleaned out Ty's desk, and soon there would be little left of him until someone hung up a plaque somewhere in remembrance of all he gave to the station. It would never feel like enough.

The memorial service was that morning.

I'd taken the next couple of days off to get my head on straight, giving me a long weekend to make it through. I stood in front of the church and stared up at the climbing spires as if on their way to someplace grander. I was envious, wanting desperately to escape. I swallowed, gathering my courage, a practice I'd become familiar with, and went inside. I saw several of my colleagues already seated, knowing that the rest of them had to get today's broadcasts up and on air. That was the thing. The news never stopped.

I sat alone in a pew and waited quietly with my thoughts, which began to consume me, coming faster and faster with each second that ticked by. My chest felt heavy as I watched Sandra at the front of the room. She hugged and greeted all who approached her, but the evidence of her grief was apparent in her slumped shoulders and swollen skin, red from tears. If she could make it through this service, then so could I. Yet my body rebelled. I felt nauseous all over again, and a brick sat on my lungs. Desperate for air, I had to get out of that church and hated myself for it. This was a panic attack, I realized. I'd never experienced one of those fully before. The room was getting smaller, but I didn't think I could get my legs to work. A hand slipped into mine and offered a squeeze. My eyes were fixed on the floor, but I already felt anchored with just that one touch. I could breathe. I could think. I raised my gaze to see Carrie sitting next to me, holding my hand in her lap wordlessly. Everything slowed down. Her skin against mine, the firm manner in which she held my hand, was everything. I wanted to sob with relief, but I swallowed it back, determined to stay strong. And so we sat there, just like that, as she calmed the world down for me. I was helpless to stop her. And I didn't want to. Seeing her in person, her blue eyes, soft hair, and recognizing her very familiar scent brought so much back. All of it good, and I clung to those feelings like a lifeline.

The service began, and as shocked as I was to see her there, I was also grateful for the strength it brought me. We sat there together for the rest of the service, tears falling as we said good-bye to our friend.

When the service was over, she looked over at me, smiled, and with a fresh tissue, dried my tears. "I'm really sorry about Ty," she said. She knew how close we'd gotten. "I was devastated to hear."

I nodded, finding my raspy voice. "Thank you." I stared right at her, still absorbing her presence and the undeniable effect it had on me. Her hair was up, and she wore a dark green dress that really brought out the radiance of her eyes, which were kind.

As the church emptied, our colleagues seemed to give us our space. "I wasn't expecting to see you here," I said as we walked out. "I should have called you. I'm really sorry about that."

"Doesn't matter now, okay? And I had to come. Whether you wanted to see me or not, I had to be in the room for you. Then I saw the state you were in and thought you might need the support."

"I did." I exhaled, giving the conversation space to stretch and breathe. I looked over at her. "There's a part of me that's so upset with you for wanting the job, and there should be a big part of you that hates me for pulling so far away."

"I want to be here anyway. Is the angry part of you okay with that?" she asked.

"It's not the time to push people away." The opposite, really. Life was precious. I imagined for a small moment if I'd lost Carrie in the way I'd lost Ty and immediately shoved away the thought. Too much. One thing at a time.

She nodded. "I agree." A pause. "Will it be weird for you if I attend the gathering? If you'd rather I not, that's okay. Ty was your friend first and foremost."

There was an informal reception afterward with lunch and drinks, a time for people to come together on such a hard day. "No, no. Come. Please. You have every right to be there."

"Okay. I will. Thanks."

"And Carrie? For what it's worth, I'm sorry for how I behaved. I don't like myself very much because of it."

"Thank you," she said. A haunted look crossed her features, and my stomach dropped, watching her walk to her rental. If she'd put me through a lot, I'd certainly done it right back. I hated that knowledge. It hadn't been real until now as I witnessed the effects in person. I'd told her to go to Seattle and then punished her for it.

An hour later, covered dishes dotted every available surface of Ty's aunt's home. Ice cream flavored punch, topped off with whiskey in certain glasses, flowed. Friends and family mingled, got to know each other, and exchanged stories and memories of Ty. It was nice in so many ways to laugh with the people who loved him most. Sandra hugged me and thanked me for being a friend. I swore to her that we would stay in touch and still get those noodles together.

"He adored you," Sandra said. "I hope you know that. Rooted for your success each step of the way."

I nodded. "He was a big part of it."

"Thank you for being here. Call me soon."

"I will."

Throughout the reception, Carrie gave me space. But no matter how much I tried to focus on whatever conversation I was in, I always knew where she was in the room. She was a phantom from a life that felt so far away now...but so wonderful, too. As soon as I'd shove thoughts of Carrie to the side, I'd catch a glimpse of her smiling across the room, and I'd be right back in the thick of it, wondering how we'd gotten here and then remembering the awful details full on. She'd left me, and then I'd left her right back.

At some point, mid-reception, I'd looked around to find Carrie had gone home. Everything, to my annoyance, seemed much dimmer after that. The air had been let out of the world.

Lying on my couch that night and decompressing after such an emotionally charged day, I imagined what it was going to take to get me back to...me. Micky, mimicking my energy, lay on his back with all four legs standing straight in the air. "You doin' dead bug?" I asked. He didn't move. "I completely feel you on that." Because after today, I had nothing left to give. I'd cried my eyes out at a funeral, had a panic attack, and seen the woman who'd broken my heart after months apart. Dead bug was looking like my new favorite pose.

My phone buzzed, but I didn't have the energy to even look. "Go away," I said blandly. "Don't you buzz at me."

Shortly after that, there was a knock at the door. Perfect. Was there no peace? I stalked my way to open it, unsure what I would say to... had to be Sarah. I swung the door open and paused. There she stood, in jeans and a long-sleeved turquoise top that looked incredibly soft. My fingers itched to find out. Her hair was down and her expression earnest.

Carrie.

She opened her mouth and closed it, saying nothing. For a weighted moment, we simply stared at each other as my heart thudded, ignoring my brain. When she took my hand and gave it a soft tug, pulling me to her, I didn't resist. I closed my eyes when she leaned in to receive her kiss. Everything went soft. Me, the room, the door, the universe, and most especially, my resolve. As our lips moved together the way they always did, I came back to myself. I pressed closer, deepening the kiss, needing her now more than I thought humanly possible. I needed this in every way. My arms were around her waist and holding her firmly against my body as we kissed. And kissed. And kissed. I was lost in her, and for this short period of time, more than okay with that. I had zero strength to fight myself because having her in my arms was everything.

"Skyler," she whispered moments later when we came up for air. Everything in me had come alive. I opened my eyes and held her gaze, drunk on the connection I desperately missed and now craved, and went in again without hesitation, hungry for more, more, more. I caught her lips with mine and sank into the kiss, which was anything but timid. Not enough. I pulled her into the apartment, kissing her the entire way. She kicked the door closed behind us. I unbuttoned her shirt in my living room, tossing her bra to the floor within seconds, too. Her breasts fell into my hands, and I squeezed gently. I turned her around, kissed her neck, and cupped her breasts from behind, moving my hips against her backside. She murmured her approval, eyes closed. I kissed her neck without reserve. She angled it to give me more access and snaked her arm up and into my hair, grabbing a fistful of it. We were on fire, and she'd been in the room for under a minute.

"Off," I whispered and gave her jeans a tug. She obeyed and slid them down her legs, leaving them on my floor. I pushed my hand down the back of her panties, reaching under and around into warmth and wetness, and listened to the sounds she made as I stroked her slowly yet firmly toward release, on a total mission, her hands flat against the wall as I took her higher. This wasn't about tenderness. It was primal, lust-driven sex, and we seemed to be in sync on that.

"More," she breathed, rocking her hips, pushing back against me. I could oblige.

I turned her to face me, my eyes drawn to her slightly swaying exposed breasts. With her back to the wall, I returned to my goal, this time sliding my fingers firmly inside to the sound of her gasp and whimper. She began to ride my hand, but no, I needed that control.

With one arm around her waist, I began to move in and out in my own rhythm, thrusting firmly, watching her breasts as she climbed. I leaned down and pulled a nipple into my mouth and sucked, skidding across it with my teeth, which had an enormous effect on Carrie, who cried out as her back arched. I didn't stop, though, I couldn't.

"Wait," she said. "It's happening too fast."

"No, it's not." My thumb circled her and then moved across her most sensitive spot slowly and then again until I felt her jerk, her speed picking up. *There we go.* It felt like a challenge to keep her there, hovering, so I pulled back my attention. I kissed her mouth gently, pulled my fingers out, and stroked between her legs ever so softly. She pulled back from the kiss, eyes still closed, lips parted, and breathing more than a little ragged. "What are you doing to me?" she murmured, drunk.

I sank to my knees, parted her legs, and pulled her into my mouth. My tongue had only just started to go to work when she cried out, bucked her hips, and went still. I did what I could to prolong her pleasure, refusing to withdraw my efforts. After a long moment she joined me on the floor, shaking her head, trembling. I pulled her into my arms and held on. We stayed just like that on the floor of my living room for who knew how long. Finally, she stood, took my hand, and walked me to the bedroom, where she systematically removed every piece of clothing I had on and climbed on top. I was already so far along, so ready for her touch, that it didn't take much to send me over the edge. With a well-placed thigh between my legs, she was easily able to rock me to oblivion as I stared up into beautiful blue eyes.

After, we lay facing each other in my bed, tucked beneath the sheets that felt cool against my naked and sensitive skin. Occasionally, I'd touch her face, or she'd move a stray strand of hair off my forehead. It was almost as if we were drinking each other in after such a long time apart.

"I know this doesn't fix anything," she said, finally. "But I've really missed you. This." She palmed my breast.

I sighed. "Me, too." I could admit that part.

"You didn't call back."

"Yeah. I couldn't. I should have."

"I know."

The small collection of words we said to each other that night could fit on a Post-it. We communicated in other ways. Caresses, stares, and silence. We came together, making love several more times that night, until we fell asleep wrapped in each other's arms. I understood as I drifted off that tonight was stolen. I hadn't forgiven Carrie, but that didn't mean I'd stopped loving her. She wasn't coming back, but it didn't mean her feelings didn't still linger. It was simply an impossible love, and I needed to remember that. Stolen or not, it was a night that was etched in my memory forever.

When the sun woke us the next morning, Carrie quietly assembled herself and, with a final hug and soft smile, let herself out of my apartment.

In many ways, it was the good-bye we never truly got.

I took a shower, made coffee, snuggled my dog, and stared ahead at the new, strange life stretched out in front of me.

CHAPTER TWENTY

As I cruised the Pacific Coast Highway on my way to host a fundraising event for one of the San Diego animal sanctuaries, I turned my music up way too loud on purpose. Lately, the practice had served as a mechanism for motivating me for what was ahead. The volume consumed me, harnessed me a shot of adrenaline, and got me into moose mode, ready to take on the world. I tried to sing loudly with the lyrics but didn't know them. "Learn new songs," I shouted to myself as a form of reminder.

I was changing a lot these days. I'd started taking tennis lessons for exercise now that spring was not far off. I wasn't half bad and planned to join a beginners' league. I'd also asked my aunt Yolanda to teach me how to cook a few of her favorite dishes, so I could improve upon my very basic cooking skills and impress the guests I planned to invite over and dazzle. Did I mention I was trying to make more friends? At the station, outside events, wherever. Micky was becoming the popular kid at the dog park himself, and Grace used me as her sounding board for her now full-fledged romance with Bobby. My life was feeling fuller, and that was by design. When I stayed busy and connected to tasks, it didn't leave time to reminisce about…before. Notice the gaps that had never really filled after losing two people close to me.

Over the roar of Gaga on the radio, my screen showed an incoming call. I clicked through.

"You close?" Rory asked, his voice coming through my new car's speakers. A pretty black Infiniti. "Dogs make me nervous."

"Then you have no soul."

"That's what my ex says."

"Oh, Rory." I sighed. He meant well, but Rory was Rory. Good-looking but relatively simple. I had his back, though, as my partner behind that desk. "Give me five." I paused, stared, my jaw falling open. "What the hell?"

"What's wrong?"

"Rory. I'm fine, but I gotta go." I didn't wait for his response before ending the call. My attention had been yanked to the billboard looming to my right. A giant ad. Carrie holding a glass of white wine and smiling knowingly at me. *Soon, San Diego.* Then she was gone. The speed limit had not afforded me a long enough study.

Soon, San Diego? What in the world did *Soon, San Diego* mean?

The drive took on a new mood—befuddlement. My shock dominated everything, my curiosity was in overdrive, and I had a million questions for my empty car. Why was Carrie on a San Diego billboard? Was this a new project? Because it looked very much like the old project, the show she'd been tapped to host. Right here. In town. I took a deep breath, but it didn't settle me at all. Maybe she was planning to shoot a few episodes here and there on a spare weekend, in between her workweeks in Seattle. It seemed overly ambitious to tackle both, but if anyone could do it, Carrie could.

At the fundraiser, I turned on the charm as best I could but was decidedly un-moose-like. My mind was a jumble, and I bit the inside of my lip far too often.

"You do that a lot."

"Do what?" I asked Rory.

"Right before we go on air, or if you're nervous about something, you chew on your lip. Telltale sign." He laughed.

"Sue me," I said absently. "Hey. Have you heard anything about Carrie's new show?"

"As in your ex? Shouldn't you know more about that than me?" I'd yet to think of Carrie as my ex, but I guess she technically was. We didn't speak. We weren't together anymore. "But yeah, I've heard about it."

I squinted at him. His hair was too perfect tonight, slicked back like a Ken doll. "Why haven't you said anything?"

He shrugged and looked off into the distance, adjusting his cuff links. "Romance. Touchy subject. Not my territory."

I ignored the stupid take. "Tell me what you know, or I will kill you right here."

He sighed. "The show is called *The Secret Sauce*, and it's a local take on food and wine and shit. Carrie's hosting and acts as a tour guide. They shot the pilot this weekend at that new seafood restaurant, The Ark. Something like that."

"You know a lot."

"I pay attention when people talk."

Interesting that they'd strategically not been talking around me. I felt myself get excited and then shut it the hell down. Even if Carrie was back in town, so what? It didn't necessarily mean that she was back for any reason other than she didn't like the weather up there. No. I would not let this affect me the way it had the potential to. I also needed to prepare myself for the very real possibility that she was dating. She had every right to be. Did I drive by that billboard one more time on my way home? Maybe it was twice. But I had time to spare, and it meant nothing. She did look beautiful up there, though. Her hair was a lot more like her everyday look, different from her news hairstyles, softer with the wavy curls I knew were natural. Pretty.

My phone hadn't so much as pinged with a text from her, though, so there was really nothing for me to battle anyway. It was up to me to just live my life and remember to breathe. That's all I had to do.

❖

It got harder when, like a ghost, Caroline McNamara walked through our newsroom that following Thursday, causing my world to skid to a stop like a needle on a scratched record. My lips parted as I watched her walk down the hallway across from my desk. What in the hell was happening?

I didn't delay. "What the hell is happening?" I asked Carlos, spinning around in my chair to face his desk, three over.

He followed my gaze and his eyebrows shot up. "Oh, right, right. Her new food show is partnering with our parent company. An offshoot."

"Get out. Sylvan is a producer?"

"That's what I heard. That gives them access to resources here. My guess is they're shooting some sort of promo spot this afternoon."

Hence her presence, which was clearly felt by all. There were waves, hugs, excited exclamations. I stood as she approached my desk wearing white pants and a white denim jacket over a strappy pink top. Whoever had styled her for the shoot had hit it out of the park.

"Hey, Skyler," she said. I easily picked up on her trepidation. Couldn't blame her.

I smiled warmly to let her know I was fine with her presence. No big deal. Just Thursday. A Thursday that turned my world on its head. "I heard someone has a new show."

She nodded. "I imagine that's unexpected, huh?"

"You could say that." It was the most conservative answer I could come up with.

"Hey, Carrie. We're ready for you." It was that Sherry woman, one of the producers.

Carrie glanced over her shoulder. "I better go."

As she turned, I had to ask. "Um, who's anchoring the Seattle news tonight?"

She didn't hesitate. "Got me. My last day was Friday."

"How?" It wasn't my most eloquent of sentences. I'd have to work on my prose.

"I had a sixty-day opt out written into my contract. No questions asked. And I exercised it." A pause. "The bigger question is *why*."

"Okay. Why?"

"You," she said simply, with the softest smile ever. Everything in me went still.

"Carrie, you ready?" Sherry asked.

She snapped out of it, widening her eyes. "Yes, coming. Bye, Skyler." And she was off, stalking away briskly, leaving me stunned and at a loss.

Huh.

Maybe she wasn't dating anyone after all. And what was I supposed to do with this exactly?

"What in the world just happened there?" Carlos asked, sidling up next to me with his hands in his pockets.

"You saw that, too, huh?" My gaze was still trained on the hallway.

"Everyone saw it."

I looked around the normally bustling newsroom that had gone noticeably quiet. Lots of eyes were trained directly on me. I offered them a shoo sign. "Nothing to see here, folks."

Mila raised an eyebrow at me in amused challenge and answered her phone. Devante whistled his way back to his office, and Kristin smothered a smile as she approached my desk.

"Want to go over the running order?"

"I do."

And just like that, I went back to work. But the ground beneath my feet felt changed with Carrie in town. The sun landed differently on my skin. At first, I found it all a little exhilarating, but that quickly shifted to annoyance at her ability to waltz in and out of my orbit whenever she wanted and still have a noticeable effect. In my mind, she didn't deserve that kind of power, and I wanted to snatch it away. In fact, I would.

"Oh, I saw a billboard of your girlfr—I mean, Carrie," Grace said. "From the news." I'd come over for dinner, and Grace, who was supposed to be heading out for a date with Bobby, had announced she'd be joining us for cheeseburgers and truffle fries instead.

"I know. I saw it, too." I shrugged. "Apparently, she's back in town to host a new show. No big deal."

I saw Emory and Sarah exchange a glance over the sizzling pan. I planned to call them on it later. Assure them that I was steady on my feet.

"That's so great. Do you think you'll get back together?" Grace asked unabashedly.

I stared at her, forgetting momentarily the ask-you-anything quality of teenagers. "No. I don't think that's very likely."

"Oh." She seemed confused. "Really? Why? I thought it was a geography issue or something."

"Yes, but it goes a little deeper." I decided to change the subject. "Anyway, what happened to your date?"

With a tilt of her head, she signaled me to follow her, likely out of earshot of the moms. Once we were a safe distance away on the couch, she leveled with me in a quiet voice. "Bobby and I had a fight. It's prob over between us. It's whatever."

"Oh no. Why? What was the fight about?"

"They got all weird when I mentioned that my feelings were getting stronger."

"Define weird."

She huffed. "They didn't call me that night like usual and when I asked about it said that I stressed them out or whatever. Then I heard Melinda Harbinger say that she was texting Bobby the night before."

"And what did they say about that?"

"That they were just being stupid and it was me they liked. But that they freaked and didn't know what to do when things started getting serious."

I paused. "Do you believe them?"

She sat back against the couch in frustration. "I think so, but it all just makes me mad, so I canceled tonight."

"And how does that feel?"

She sat back up. "It sucks. I'm going to spend it practicing my tuba and marching band steps alone in my room. My mom will love it."

"Oh, me, too," Emory called from the kitchen. "That's my favorite."

"You're eavesdropping?" Grace called back.

"Always!" Sarah answered.

Grace rolled her eyes with a smile. She loved them in spite of it, clearly.

I regrouped us. "Just my two cents. Maybe Bobby handled the situation poorly but is still worth your time." I shrugged. "But what do I know?"

"Yeah."

"I tend to believe in second chances when the person meant well."

"Maybe." She didn't seem fully convinced.

"Come eat these burgers," Emory called.

As we gathered around the less formal dining table in the kitchen for fantastic comfort food, Sarah smiled at me pointedly. "Sometimes those that handle things poorly are still worth your time, huh?"

I frowned at her until the larger meaning settled. I blew her off. "Yeah, yeah. Okay."

"I'm serious," she said quietly in a private moment, while Emory and Grace chatted about the fry seasoning. "Maybe listen to some of your own advice, and see where it gets you."

"My situation is a little different."

"Yeah, the two of you are grown-ass adults and should have a much easier time sorting your whole thing out. You both screwed up. Forgive each other and be in love already."

"Since when do you say *grown-ass*?"

"I know." She sighed. "I have a teenager now. Can you believe it?"

I grappled. "No, because life will not stop surprising me. I keep begging it to."

She handed me the bowl of glorious fresh Parmesan for my fries. "Figure out how to be the llama or whatever."

"The moose. Why would I be a llama? They don't even have antlers, Sarah."

"Fine. Moose it up. And stop dragging your feet." She was fussing at me. At *me*. As if *I'd* done something wrong.

"No way. As far as Carrie is concerned, there will be no moosing."

"All because she made a bad call, like Bobby?"

Grace nodded wholeheartedly, now listening in. "I definitely think I'll be forgiving Bobby now that I'm thinking more clearly about it."

"How convenient." I stared at her and then back to Sarah. "Carrie's off-moose-limits to me. I don't even look at the billboard when I pass it anymore. I'm that good."

Sarah regarded me and her gaze flicked to Emory. "I remember saying something similar once upon a time." She gestured to my plate. "And now she makes me the best hamburger I've ever had."

Emory smiled triumphantly, and I sighed, wondering why things had to be so complicated, and how in the hell could I snag this burger recipe?

❖

"Dammit all."

I was standing beneath a stream of amazingly warm water that following Monday morning when my phone began buzzing insistently on my bathroom counter. Micky stared at it and back at me with alarm in his eyes that said I was about to miss out on something crucial, and what should he do?

"It's probably not important," I called to him, but my curiosity got the better of me, and I hopped out of the shower, closed my eyes to the immediate shiver, and saw I had a voice mail waiting. From Carrie. I blew out a breath and listened, because I had no will power to wait another second.

"Hi, Skyler. I'm calling in an official capacity. The station would love for you to appear on *The Secret Sauce* as part of our cross-promotion. I don't know if you heard, but Sylvan is a producing partner on the show. Can we talk about the possibility and, if you're interested, schedule an afternoon to shoot? And I just caught the time. You're in the shower. Which is lovely."

I had instant flashes of us in the shower, of her worshipping my body, and the sight of suds sliding off her. Suddenly that chill in the air was gone, and I was decidedly hot. Choosing to be an adult, I called her back. "Hey, it's Skyler."

"Sorry for interrupting the shower." Her voice tickled my ear in the best way.

"Not a problem."

"If you want to get dressed first, you can." She knew me well enough to know that I was standing there naked.

I rolled my lips in. "When did you have in mind for the shoot? And what do you pay?" Nice one. Keep it about the work.

She laughed. "We were looking at episode five. We'd shoot later this week, maybe do a wine pairing segment in my back garden. Trust me, we'll meet your minimum and more."

"Good. Sounds great as long as we can work around my schedule at the station."

"Luckily, I know it well. Talk to you soon, okay?" It was so natural, having this conversation, so easy. It shouldn't be.

A pause. "I just want to be clear that I'm accepting because of professional obligations and as a courtesy to you, of course."

"Got it. You want zero to do with me, personally."

"I didn't say that." But my guard was certainly up. "I'm sure we'll be fine, existing within the overlap in our jobs. We're both adults."

She didn't hesitate. "We more than exist to each other, whether you want that or not. But I get that you're upset with me. Just know that I'm back here because this is where I want to be."

I didn't know what to say. She wasn't wrong about the first part. "Still."

She sighed, and I heard defeat creep into her voice. "Still." Maybe the controlled confidence she projected didn't run so deep. For some reason, that resonated. The vulnerability. And why wouldn't it be there? I'd always known her to be a soft-hearted person underneath the badass face of the news.

"Hey," I tossed in. "Maybe it'll be fun, the shoot."

"I hope so," she said. "I better let you get on with your morning."

We said good-bye, I clicked off the call, and I caught sight of myself in the mirror. I was very aware of my body. It was like her voice alone could wake me the hell up. My skin felt wonderfully prickly, my nipples were taut and sensitive, and the lower portions should just shut the hell up. I ran a hand all the way to my inner thigh and closed my eyes at the images of her and the movie in my mind. If only we'd come with a different ending.

I heard my own advice to Grace. The same shred Sarah had thrown back at me. Maybe she had just made a bad call? Was that possible? Maybe I mattered more to her than I thought. After doing so much convincing of myself otherwise, it was hard to imagine.

Maybe. Maybe. Maybe.

The word should come with a warning label and an insurance policy.

I knew one thing for sure. She and I had unfinished business, and I could run, but I couldn't hide from Carrie forever.

Chapter Twenty-one

A nd Skyler, I think we'll have you over here," the director—Scott—
said, indicating a chair at the small table with *The Secret Sauce*
logo set up in Carrie's backyard, which still felt a little like mine. I wore
a blue sundress, picked out for me by wardrobe from the three options
I'd brought with me. Sherry was there along with an entire crew. People
bustled, chatted quietly with each other, and took lighting readings.
Hair and makeup had really come through as well. A sophisticated
operation. I was highly impressed by the setup.

"This is great," I told Scott, taking the seat he indicated. An intern
appeared on my side and offered me a water with lime. *Well, well.*

Carrie would be seated to my right, and our sommelier for the day,
Ray, would come and go between our chat sessions to usher us through
another small bite and wine pairing. It was a relaxed, unscripted format
under a structured umbrella. I liked it already and could see Carrie's
hand in all of it. I watched her have her makeup touched up just feet
away. I didn't want to say I told you so, but I had. She was in her
element.

"You've added those," I said, indicating the snaking vines with
orange blossoms along the back wall of her yard. "They're nice."

"Yeah, not too long ago. I like the pop of color."

It was strange being back there in the place I'd created so many
wonderful memories, only to feel like a visitor. In fact, I didn't like it.
I smiled at her, but my stomach flip-flopped. I was feeling at sea. "You
always had great intuition."

"Shall we get started on segment one?" Scott asked, interrupting.
I was told they'd already shot the intro.

We nodded, and after a brief chat with him about goals for the
conversation, we got started.

Carrie kicked us off, and after introducing me to the viewers, turned to me directly. "Now, Skyler, you and I know each other pretty well, and I'm aware of your appreciation of a good glass of wine."

I grinned. "Now don't mistake that for knowledge."

"Well, not to worry. I think we're going to get a bit of help with that shortly. You're gonna love Ray."

And we were off, a casual back-and-forth that actually flowed really well. Carrie had an impressive ability to put her guests at ease immediately. It was a really fun conversation, one that I never would have allowed to happen informally. But now that it had? It was really wonderful to talk with Carrie casually again, like water to the thirsty. The show had granted me a certain permission that I didn't grant myself. We moved onto segment two, and the wine flowed a little bit as we tasted a few varietals from a small winery in the Willamette Valley.

"I don't know about you, but I'm falling for this pinot," Carrie said.

I nodded and studied the glass for color. "It's the star today. Hey, you need a revisit over there?" I asked, surveying her empty glass. "Can we get her a revisit?" I asked Ray, who happily appeared and topped her glass.

She laughed. "I guess I do. And would you believe I've been to this winery? Tangle Valley Vineyard located in the perfect little town of Whisper Wall, Oregon. Check out our website for a little discount if you want to visit. Tell them we sent you. I have a feeling they're going to take great care of you either way."

"Oh yeah? I'll have to check it out."

She placed her hand on my wrist. "Well, if you do, don't miss the little biscuit café up the street."

I flashed on her telling me about that place the morning she made me those amazing biscuits after a steamy night together. I gave my head the smallest of shakes to clear the images that struck because I was on camera, for God's sake. Then I decided it didn't matter. If I was gonna take a risk, why not make it big? Because for starters, I couldn't take my eyes off her. The gestures that were all her, the sparkle in her eyes that she was never stingy with. I knew Carrie's heart, and it was pure. She was a kind person who put thought into most everything she did. Wasn't she worthy of a second shot? And if she wasn't, who was? What the hell was I waiting for?

"Maybe first we can go to dinner somewhere closer. Just us." I sipped my wine and waited.

She studied me, clearly caught off guard. Her lips parted, and her eyes searched mine as if wondering if she'd heard me right.

"Officially," I added. "A date."

She blinked. "Are you asking me on a date right here on television?"

I smiled softly. "I am. Would you like to go?"

She touched her cheek and it was adorable. "I might be blushing."

"Totally allowed." In my peripheral I saw Scott's mouth hanging open. Sherry stood off to the side watching in rapt amazement.

"I would love that," she said, with a smile that matched mine. It was the end of our last segment, and it would fall to Carrie to wrap us up. She turned to the camera. "So it seems we've scored some wine tips, some details about Skyler Ruiz, and a date for the two of us. Stay tuned, San Diego. Next week we'll explore the very best eats on Mission Beach. I'm Caroline McNamara, wishing you a happily hungry week ahead. Be good to your heart, and always seek out the secret sauce."

We held for the wide shot, and when we were clear, production seemed to give us a minute, busying themselves with other tasks, keeping their distance. Carrie turned to me. "Did you mean that?"

I inclined my head to the side. "Do I look like the kind of girl who would take a punch just to get ratings?"

Thankfully, she laughed. "No. I know you're not."

"Let's do as I proposed. Let's have food at the same time. Across from each other. In public." I lifted one shoulder. "No promises. No expectations. We'll see what we may have to talk about."

She nodded, content. "We'll talk and eat."

"Both things."

"Hey, that last part?" Scott asked, approaching with a question on his face. "Were you wanting us to cut around the uh…?"

"Skyler asking me out?" Carrie said brazenly. Against my better judgment, I allowed the flutter it brought on.

He blinked and offered a subtle nod, careful where he stepped.

"Air it," Carrie said, a little bit to my surprise. "This show is about real life. In all capacities."

"Got it," he said and held his hands up. "All for it, by the way. Just want to put that out there. That's great TV."

Well, at least we'd made a moment, if nothing else.

I stood. "Looks like we're all taking a few risks today. Thank you for having me."

"Thank you for coming. It was fun." Oh, the chemistry when our gazes held. Blazing hot as ever. It never waned. It never got old. It covered everything in its potency like glitter in the air.

"What about tomorrow?" I asked, riding the wave of the overly brave.

"What about *tonight*?" Oh, she'd upped the ante.

"Yeah?" It made me nervous, what I was doing. I did it anyway. She nodded. "Yeah."

So we were doing this. "Pick me up at seven. Don't be late." She never was. It was something fun to say.

Seven would give me a couple of hours to find a suitable outfit that showed off my shape, transition my hairstyle so it wouldn't be the same as the shoot, and get my head…ready. Heartbreak or home run. Tonight could truly go a lot of ways, and I needed to be prepared for the feelings that came with all of them. Was there a *What have I done* moment once I was alone behind the wheel of my car? Most definitely. But it felt like I had very little to lose, and maybe a lifetime to gain. So I shut it the hell down, put the car in drive, and channeled the moose I knew I could be. After all, love wasn't for the faint of heart.

Carrie picked me up right on time, wearing a white sweater dress and light brown boots with a heel. I was captivated by her look, stealing glances even moments after we'd greeted each other. Also, I could live in the soft aroma of her shampoo, and there it was as soon as I opened my door, a wonderful floral combination that took me places too good to examine in the present. There was a dinner to get to. "You look pretty."

"Thank you. But you…you take my breath away in this," she said, indicating the black belted cocktail dress I'd selected. We were a black and white fashion duo tonight, and somehow it felt fitting. I liked the juxtaposition.

"Thank you."

"Shall we?" I saw her eyeing Micky through the open door behind me. Similarly, he seemed to have discovered his best friend was near, and the shrieking had commenced. "Go ahead," I told her and stepped out of their way.

They reunited like family members separated for decades. She scooped the little sucker into her arms, cradled him like a baby, and gave him a few twirls. He wagged his body and licked every part of her he could. The display was really something to behold, and it was a shame I was the only one to witness it. What an impactful connection they had. "I hope you're doing okay," I heard her whisper to him. "I miss you so much. Do you know that?" He swiped her chin with his tongue lovingly, and she didn't even bat an eye. Another great quality of hers. She'd get dirty in the mud, tending to her garden, and let my mutt kiss all over her.

"Now we can go," she said, placing Micky gently on his favorite throw pillow. He'd be asleep in a ball within five minutes.

We made our way down the sidewalk as the chilly night air fueled the tiny bolts of tension mixed with anticipation that danced between us. Fear. Hope. Relief. Then she did something unexpected. She took my hand and held it all the way to the car. That simple gesture served to connect us and steady me. I felt the loss when I climbed into the passenger's seat and spent the rest of the car ride watching her profile whenever I got the chance. Obsessing about the way her hair curled and gently touched her neck on its way down to where it rested beyond her shoulders. I missed how soft it was.

"I'm maybe more excited than I've let on," Carrie said as we drove to the restaurant she'd picked out for us. "Gotta play it cool, you know."

"Yeah? I'm nervous."

"I'm that, too. I was just so taken aback when you asked me to dinner. Up until then, you'd shown no real signs of reconsidering…us."

I had to choose my words carefully here because this was delicate ground. "We had something really good. The least I could do is…try."

"And how's it going?"

"Well, you danced with my dog and told me I looked pretty. But I'm still grappling with the stuff from months ago."

She pulled the car into a parking space. "Here's the thing." She looked around, clearly agitated. "Um…let's get out of the car."

I frowned and did as she asked, curious. The parking lot of the restaurant wasn't full, but there were handfuls of nicely dressed people coming and going from beneath the maroon awning that marked the entrance. Carrie didn't care.

"I'm trying to imagine sitting in a restaurant and exchanging witty banter, flirting with you, and talking about the amazing qualities of the food when none of that matters."

"It doesn't?" I frowned, trying to follow.

"All that matters is you understanding something very important, and I can't go another minute until you do."

"Okay." My heart squeezed uncomfortably because we were

entering territory that left me feeling exposed, without armor. She placed her palm flat against mine and threaded our fingers. "You're everything." She paused to let the words work. "You're not a piece of the puzzle for me. Not one of a handful of details. Not a contributing factor. But my *everything*." She swallowed and I could see how nervous she was. This was a woman who went in front of thousands of people daily, unflappable and calm. Nothing like the vulnerable, flustered, heart-on-her-sleeve version I saw standing in front of me. But it was the words she spoke that toppled my resistance. I meant that much? I was crying. I wasn't sure when I started, but there were tears streaming down my face. She pressed on. "And somewhere along the way, in my quest to find my place in my unexpected new life, I forgot to inform you of my feelings, and to make choices that would reflect them." She shook her head in annoyance as if marveling at her own idiocy. "Once the dust settled, it was so obvious to me that I'd taken a wrong turn, and how I'd screwed everything up and miscommunicated myself. I'm so sorry for that, Skyler. So I got the hell out of Seattle, which is probably the end of my newscasting career forever."

I winced and she held up a hand.

"That doesn't even matter to me as long as you know the deep-down truth, which is that if I lost you forever, I would be losing *everything*. Do you know that?" Her brow was dropped, and she searched my face for any kind of clue.

I nodded and wiped the tears because I could actually feel the sincerity flowing off her in waves. I mattered that much to her. Me. "I can identify. When you walked out the door, I felt like my whole heart got up, left the room, and flew to Seattle."

"Biggest mistake of my life and not one I'll ever make again. Where you go, I go, if you ever give me that opportunity again." She kissed the back of my hand. "Because nothing in life shines without you there." She let go of my hand and took a step back. "And it's not something you have to decide now or today or next week. We can take our time. We can—"

"I want an us. And I should have wanted us regardless of where you lived. I should have been stronger. I should have fought for what mattered. Not geography, but you. I was a jerk, and I'm so sorry for the way I acted. I clearly have a few insecurities to work on. But I want us. I do."

She went still, mid-gesture. Silence. "Are you sure you know that?" She was clearly prepared to work to convince me, to put in her time. For a moment, I imagined her wooing me with gestures. Courting me slowly, properly. But this was a two-way street, and that wouldn't be fair. It's also not what I needed. She was.

My tears welled again. "I miss you so much. And you came back. I didn't expect that."

"I had to. You were here."

I grinned. "And let's be honest. Micky was."

She laughed. "Definitely part of the package. You're lucky I wasn't camped outside your apartment with a thermos of spiced rum and a poster board that said *Love me*."

I softened, took a moment. "Well, I do love you."

She exhaled, and this time it was Carrie who lost the battle to tears. "Yeah? Because I love you so much and want to wake up every morning and look into your eyes and say it. I will spend my life trying to make you happy, Skyler. I never want you to doubt my feelings ever again."

"Yes, please. Does that mean biscuits in a sexy robe?"

"At least every weekend. And I may be ahead of myself, but do you really need your apartment? I have tons of closet space and am willing to share."

I paused because a family of four walking by was very interested in our conversation and heading our way.

"Big fans. Can we get a photo?"

I laughed and looked to Carrie, both of us a pile of emotion. "I feel like this might be a moment worth documenting."

We stood together and smiled with the family. "I can't believe we're meeting both of you," one of the moms said. "Our favorite newswomen."

"Can you send me that photo?" I asked, realizing it had captured a true moment. I gave her my work email. I wanted to remember today.

The woman brightened. "Of course! Enjoy your night."

I turned back to Carrie, alone again. "So you wanna shack up, huh?"

"In a heartbeat."

"Well." I slid a strand of hair behind my ear, enjoying the way she watched me do it. "Why don't we eat and flirt and banter and talk about the amazing quality of the food and then take it from there? Also, that's code for likely yes. Let's just check a few boxes first."

She didn't hesitate. She kissed me like a pro in that very parking lot, and not just a quick one either. I leaned back against the car, and she melded herself to me right there in public. Everything was right with the world. I hadn't been breathing until this moment, holding my breath until we were back where we were supposed to be. The air here was wonderful, plentiful, and the best kind of high.

"Mmm. What about a fast dinner?" I asked around the kiss. "I'm a speedy eater."

"I vote for that. Appetizers?"

"Well, we're not skipping dessert. How about dessert followed by…another kind of dessert."

"You have the best brain. And lips. Come here." The woman I loved leaned down and kissed me silly up against a car in a restaurant's parking lot in a city in which we were both well-known. She wasn't afraid or ashamed to do that, to pick me, to love me in front of the whole world, and that made my heart swell immensely.

After the fastest consumption of scallops and a flourless chocolate cake with two scoops of vanilla ice cream, we were back at her place in bed, battling for control.

"You're a tiger tonight," Carrie whispered, as I tossed the white sweater dress over my shoulder and stared down at her in the pale blue bra and panties that were about to be next. "And I'm not complaining at all." She was right. My newfound confidence guided me forward as I worshiped her body. Slowly, deliberately, and without a shred of trepidation. We were an *us*, and I had this firm inkling that we always would be. There were just some things in life that felt right. You knew when that click of perfection happens, and that night, everything fell into its rightful spot beneath the watchful eyes of the fates and the stars. Our click. Hell, I even sounded like a sappy romantic but wouldn't change a thing. We made love more than a few times that night, savoring the excitement and celebration that came with a reunion.

"I love you," I whispered in her ear when we cuddled up in a sliver of moonlight.

"Never stop," she said, covering my arms with hers. "Because nothing shines without you. Remember that." She leaned back and kissed me softly. "I love you so much, Skyler Ruiz."

I smiled, fulfilled from outside in and looking forward to every single day ahead. Judgment and scrutiny at work? Bring 'em on. I had something wonderful to come home to. A punch in the face? Lay it on me. Didn't matter.

I had Carrie and she had me.

Epilogue

Strawberries in the summer hit the spot. Strawberries tossed into a pitcher of lemonade exploded with flavor. Strawberry cake? Excellent. Milkshakes were even better. That's why the Peak of Berries Festival in the small town of Tanner Peak was a true celebration, especially now that I could simply enjoy the festival as an attendee and not have to cover the event. Eat the food. Play the games. Stroll the stroll.

Speaking of work, Carrie had just wrapped shooting a segment for *The Secret Sauce* underneath the festival pavilion in front of a live audience. The show had really taken off. Her viewership was through the roof, blowing past expectations, which offered the show a much bigger budget, and an up-front order for more episodes.

"Good God. Did you see the size of the strawberry milkshake? It has cake coming out the top," Carrie asked, coming down the steps. "It was so good, too." She shook her head in wonder. "This festival is insane. I can't believe I've never attended it before. And you were right. It's perfect for the show. Kiss me."

I did as I was asked and grinned against her lips, tasting the strawberry milkshake. "I have a few secrets to pass on. Have you seen my family?"

Carrie nodded and glanced behind her. "Grace is walking around with Micky, who's prancing, by the way. He adores it here. You can tell. He's already had, like, six strawberries."

"Love you guys," a passerby said from beneath a giant strawberry hat. "We're from San Diego and watch *The Secret Sauce* each week. Glad she agreed to go on that date, huh, Skyler?"

"Asking was a good move," I called back and squeezed her hand.

"And so very public. You had guts."

"Well, the payoff was pretty great."

Carrie turned to me. "I'm hoping for the same payoff."

I squinted "From what?"

She grinned. "The segment is not quite over. Did I mention we're still rolling?"

"No." I studied her, mystified. "What's going on?"

"Why don't we walk back up the stairs? Here we go." She took my hand and led the way, as I followed, struggling to piece together the puzzle. My stomach contained a swarm of butterflies, but I wore a big smile, too. I knew I was safe with Carrie. That everything would be okay.

Moments later, we were on the small stage that they'd used to shoot the show, and to my surprise, the audience was still very much in their seats. Had that ending applause been fake? What was going on?

"Let's say hi to these nice people." The lavalier mic I didn't even realize Carrie was wearing went hot on that last sentence and her voice amplified to the live audience. This was all very surreal, and my mind couldn't seem to catch up to the action as it unfolded. "Does everyone remember Skyler?" she asked the audience, who broke into applause in response. I smiled and waved. "Well, I like to make my guests comfortable on *The Secret Sauce*, so why don't you have a seat on this couch." I looked behind me at the set they'd used for the show: a couch, a comfy chair, and a coffee table. I grinned and took a seat. Carrie sat down next to me for what was apparently an off-the-cuff segment. Now I was wishing I'd sampled more of the food before she'd gotten to me.

"Skyler, do you remember when you appeared on *The Secret Sauce* for the first time?"

A crew member in black appeared out of nowhere and handed me a handheld mic. Impressive, sir. "I do. We had a great time tasting wine from Napa and the Willamette Valley." I looked around. "Is there strawberry wine? Are we about to break some out?"

"I'd like to break this out instead," Carrie said and produced a small velvet box. My eyes went wide. My heart stopped. We loved each other, the kind of love that you read about. Our days were spent sending supportive, sexy, and playful text messages back and forth until we both returned home, kicked off our shoes, and shared a God-it's-good-to-see-you kiss before a late-night dinner. Weekends were for either lounging around outside or heading out on an impromptu adventure, which were the best kind. Nights were the best, both for the sex and the times we skipped it for cuddling and catching up. I never wanted any of it to end, and if that little box was what I thought it was, Carrie didn't either. The emotion had already taken hold, and I felt my throat constrict, strangled in the best way. Everything I felt for her, for us, welled to the surface and grabbed hold of my heart in its fluttery, happy grip.

Carrie got up from the couch and sank to one knee as the audience went absolutely wild. She pulled the box open to display a breathtaking pear-shaped diamond in a halo setting. The tears hit. "Skyler Ruiz, you gorgeous woman." That pulled a collective *awww* and the room went quiet. "From the moment you traipsed into the newsroom at KTMW, my life was never the same. I never want it to be. You changed all that I value for the better and made the world the best damn place to be. I'm obsessed with you. What's more? I'm madly, wildly, passionately in love with you, and the only thing left to do is make it official. I want to shout it from the rooftops. I want forever with you. What do you say? Skyler, will you please, please marry me?"

I knew the answer without having to think. For the sake of the audience, I let the silence linger before raising the microphone to my mouth, my hand shaking. "Yes."

Carrie stood, a huge grin erupting on her beautiful face. She moved toward me. I couldn't wait. Closing the distance, I threw my arms around her neck with gusto. She caught my mouth in a kiss as the people clapped, hooted, and hollered and the cameras rolled. "Yes," I whispered again. "Yes. Yes. Yes."

We watched that video a lot to relive one of the best moments of our lives. I say *one of* because there have been so many, especially ever since we tied the knot. That beach wedding I'd always yearned for turned out to be one of the most beautiful days of the year. The photos were gorgeous and the memories even better. Caroline McNamara was now my wife, and I would never get used to it. Each new day was special for its own separate reason, and I've never been made to feel more special.

"Shall we jet up the coast to that little winery in Oregon this weekend? There's now a fantastic new resort practically next door. I want you to think couples massages, wine tasting, and a cute little town to explore."

I felt myself light up. "Sold. Make the reservation." Paused. "But I think you're just after more of those biscuits you lust after."

"I want to introduce them to my wife, who, by the way, happens to be really hot in this businessy dress she's wearing." She touched the fabric of my dusty-blue belted number. "The station has you in the best clothes lately. This color is perfection."

The ratings for both the five and ten were high. We were riding the wave, which allowed for a nice bump in my wardrobe budget. Not that I had anything to brag about over Carrie, who had conquered the San Diego leisure market soundly, driving her star all the higher. We were an *it* couple in town, which came with a lot of invitations and attention, most of which we politely declined for quiet time on our own.

Emory and Sarah had become our go-to couple for game nights on the weekends. Emory, having been given a clean bill of health, dominated most any game we played. She also allowed us to see her vulnerable side when she lost. That was still new. When we were deemed cool enough, sometimes Grace and Bobby joined us and shared their cuteness. We exchanged adoring looks over their heads, sparing them the attention.

I looked down at the dress Carrie had complimented. "This old thing?" I raised an eyebrow. "Are you thinking about taking it off me?" She was. I knew her looks.

Carrie, objectifying me blatantly, grinned and nodded, which made me laugh and my stomach flutter for what I knew was coming. As she kissed my neck, I grinned. "I think you should book it. The trip. Take me to wine country and spoil me properly. There might even be some spoiling back."

She popped back up. "Yeah? We could have so much fun there."

"Mm-hmm. I wanna go to wine country with you. Maybe steal some kisses between the vines."

"You think you can score an extra day off? We can make it a three-day weekend. That third day could make a difference. It could change our lives."

"You are raising the stakes right now." More kissing. "I will tell Tam the world is ending and I must save it. Back Tuesday, Tam. Send in Lisette."

"Brilliant. Now come here with this dress."

Happily ever after was a cliché I used to fantasize about with one foot firmly in the land of realism. I was aware that those kinds of endings lived only in movies and hyperbolic stories about people's grandparents. I was a newswoman, after all, and dealt with facts and harsh realities on a daily basis. All of that went out the window when Carrie stepped into the picture. Because we were *living* happily ever after, and each passing day staggered me with the amount of love that flowed. Little things like notes tucked into work bags, foot massages at night, and discreet hand-holding under the table when in groups. Our secret world. The best part? Going home together, retreating from the world to just…be. The solid ground beneath my feet and the pitter-patter of my heart left me the happiest I'd ever been in my life.

I'd found my person. I'd found my life. I'd found my reason to get up in the morning.

The news had never been better.

About the Author

Melissa Brayden (www.melissabrayden.com) is a multi-award-winning romance author, embracing the full-time writer's life in San Antonio, Texas, and enjoying every minute of it.

Melissa is married and working really hard at remembering to do the dishes. For personal enjoyment, she spends time with her Jack Russell Terriers and checks out the NYC theater scene as often as possible. She considers herself a reluctant patron of spin class, but would much rather be sipping merlot and staring off into space. Bring her coffee, wine, or doughnuts and you'll have a friend for life.